# 19th & 20th Century
# Short Stories

Selected and edited by
## David Adams

Oxford University Press

# OXFORD
UNIVERSITY PRESS

Great Clarendon Street, Oxford OX2 6DP

Oxford University Press is a department of the University of Oxford.
It furthers the University's objective of excellence in research, scholarship,
and education by publishing worldwide in

Oxford New York

Athens Auckland Bangkok Bogotá Buenos Aires Calcutta
Cape Town Chennai Dar es Salaam Delhi Florence Hong Kong Istanbul
Karachi Kuala Lumpur Madrid Melbourne Mexico City Mumbai
Nairobi Paris São Paulo Singapore Taipei Tokyo Toronto Warsaw

with associated companies in Berlin Ibadan

OXFORD is a registered trade mark of Oxford University Press
in the UK and in certain other countries

First published 1998
Reprinted 1998, 2000

ISBN 0 19 831400 0

Typeset by AFS Image Setters Ltd., Glasgow
Printed and bound in Great Britain

Cover illustration: 'Richmond Bridge' by Tissot.
The publishers would like to thank the W.B. Ruger Collection, USA/Bridgeman Art Library
for permission to reproduce this image.

Also available in the *Oxford Literature Resources* series:

# Contents

# Acknowledgements

The editor and publisher are grateful for permission to include the following copyright material in this collection.

**Thomas Hardy:** 'Old Mrs Chundle' and 'The Superstitious Man' reprinted from *Thomas Hardy: Collected Short Stories* (Macmillan, Papermac), by permission of the publishers.

**L.P. Hartley:** 'Night Fears' reprinted from *Night Fears and Other Stories* (1924), by permission of The Society of Authors as the Literary Representative of the Estate of L.P. Hartley.

**James Joyce:** 'Eveline', © The Estate of James Joyce, reprinted from *Dubliners* (Cape, 1967), by permission of The Wylie Agency.

**Mary Lavin:** 'The Will', first published in *The Long Ago and Other Stories* (1944), reprinted from *The Stories of Mary Lavin, Volume I* (Constable, 1964) and also *In A Cafe* edited by Elizabeth Walsh Peavoy, (Townhouse, Dublin, 1995), by permission of Elizabeth Walsh Peavoy.

**D.H. Lawrence:** 'The Rocking-Horse Winner' reprinted from *D.H. Lawrence: The Complete Short Stories* (Heinemann), by permission of Laurence Pollinger Limited and the Estate of Frieda Lawrence Ravagli.

**James Thurber:** 'The Secret Life of Walter Mitty', Copyright © 1942 by James Thurber, Copyright © renewed 1970 by Helen Thurber and Rosemary A. Thurber, reprinted from *A Thurber Carnival* (Penguin, 1953) by permission of Rosemary A. Thurber and the Barbara Hogeson Agency.

**Eudora Welty:** 'A Visit of Charity', Copyright © 1941 by Eudora Welty, renewed 1969 by Eudora Welty, first appeared in *Decision*, April 1941, reprinted from *A Curtain of Green and Other Stories*, contained within *The Collected Stories of Eudora Welty*, (Marion Boyars Publishers Ltd), by permission of the publishers.

# Preface

The latest GCSEs in English and English Literature have brought with them some new challenges for students and teachers, and placed renewed emphasis on a few old ones. The aim of this book is to help both teachers and students meet these challenges, old and new, and hopefully to provide some entertaining and thought-provoking reading along the way.

The problems faced by students in tackling pre-twentieth century texts are all too familiar. They are put off by what they see as the interminable length of the books, by the incomprehensible language, the unfamiliar settings, the inexplicable mannerisms of the characters, not to mention the fact that nothing ever seems to happen. The pre-twentieth century stories in this anthology are chosen to try to counter these objections. The story-lines and themes have been chosen to be relevant to today's readers, and to appeal to a range of interests. The stories are relatively short and in accessible language, though where unfamiliar words and phrases occur, footnotes are provided. Background details to the stories are explained in the social, historical, and cultural sections of the activities, which ideally should be read before the stories.

Once the difficulties of reading a pre-twentieth prose text are overcome, the GCSEs present the challenge of selecting an appropriate text with which to compare it. The twentieth-century texts in this anthology match the pre-twentieth century texts both in genre and in theme. These too have footnotes and background notes. The pairings have been selected to focus on one particular aspect of the texts. Social issues, about the care of the elderly, appear in *Old Mrs Chundle* and *A Visit of Charity*, and are particularly relevant at a time when society is replacing institutional care of its vulnerable members with 'care in the community'. The nature of heroism is examined in *The Sexton's Hero* and *The Will*, which focus on whether it has to involve dramatic and dangerous acts, or whether it can involve an individual struggle with principle. Romance and the position of women in society are explored in *Malachi's Cove* and *Eveline*. Again both stories reflect very different beliefs to ones that today's society holds. The supernatural appears in *The Superstitious Man's Story* and *Night-Fears*, showing a changing attitude to the 'unknown' in our lives. Finally, fantasy appears in different forms through the escapist characters in *The Poor Relation's Story* and *The Secret Life of Walter Mitty*, and again through supernatural means in *The Bottle Imp* and *The Rocking-horse Winner*.

All the stories in the anthology fulfil the requirements specified by the National Curriculum. The pre-twentieth century texts were all written by authors on the prescribed list and all the twentieth-century texts are by authors with a 'well-established critical reputation'. Indeed, Lawrence and Joyce are actually named in the National Curriculum list.

Another requirement of the latest GCSEs is the skill of written comparison. Often students display a sound knowledge orally of texts studied, but have trouble expressing their understanding in a formal essay. The activities that accompany each pairing are designed to guide the student through a close reading of the texts towards a formal comparative essay.

The activities for each pairing are divided into three sections. The first section, 'Understanding the Stories', presents questions and tasks that students should attempt in pairs or groups, discussing their answers and keeping detailed notes. The tasks cover the following areas: plot, character, theme, genre, viewpoint, structure, and form. They also present questions to prepare students for the topics they are about to read about in the stories. (Line references are given to help students to focus on appropriate sections of the texts.) The second section, 'Interim Activities', offers a brief choice of extended assignments that serve the dual purpose of consolidating students' knowledge of the stories and of producing a piece of coursework to cover other examination criteria. The final section, entitled 'Wider Reading Coursework Assignments', provides two essay questions – one for Foundation Tier and one for Higher Tier – and structured guidelines to cover the wider reading requirements of the coursework.

If students' enthusiasm is kindled by any of the stories that they read in the anthology, there is a Wider Reading list at the end of the book that will enable them to take their enjoyment of the genre or the theme further.

The activities have been written so that a student could take the book away and work independently on the exercises to produce an essay, but that is not the ideal way to use it. Any book of this nature is naturally restricted in the amount of information and the type of activity that can be included in it, and not all of the activities are easily accessible to students of all abilities. Further enticing and fruitful avenues of exploration can be pursued by encouraging students to discover other points of comparison between the existing pairings, or to create new pairings of their own either from within the text or by using short stories from the Wider Reading list.

It is also possible to combine study of twentieth-century short stories in the NEAB anthology with some of the pre-twentieth century short stories here. The subjects and themes in these stories link well with some stories in the NEAB anthology. And yet while the activities and tasks have been designed to suit the NEAB syllabus requirements, they could also be easily adapted to other syllabuses.

*David Adams*

# *Care in the Community*

# Old Mrs Chundle

*Thomas Hardy*

The curate[1] had not been a week in the parish, but the autumn morning proving fine, he thought he would make a little water-colour sketch, showing a distant view of the Corvsgate ruin two miles off, which he had passed on his way hither.[2] The sketch occupied him a longer time than he had anticipated. The luncheon hour drew on, and he felt hungry.

Quite near him was a stone-built old cottage of respectable and substantial build. He entered it, and was received by an old woman.

'Can you give me something to eat, my good woman?' he said.

She held her hand to her ear.

'Can you give me something for lunch?' he shouted. 'Bread and cheese     10
– anything will do.'

A sour look crossed her face, and she shook her head. 'That's unlucky,' murmured he. She reflected and said more urbanely,[3] 'Well, I'm going to have my own bit o' dinner in no such long time hence. 'Tis taters and cabbage, boiled with a scantling o' bacon. Would ye like it? But I suppose 'tis the wrong sort, and that ye would sooner have bread and cheese.'

'No, I'll join you. Call me when it is ready. I'm just out here.'

'Ay, I've seen ye. Drawing the old stones, baint ye?'

'Yes, my good woman.'                                                   20

'Sure 'tis well some folk have nothing better to do with their time. Very well, I'll call ye, when I've dished up.'

He went out and resumed his painting; till in about seven or ten minutes the old woman appeared at her door and held up her hand. The curate washed his brush, went to the brook, rinsed his hands and proceeded to the house.

'There's yours,' she said, pointing to the table. 'I'll have my bit here.' And she denoted the settle.[4]

'Why not join me?'

---

[1] *curate* – an assistant priest or vicar of a parish
[2] *hither* – to here; (on his way to taking up his new post)
[3] *urbanely* – with polite manners
[4] *settle* – a long wooden seat with a high back

1

30    'Oh, faith, I don't want to eat with my betters – not I.' And she continued firm in her resolution, and eat apart.

The vegetables had been well cooked over a wood fire – the only way to cook a vegetable properly – and the bacon was well boiled. The curate ate heartily: he thought he had never tasted such potatoes and cabbage in his life, which he probably had not, for they had been just brought in from the garden, so that the very freshness of the morning was still in them. When he had finished he asked her how much he owed for the repast, which he had much enjoyed.

'Oh, I don't want to be paid for that bit of snack 'a b'lieve!'

40    'But really you must take something. It was an excellent meal.'

' 'Tis all my own growing, that's true. But I don't take money for a bit o' victuals.[5] I've never done such a thing in my life.'

'I should feel much happier if you would.'

She seemed unsettled by his feeling, and added as by compulsion, 'Well, then; I suppose twopence won't hurt ye ?'

'Twopence?'

'Yes. Twopence.'

'Why my good woman, that's no charge at all. I am sure it is worth this, at least.' And he laid down a shilling.

50    'I tell 'ee 'tis *twopence*, and no more!' she said primly. 'Why, bless the man, it didn't cost me more than three halfpence, and that leaves me a fair quarter profit. The bacon is the heaviest item; that may perhaps be a penny. The taters I've got plenty of, and the cabbage is going to waste.'

He thereupon argued no further, paid the limited sum demanded, and went to the door. 'And where does that road lead ?' he asked, by way of engaging her in a little friendly conversation before parting, and pointing to a white lane which branched from the direct highway near her door.

'They tell me that it leads to Enckworth.'

'And how far is Enckworth?'

60    'Three miles, they say. But God knows if 'tis true.'

'You haven't lived here long, then?'

'Five-and-thirty year come Martinmas.'[6]

'And yet you have never been to Enckworth?'

'Not I. Why should I ever have been to Enckworth ? I never had any business there – a great mansion of a place, holding people that I've no more doings with than with the people of the moon. No, there's on'y two places I ever go to from year's end to year's end: that's once a fortnight to Anglebury, to do my bit o' marketing, and once a week to my parish church.'

---

[5] *victuals* – (pronounced 'vittles') food

[6] *Martinmas* – the feast of St Martin, the 11th November

'Which is that?'                                                                70

'Why, Kingscreech.'

'Oh – then you are in my parish?'

'Maybe. Just on the outskirts.'

'I didn't know the parish extended so far. I'm a newcomer. Well, I hope we may meet again. Good afternoon to you.'

When the curate was next talking to his rector[7] he casually observed: 'By the way, that's a curious old soul who lives out towards Corvsgate – old Mrs – I don't know her name – A deaf old woman.'

'You mean old Mrs Chundle, I suppose.'

'She tells me she's lived there five-and-thirty years, and has never     80 been to Enckworth, three miles off. She goes to two places only, from year's end to year's end – to the market town, and to church on Sundays.'

'To church on Sundays. H'm. She rather exaggerates her travels, to my thinking. I've been rector here thirteen years, and I have certainly never seen her at church in my time.'

'A wicked old woman. What can she think of herself for such deception!'

'She didn't know you belonged here when she said it, and could find out the untruth of her story. I warrant she wouldn't have said it to me!'   90 And the rector chuckled.

On reflection the curate felt that this was decidedly a case for his ministrations,[8] and on the first spare morning he strode across to the cottage beyond the ruin. He found its occupant of course at home.

'Drawing picters again?' she asked, looking up from the hearth, where she was scouring the fire-dogs.[9]

'No, I come on a more important matter, Mrs Chundle. I am the new curate of this parish.'

'You said you was last time. And after you had told me and went away I said to myself, he'll be here again sure enough, hang me if I didn't. And  110 here you be.'

'Yes. I hope you don't mind?'

'Oh, no. You find us a roughish lot, I make no doubt?'

'Well, I won't go into that. But I think it was a very culpable – unkind thing of you to tell me you came to church every Sunday, when I find you've not been seen there for years.'

'Oh, did I tell 'ee that?'

'You certainly did.'

[7] *rector* – the head priest or vicar of a parish

[8] *ministrations* – the services of ministers of religion

[9] *fire-dogs* – metal supports for logs of wood in a fire

'Now I wonder what I did that for?'

120 'I wonder too.'

'Well, you could ha' guessed, after all, that I didn't come to any service. Lord, what's the good o' my lumpering[10] all the way to church and back again, when I'm as deaf as a plock?[11] Your own commonsense ought to have told 'ee that 'twas but a figure o' speech, seeing you was a pa'son.'

'Don't you think you could hear the service if you were to sit close to the reading-desk and pulpit?'

'I'm sure I couldn't. Oh no – not a word. Why I couldn't hear anything even at that time when Isaac Coggs used to cry the Amens out loud

130 beyond anything that's done nowadays, and they had the barrel-organ for the tunes – years and years agone, when I was stronger in my narves than now.'

'H'm – I'm sorry. There's one thing I could do, which I would with pleasure, if you'll use it. I could get you an ear-trumpet. Will you use it?'

'Ay, sure. That I woll. I don't care what I use – 'tis all the same to me.'

'And you'll come?'

'Yes. I may as well go there as bide[12] here, I suppose.'

The ear-trumpet was purchased by the zealous young man, and the

140 next Sunday, to the great surprise of the parishioners when they arrived, Mrs Chundle was discovered in the front seat of the nave of Kingscreech Church, facing the rest of the congregation with an unmoved countenance.[13]

She was the centre of observation through the whole morning service. The trumpet, elevated at a high angle, shone and flashed in the sitters' eyes as the chief object in the sacred edifice.

The curate could not speak to her that morning, and called the next day to inquire the result of the experiment. As soon as she saw him in the distance she began shaking her head.

150 'No, no,' she said decisively as he approached. 'I knowed 'twas all nonsense.'

'What?'

' 'Twasn't a mossel[14] o' good, and so I could have told 'ee before. A wasting your money in jimcracks[15] upon a' old 'ooman like me.'

'You couldn't hear! Dear me – how disappointing.'

---

[10] *lumper* – (dialect) to blunder along
[11] *plock* – (dialect) block
[12] *bide* – (old-fashioned) stay
[13] *unmoved countenance* – her face showed no feelings
[14] *mossel* – morsel; a tiny bit
[15] *jimcracks* – (dialect) a useless device

'You might as well have been mouthing at me from the top o' Creech Barrow.'[16]

'That's unfortunate.'

'I shall never come no more – never – to be made such a fool of as that again.'                                                                        160

The curate mused. 'I'll tell you what, Mrs Chundle. There's one thing more to try, and only one. If that fails I suppose we shall have to give it up. It is a plan I have heard of, though I have never myself tried it; it's having a sound tube fixed, with its lower mouth in the seat immediately below the pulpit, where you would sit, the tube running up inside the pulpit with its upper end opening in a bell-mouth[17] just beside the book-board.[18] The voice of the preacher enters the bell-mouth, and is carried down directly to the listener's ear. Do you understand?'

'Exactly.'

'And you'll come, if I put it up at my own expense?'                            170

'Ay, I suppose. I'll try it, e'en though I said I wouldn't. I may as well do that as do nothing, I reckon.'

The kind-hearted curate, at great trouble to himself, obtained the tube and had it fitted vertically as described, the upper mouth being immediately under the face of whoever should preach, and on the following Sunday morning it was to be tried. As soon as he came from the vestry the curate perceived to his satisfaction Mrs Chundle in the seat beneath, erect and at attention, her head close to the lower orifice[19] of the sound-pipe, and a look of great complacency that her soul required a special machinery to save it, while other people's could be saved in a common-   180
place way. The rector read the prayers from the desk on the opposite side, which part of the service Mrs Chundle could follow easily enough by the help of the prayer-book; and in due course the curate mounted the eight steps into the wooden octagon,[20] gave out his text, and began to deliver his discourse.

It was a fine frosty morning in early winter, and he had not got far with his sermon when he became conscious of a steam rising from the bell-mouth of the tube, obviously caused by Mrs Chundle's breathing at the lower end, and it was accompanied by a suggestion of onion-stew. However, he preached on awhile, hoping it would cease, holding in his   190
left hand his finest cambric[21] handkerchief kept especially for Sunday morning services. At length, no longer able to endure the odour, he

---

[16] *Creech Barrow* – a hill in the area

[17] *bell-mouth* – a large opening in the shape of a bell

[18] *book-board* – a place to put a book while reading from it

[19] *orifice* – hole; opening

[20] *octagon* – the eight-sided pulpit from which the curate preaches his sermons

[21] *cambric* – a fine white linen

lightly dropped the handkerchief into the bell of the tube, without stopping for a moment the eloquent flow of his words; and he had the satisfaction of feeling himself in comparatively pure air.

He heard a fidgeting below; and presently there arose to him over the pulpit-edge a hoarse whisper: 'The pipe's chokt!'

'Now, as you will perceive, my brethren,'[22] continued the curate, unheeding the interruption; 'by applying this test to ourselves, our
200    discernment of—'

'The pipe's chokt!' came up in a whisper yet louder and hoarser.

'Our discernment of actions as morally good or indifferent will be much quickened, and we shall be materially helped in our—'

Suddenly came a violent puff of warm wind, and he beheld his handkerchief rising from the bell of the tube and floating to the pulpit floor. The little boys in the gallery laughed, thinking it a miracle. Mrs Chundle had, in fact, applied her mouth to the bottom end, blown with all her might, and cleared the tube. In a few seconds the atmosphere of the pulpit became as before, to the curate's great discomfiture. Yet stop the
210    orifice again he dared not, lest the old woman should make a still greater disturbance and draw the attention of the congregation to this unseemly[23] situation.

'If you carefully analyse the passage I have quoted,' he continued in somewhat uncomfortable accents, 'you will perceive that it naturally suggests three points for consideration—'

('It's not onions: it's peppermint,' he said to himself.)

'Namely, mankind in its unregenerate state—'

('And cider.')

'The incidence of the law, and loving-kindness or grace, which we will
220    now severally consider—'

('And pickled cabbage. What a terrible supper she must have made!')

'Under the twofold aspect of external and internal consciousness.'

Thus the reverend gentleman continued strenuously for perhaps five minutes longer; then he could stand it no more. Desperately thrusting his thumb into the hole, he drew the threads of his distracted discourse together, the while hearing her blow vigorously to dislodge the plug. But he stuck to the hole, and brought his sermon to a premature close.

He did not call on Mrs Chundle the next week, a slight cooling of his zeal for her spiritual welfare being manifest; but he encountered her at
230    the house of another cottager whom he was visiting; and she immediately addressed him as a partner in the same enterprise.

'I could hear beautiful!' she said. 'Yes; every word! Never did I know

---

[22] *brethren* – (old-fashioned) plural of brother, used by religious groups
[23] *unseemly* – inappropriate; indecent

such a wonderful machine as that there pipe. But you forgot what you was doing once or twice, and put your handkerchief on the top o' en, and stopped the sound a bit. Please not to do that again, for it makes me lose a lot. Howsomever,[24] I shall come every Sunday morning reg'lar now, please God.'

The curate quivered internally.

'And will ye come to my house once in a while and read to me?'

'Of course.'                                                                  240

Surely enough the next Sunday the ordeal was repeated for him. In the evening he told his trouble to the rector. The rector chuckled.

'You've brought it upon yourself,' he said. 'You don't know this parish so well as I. You should have left the old woman alone.'

'I suppose I should!'

'Thank Heaven, she thinks nothing of my sermons, and doesn't come when I preach. Ha, ha!'

'Well,' said the curate somewhat ruffled, 'I must do something. I cannot stand this. I shall tell her not to come.'

'You can hardly do that.'                                                     250

'And I've half-promised to go and read to her. But – I shan't go.'

'She's probably forgotten by this time that you promised.'

A vision of his next Sunday in the pulpit loomed horridly before the young man, and at length he determined to escape the experience. The pipe should be taken down. The next morning he gave directions, and the removal was carried out.

A day or two later a message arrived from her, saying that she wished to see him. Anticipating a terrific attack from the irate old woman, he put off going to her for a day, and when he trudged out towards her house on the following afternoon it was in a vexed mood. Delicately nurtured man    260
as he was, he had determined not to re-erect the tube, and hoped he might hit on some new *modus vivendi*,[25] even if at any inconvenience to Mrs Chundle, in a situation that had become intolerable as it was last week.

'Thank heaven, the tube is gone,' he said to himself as he walked; 'and nothing will make me put it up again!'

On coming near he saw to his surprise that the calico[26] curtains of the cottage windows were all drawn. He went up to the door, which was ajar; and a little girl peeped through the opening.

'How is Mrs Chundle?' he asked blandly.                                       270

'She's dead, sir,' said the girl in a whisper.

---

[24] *howsomever* – (dialect) however

[25] modus vivendi – (Latin: 'a way of living') an arrangement

[26] *calico* – plain white cotton cloth

'Dead? . . . Mrs Chundle dead?'

'Yes, sir.'

A woman now came. 'Yes, 'tis so, sir. She went off quite sudden-like about two hours ago. Well, you see, sir, she was over seventy years of age, and last Sunday she was rather late in starting for church, having to put her bit o' dinner ready before going out; and was very anxious to be in time. So she hurried overmuch, and runned up the hill, which at her time of life she ought not to have done. It upset her heart, and she's been poorly all the week since, and that made her send for 'ee. Two or three times she said she hoped you would come soon, as you'd promised to, and you were so staunch and faithful in wishing to do her good, that she knew 'twas not by your own wish you didn't arrive. But she would not let us send again, as it might trouble 'ee too much, and there might be other poor folks needing you. She worried to think she might not be able to listen to 'ee next Sunday, and feared you'd be hurt at it, and think her remiss.²⁷ But she was eager to hear you again later on. However, 'twas ordained²⁸ otherwise for the poor soul, and she was soon gone. "I've found a real friend at last," she said. "He's a man in a thousand. He's not ashamed of a' old woman, and he holds²⁹ that her soul is worth saving as well as richer people's." She said I was to give you this.'

It was a small folded piece of paper, directed to him and sealed with a thimble.³⁰ On opening it he found it to be what she called her will, in which she had left him her bureau, case-clock, four-post bedstead, and framed sampler – in fact all the furniture of any account that she possessed.

The curate went out, like Peter at the cock-crow.³¹ He was a meek young man, and as he went his eyes were wet. When he reached a lonely place in the lane he stood still thinking, and kneeling down in the dust of the road rested his elbow in one hand and covered his face with the other.

Thus he remained some minutes or so, a black shape on the hot white of the sunned trackway; till he rose, brushed the knees of his trousers, and walked on.

---

²⁷ *remiss* – at fault

²⁸ *ordained* – fated

²⁹ *holds* – believes

³⁰ *sealed with a thimble* – the will has been sealed with hot wax and the wax stamped with a thimble end

³¹ *Peter at the cock-crow* – St Peter realized that he had betrayed Jesus when he heard the cock crowing

# A Visit of Charity

*Eudora Welty*

It was mid-morning – a very cold, bright day. Holding a potted plant before her, a girl of fourteen jumped off the bus in front of the Old Ladies' Home, on the outskirts of town. She wore a red coat, and her straight yellow hair was hanging down loose from the pointed white cap all the little girls were wearing that year. She stopped for a moment beside one of the prickly dark shrubs with which the city had beautified the Home, and then proceeded slowly toward the building, which was of whitewashed brick and reflected the winter sunlight like a block of ice. As she walked vaguely up the steps she shifted the small pot from hand to hand; then she had to set it down and remove her mittens before she   10 could open the heavy door.

'I'm a Campfire Girl. . . .[1] I have to pay a visit to some old lady,' she told the nurse at the desk. This was a woman in a white uniform who looked as if she were cold; she had close-cut hair which stood up on the very top of her head exactly like a sea wave. Marian, the little girl, did not tell her that this visit would give her a minimum of only three points in her score.

'Acquainted with any of our residents?' asked the nurse. She lifted one eyebrow and spoke like a man.

'With any old ladies? No – but – that is, any of them will do,' Marian   20 stammered. With her free hand she pushed her hair behind her ears, as she did when it was time to study Science.

The nurse shrugged and rose. 'You have a nice *multiflora cineraria*[2] there,' she remarked as she walked ahead down the hall of closed doors to pick out an old lady.

There was loose, bulging linoleum[3] on the floor. Marian felt as if she were walking on the waves, but the nurse paid no attention to it. There was a smell in the hall like the interior of a clock. Everything was silent until, behind one of the doors, an old lady of some kind cleared her throat like a sheep bleating. This decided the nurse. Stopping in her tracks, she   30 first extended her arm, bent her elbow, and leaned forward from the hips – all to examine the watch strapped to her wrist; then she gave a loud double-rap on the door.

[1] *Campfire Girl* – US equivalent to a Girl Guide
[2] multiflora cineraria – the scientific name for the potted plant that Marian carries
[3] *linoleum* – a cheap floor covering

9

'There are two in each room,' the nurse remarked over her shoulder.

'Two what?' asked Marian without thinking. The sound like sheep's bleating almost made her turn around and run back.

One old woman was pulling the door open in short, gradual jerks, and when she saw the nurse a strange smile forced her old face dangerously awry.[4] Marian, suddenly propelled by the strong, impatient arm
40  of the nurse, saw next the side-face of another old woman, even older, who was lying flat in bed with a cap on and a counterpane[5] drawn up to her chin.

'Visitor,' said the nurse, and after one more shove she was off up the hall.

Marian stood tongue-tied; both hands held the potted plant. The old woman, still with that terrible, square smile (which was a smile of welcome) stamped on her bony face, was waiting. . . . Perhaps she said something. The old woman in bed said nothing at all, and she did not look around.

50  Suddenly Marian saw a hand, quick as a bird claw, reach up in the air and pluck the white cap off her head. At the same time, another claw to match drew her all the way into the room, and the next moment the door closed behind her.

'My, my, my,' said the old lady at her side.

Marian stood enclosed by a bed, a washstand and a chair; the tiny room had altogether too much furniture. Everything smelled wet – even the bare floor. She held on to the back of the chair which was wicker and felt soft and damp. Her heart beat more and more slowly, her hands got colder and colder, and she could not hear whether the old women were
60  saying anything or not. She could not see them very clearly. How dark it was! The window shade was down, and the only door was shut. Marian looked at the ceiling. . . . It was like being caught in a robbers' cave, just before one was murdered.

'Did you come to be our little girl for a while?' the first robber asked. Then something was snatched from Marian's hand – the little potted plant.

'Flowers!' screamed the old woman. She stood holding the pot in an undecided way. 'Pretty flowers,' she added.

Then the old woman in bed cleared her throat and spoke. 'They are
70  not pretty,' she said, still without looking around, but very distinctly.

Marian suddenly pitched against the chair and sat down in it.

'Pretty flowers,' the first old woman insisted. 'Pretty – pretty . . . '

Marian wished she had the little pot back for just a moment – she had

---

[4] *awry* – crooked

[5] *counterpane* – a decorated cover for a bed

forgotten to look at the plant herself before giving it away. What did it look like?

'Stinkweeds,' said the other old woman sharply. She had a bunchy white forehead and red eyes like a sheep. Now she turned them toward Marian. The fogginess seemed to rise in her throat again, and she bleated, 'Who – are – you?'

To her surprise, Marian could not remember her name. 'I'm a Campfire Girl,' she said finally. 80

'Watch out for the germs,' said the old woman like a sheep, not addressing anyone.

'One came out last month to see us,' said the first old woman.

A sheep or a germ? wondered Marian dreamily, holding on to the chair.

'Did not!' cried the other old woman.

'Did so! Read to us out of the Bible, and we enjoyed it!' screamed the first.

'Who enjoyed it!' said the woman in bed. Her mouth was unexpectedly small and sorrowful, like a pet's. 90

'We enjoyed it,' insisted the other. 'You enjoyed it – I enjoyed it.'

'We all enjoyed it,' said Marian, without realizing that she had said a word.

The first old woman had just finished putting the potted plant high, high on the top of the wardrobe, where it could hardly be seen from below. Marian wondered how she had ever succeeded in placing it there, how she could ever have reached so high.

'You mustn't pay any attention to old Addie,' she now said to the little girl. 'She's ailing[6] today.'

'Will you shut your mouth?' said the woman in bed. 'I am not.' 100

'You're a story.'

'I can't stay but a minute – really, I can't,' said Marian suddenly. She looked down at the wet floor and thought that if she were sick in here they would have to let her go.

With much to-do[7] the first old woman sat down in a rocking chair – still another piece of furniture! – and began to rock. With the fingers of one hand she touched a very dirty cameo pin[8] on her chest. 'What do you do at school?' she asked.

'I don't know . . .' said Marian. She tried to think but she could not.

'Oh, but the flowers are beautiful,' the old woman whispered. She seemed to rock faster and faster; Marian did not see how anyone could rock so fast. 110

---

[6] *ailing* – unwell

[7] *to-do* – fussing

[8] *cameo pin* – a brooch made out of a precious stone, no longer fashionable

'Ugly,' said the woman in bed.

'If we bring flowers—' Marian began, and then fell silent. She had almost said that if Campfire Girls brought flowers to the Old Ladies' Home, the visit would count one extra point, and if they took a Bible with them on the bus and read it to the old ladies, it counted double. But the old woman had not listened, anyway; she was rocking and watching the other one, who watched back from the bed.

120 'Poor Addie is ailing. She has to take medicine – see?' she said, pointing a horny finger at a row of bottles on the table, and rocking so high that her black comfort shoes lifted off the floor like a little child's.

'I am no more sick than you are,' said the woman in bed.

'Oh yes you are!'

'I just got more sense than you have, that's all,' said the other old woman, nodding her head.

'That's only the contrary way she talks when *you all* come,' said the first old lady with sudden intimacy. She stopped the rocker with a neat pat of her feet and leaned toward Marian. Her hand reached over – it felt
130 like a petunia leaf, clinging and just a little sticky.

'Will you hush! Will you hush!' cried the other one.

Marian leaned back rigidly in her chair.

'When I was a little girl like you, I went to school and all,' said the old woman in the same intimate, menacing voice. 'Not here – another town. . . . '

'Hush!' said the sick woman. 'You never went to school. You never came and you never went. You never were anywhere – only here. You never were born! You don't know anything. Your head is empty, your heart and hands and your old black purse are all empty, even that little
140 old box that you brought with you you brought empty – you showed it to me. And yet you talk, talk, talk, talk, talk all the time until I think I'm losing my mind! Who are you? You're a stranger – a perfect stranger! Don't you know you're a stranger? Is it possible that they have actually done a thing like this to anyone – sent them in a stranger to talk, and rock, and tell away her whole long rigmarole?[9] Do they seriously suppose that I'll be able to keep it up, day in, day out, night in, night out, living in the same room with a terrible old woman – forever?'

Marian saw the old woman's eyes grow bright and turn toward her. This old woman was looking at her with despair and calculation in her
150 face. Her small lips suddenly dropped apart, and exposed a half circle of false teeth with tan gums.

'Come here, I want to tell you something,' she whispered. 'Come here!'

---

[9] *rigmarole* – nonsense

Marian was trembling, and her heart nearly stopped beating altogether for a moment.

'Now, now, Addie,' said the first old woman. 'That's not polite. Do you know what's really the matter with old Addie today?' She, too, looked at Marian; one of her eyelids drooped low.

'The matter?' the child repeated stupidly. 'What's the matter with her?'                                                                                      160

'Why, she's mad because it's her birthday!' said the first old woman, beginning to rock again and giving a little crow as though she had answered her own riddle.

'It is not, it is not!' screamed the old woman in bed. 'It is not my birthday, no one knows when that is but myself, and will you please be quiet and say nothing more, or I'll go straight out of my mind!' She turned her eyes toward Marian again, and presently she said in the soft, foggy voice, 'When the worst comes to the worst, I ring this bell, and the nurse comes.' One of her hands was drawn out from under the patched counterpane – a thin little hand with enormous black freckles. With a    170
finger which would not hold still she pointed to a little bell on the table among the bottles.

'How old are you?' Marian breathed. Now she could see the old woman in bed very closely and plainly, and very abruptly, from all sides, as in dreams. She wondered about her – she wondered for a moment as though there was nothing else in the world to wonder about. It was the first time such a thing had happened to Marian.

'I won't tell!'

The old face on the pillow, where Marian was bending over it, slowly gathered and collapsed. Soft whimpers came out of the small open    180
mouth. It was a sheep that she sounded like – a little lamb. Marian's face drew very close, the yellow hair hung forward.

'She's crying!' she turned a bright, burning face up to the first old woman.

'That's Addie for you,' the old woman said spitefully.

Marian jumped up and moved toward the door. For the second time, the claw almost touched her hair, but it was not quick enough. The little girl put her cap on.

'Well, it was a real visit,' said the old woman, following Marian through the doorway and all the way out into the hall. Then from behind    190
she suddenly clutched the child with her sharp little fingers. In an affected, high-pitched whine she cried, 'Oh, little girl, have you a penny to spare for a poor old woman that's not got anything of her own? We don't have a thing in the world – not a penny for candy – not a thing! Little girl, just a nickel – a penny—'

Marian pulled violently against the old hands for a moment before she was free. Then she ran down the hall, without looking behind her and without looking at the nurse, who was reading *Field & Stream* at her desk. The nurse, after another triple motion to consult her wrist watch, asked automatically the question put to visitors in all institutions: 'Won't you stay and have dinner with *us?*'

Marian never replied. She pushed the heavy door open into the cold air and ran down the steps.

Under the prickly shrub she stooped and quickly, without being seen, retrieved a red apple she had hidden there.

Her yellow hair under the white cap, her scarlet coat, her bare knees all flashed in the sunlight as she ran to meet the big bus rocketing through the street.

'Wait for me!' she shouted. As though at an imperial command, the bus ground to a stop.

She jumped on and took a big bite out of the apple.

# Castles in the Air

## The Poor Relation's Story

*Charles Dickens*

He was very reluctant to take precedence[1] of so many respected members of the family, by beginning the round of stories they were to relate as they sat in a goodly circle by the Christmas fire; and he modestly suggested that it would be more correct if 'John our esteemed host' (whose health he begged to drink) would have the kindness to begin. For as to himself, he said, he was so little used to lead the way that really— But as they all cried out here, that he must begin, and agreed with one voice that he might, could, would, and should begin, he left off rubbing his hands, and took his legs out from under his arm-chair, and did begin.

I have no doubt (said the poor relation) that I shall surprise the assem- 10 bled members of our family, and particularly John our esteemed host to whom we are so much indebted for the great hospitality with which he has this day entertained us, by the confession I am going to make. But, if you do me the honour to be surprised at anything that falls from a person so unimportant in the family as I am, I can only say that I shall be scrupu- lously accurate in all I relate.

I am not what I am supposed to be. I am quite another thing. Perhaps before I go further, I had better glance at what I *am* supposed to be.

It is supposed, unless I mistake – the assembled members of our family will correct me if I do, which is very likely (here the poor relation looked 20 mildly about him for contradiction); that I am nobody's enemy but my own. That I never met with any particular success in anything. That I failed in business because I was unbusiness-like and credulous[2] – in not being prepared for the interested designs[3] of my partner. That I failed in love, because I was ridiculously trustful – in thinking it impossible that Christiana could deceive me. That I failed in my expectations[4] from my uncle Chill, on account of not being as sharp as he could have wished in worldly matters. That, through life, I have been rather put upon and disappointed in a general way. That I am at present a bachelor of between fifty-nine and sixty years of age, living on a limited income in the form of 30

[1] *take precedence* – to go first
[2] *credulous* – too ready to believe and trust others
[3] *interested designs* – selfish plans
[4] *my expectations* – what he expected to inherit when his uncle died

15

a quarterly allowance,[5] to which I see that John our esteemed host wishes me to make no further allusion.

The supposition as to my present pursuits and habits is to the following effect.

I live in a lodging in the Clapham Road – a very clean back room, in a very respectable house – where I am expected not to be at home in the day-time, unless poorly; and which I usually leave in the morning at nine o'clock, on pretence of going to business. I take my breakfast – my roll and butter, and my half-pint of coffee – at the old-established coffee shop
40   near Westminster Bridge; and then I go into the City – I don't know why – and sit in Garraway's Coffee House, and on 'Change,[6] and walk about, and look into a few offices and counting-houses[7] where some of my relations or acquaintances are so good as to tolerate me, and where I stand by the fire if the weather happens to be cold. I get through the day in this way until five o'clock, and then I dine: at a cost, on the average, of one and threepence. Having still a little money to spend on my evening's entertainment, I look into the old-established coffee shop as I go home, and take my cup of tea, and perhaps my bit of toast. So, as the large hand of the clock makes its way round to the morning hour again, I make my
50   way round to the Clapham Road again, and go to bed when I get to my lodging – fire being expensive, and being objected to by the family[8] on account of its giving trouble and making a dirt.

Sometimes, one of my relations or acquaintances is so obliging as to ask me to dinner. Those are holiday occasions, and then I generally walk in the Park. I am a solitary man, and seldom walk with anybody. Not that I am avoided because I am shabby; for I am not at all shabby, having always a very good suit of black on (or rather Oxford mixture,[9] which has the appearance of black and wears[10] much better); but I have got into a habit of speaking low, being rather silent, and my spirits are not high,
60   and I am sensible[11] that I am not an attractive companion.

The only exception to this general rule is the child of my first cousin, Little Frank. I have a particular affection for that child, and he takes very kindly to me. He is a diffident boy by nature; and in a crowd he is soon run over, as I may say, and forgotten. He and I, however, get on exceedingly well. I have a fancy that the poor child will in time succeed to[12] my

---

5  *quarterly allowance* – a sum of money given four times a year
6  *'Change* – The Stock Exchange
7  *counting-house* – an accounts office
8  *the family* – the family with whom he lodges
9  *Oxford mixture* – a dark grey woollen cloth
10  *wears* – lasts
11  *I am sensible* – I realize
12  *succeed to* – inherit

peculiar position in the family. We talk but little; still, we understand each other. We walk about, hand in hand; and without much speaking he knows what I mean, and I know what he means. When he was very little indeed, I used to take him to the windows of the toy-shops, and show him the toys inside. It is surprising how soon he found out that I would 70 have made him a great many presents if I had been in circumstances to do it.

Little Frank and I go and look at the outside of the Monument[13] – he is very fond of the Monument – and at the Bridges, and at all the sights that are free. On two of my birthdays, we have dined on à-la-mode beef,[14] and gone at half-price to the play, and been deeply interested. I was once walking with him in Lombard Street, which we often visit on account of my having mentioned to him that there are great riches there – he is very fond of Lombard Street – when a gentleman said to me as he passed by, "Sir, your little son has dropped his glove." I assure you, if you will 80 excuse my remarking on so trivial a circumstance, this accidental mention of the child as mine, quite touched my heart and brought the foolish tears into my eyes.

When Little Frank is sent to school in the country,[15] I shall be very much at a loss what to do with myself, but I have the intention of walking down there once a month and seeing him on a half holiday.[16] I am told he will then be at play upon the Heath; and if my visits should be objected to, as unsettling the child, I can see him from a distance without his seeing me, and walk back again. His mother comes of a highly genteel[17] family, and rather disapproves, I am aware, of our being too much 90 together. I know that I am not calculated to improve his retiring disposition;[18] but I think he would miss me beyond the feeling of the moment if we were wholly separated.

When I die in the Clapham Road, I shall not leave much more in this world than I shall take out of it; but, I happen to have a miniature[19] of a bright-faced boy, with a curling head, and an open shirt-frill waving down his bosom (my mother had it taken for me, but I can't believe that it was ever like), which will be worth nothing to sell, and which I shall beg may be given to Frank. I have written my dear boy a little letter with it, in which I have told him that I felt very sorry to part from him, though 100 bound to confess that I knew no reason why I should remain here. I have

---

[13] *the Monument* – a memorial column in the City of London
[14] *à-la-mode beef* – a cheap cut of beef
[15] *school in the country* – Frank will be sent to boarding school outside London
[16] *a half holiday* – a free half-day
[17] *genteel* – upper class and refined
[18] *retiring disposition* – shy nature
[19] *a miniature* – a small painting of a person's head and shoulders

given him some short advice, the best in my power, to take warning of the consequences of being nobody's enemy but his own; and I have endeavoured to comfort him for what I fear he will consider a bereavement, by pointing out to him, that I was only a superfluous something to every one but him; and that having by some means failed to find a place in this great assembly,[20] I am better out of it.

Such (said the poor relation, clearing his throat and beginning to speak a little louder) is the general impression about me. Now, it is a remark-
110 able circumstance which forms the aim and purpose of my story, that this is all wrong. This is not my life, and these are not my habits. I do not even live in the Clapham Road. Comparatively speaking, I am very seldom there. I reside, mostly, in a – I am almost ashamed to say the word, it sounds so full of pretension[21] – in a Castle. I do not mean that it is an old baronial habitation,[22] but still it is a building always known to every one by the name of a Castle. In it, I preserve the particulars of my history; they run thus:

It was when I first took John Spatter (who had been my clerk) into partnership, and when I was still a young man of not more than five-and-
120 twenty, residing in the house of my uncle Chill, from whom I had considerable expectations, that I ventured to propose to Christiana. I had loved Christiana a long time. She was very beautiful, and very winning in all respects. I rather mistrusted her widowed mother, who I feared was of a plotting and mercenary[23] turn of mind; but, I thought as well of her as I could, for Christiana's sake. I never had loved any one but Christiana, and she had been all the world, and O far more than all the world, to me, from our childhood!

Christiana accepted me with her mother's consent, and I was rendered very happy indeed. My life at my uncle Chill's was of a spare dull kind,
130 and my garret chamber[24] was as dull, and bare, and cold, as an upper prison room in some stern northern fortress. But, having Christiana's love, I wanted nothing upon earth. I would not have changed my lot with any human being.

Avarice was, unhappily, my uncle Chill's master-vice. Though he was rich, he pinched, and scraped, and clutched, and lived miserably. As Christiana had no fortune, I was for some time a little fearful of confessing our engagement to him; but, at length I wrote him a letter, saying how it all truly was. I put it into his hand one night, on going to bed.

As I came down-stairs next morning, shivering in the cold December

---

[20] *great assembly* – the world

[21] *full of pretension* – full of own importance

[22] *baronial habitation* – a house fit for a baron or lord

[23] *mercenary* – interested only in getting money

[24] *garret chamber* – attic bedroom

air; colder in my uncle's unwarmed house than in the street, where the  140
winter sun did sometimes shine, and which was at all events enlivened by
cheerful faces and voices passing along; I carried a heavy heart towards
the long, low breakfast-room in which my uncle sat. It was a large room
with a small fire, and there was a great bay window in it which the rain
had marked in the night as if with the tears of houseless people. It stared
upon a raw yard, with a cracked stone pavement, and some rusted iron
railings half uprooted, whence an ugly out-building that had once been a
dissecting room (in the time of the great surgeon who had mortgaged the
house to my uncle), stared at it.

We rose so early always, that at that time of the year we breakfasted by  150
candle-light. When I went into the room, my uncle was so contracted by
the cold, and so huddled together in his chair behind the one dim candle,
that I did not see him until I was close to the table.

As I held out my hand to him, he caught up his stick (being infirm, he
always walked about the house with a stick), and made a blow at me, and
said, 'You fool!'

'Uncle,' I returned, 'I didn't expect you to be so angry as this.' Nor
had I expected it, though he was a hard and angry old man.

'You didn't expect!' said he; 'when did you ever expect? When did you
ever calculate, or look forward, you contemptible dog?'  160

'These are hard words, uncle!'

'Hard words? Feathers, to pelt such an idiot as you with,' said he.
'Here! Betsy Snap! Look at him!'

Betsy Snap was a withered, hard-favoured, yellow old woman – our
only domestic[25] – always employed, at this time of the morning, in
rubbing my uncle's legs. As my uncle adjured her to look at me, he put
his lean grip on the crown of her head, she kneeling beside him, and
turned her face towards me. An involuntary thought connecting them
both with the Dissecting Room, as it must often have been in the
surgeon's time, passed across my mind in the midst of my anxiety.  170

'Look at the snivelling milksop!' said my uncle. 'Look at the baby!
This is the gentleman who, people say, is nobody's enemy but his own.
This is the gentleman who can't say no. This is the gentleman who was
making such large profits in his business that he must needs take a
partner, t'other day. This is the gentleman who is going to marry a wife
without a penny, and who falls into the hands of Jezabels[26] who are spec-
ulating on my death!'

I knew, now, how great my uncle's rage was; for nothing short of his
being almost beside himself would have induced him to utter that

---

[25] *domestic* – a house servant

[26] *Jezabels* – wicked women (after a character in the Bible)

19

180 concluding word, which he held in such repugnance that it was never spoken or hinted at before him on any account.

'On my death,' he repeated, as if he were defying me by defying his own abhorrence of the word. 'On my death – death – Death! But I'll spoil the speculation. Eat your last under this roof, you feeble wretch, and may it choke you!' You may suppose that I had not much appetite for the breakfast to which I was bidden in these terms; but, I took my accustomed seat. I saw that I was repudiated[27] henceforth by my uncle; still I could bear that very well, possessing Christiana's heart.

He emptied his basin of bread and milk as usual, only that he took it on
190 his knees with his chair turned away from the table where I sat. When he had done, he carefully snuffed out the candle; and the cold, slate-coloured, miserable day looked in upon us.

'Now, Mr. Michael,' said he, 'before we part, I should like to have a word with these ladies in your presence.'

'As you will, sir,' I returned; 'but you deceive yourself, and wrong us cruelly, if you suppose that there is any feeling at stake in this contract but pure, disinterested, faithful love.'

To this, he only replied, 'You lie!' and not one other word.

We went, through half-thawed snow and half-frozen rain, to the house
200 where Christiana and her mother lived. My uncle knew them very well. They were sitting at their breakfast, and were surprised to see us at that hour.

'Your servant, ma'am,' said my uncle to the mother. 'You divine[28] the purpose of my visit, I dare say, ma'am. I understand there is a world of pure, disinterested, faithful love cooped up here. I am happy to bring it all it wants, to make it complete. I bring you your son-in-law, ma'am – and you, your husband, miss. The gentleman is a perfect stranger to me, but I wish him joy of his wise bargain.'

He snarled at me as he went out, and I never saw him again.
210

It is altogether a mistake (continued the poor relation) to suppose that my dear Christiana, over-persuaded and influenced by her mother, married a rich man, the dirt from whose carriage wheels is often, in these changed times, thrown upon me as she rides by. No, no. She married me.

The way we came to be married rather sooner than we intended, was this. I took a frugal lodging and was saving and planning for her sake, when, one day, she spoke to me with great earnestness, and said:

'My dear Michael, I have given you my heart. I have said that I loved you, and I have pledged myself to be your wife. I am as much yours

---

[27] *repudiated* – disowned

[28] *divine* – guess

through all changes of good and evil as if we had been married on the day 220
when such word passed between us. I know you well, and know that if we
should be separated and our union broken off, your whole life would be
shadowed, and all that might, even now, be stronger in your character for
the conflict with the world would then be weakened to the shadow of
what it is!'

'God help me, Christiana!' said I. 'You speak the truth.'

'Michael,' said she, putting her hand in mine, in all maidenly devo-
tion, 'let us keep apart no longer. It is but for me to say that I can live
contented upon such means as you have, and I well know you are happy.
I say so from my heart. Strive no more alone; let us strive together. My 230
dear Michael, it is not right that I should keep secret from you what you
do not suspect, but what distresses my whole life. My mother: without
considering that what you have lost, you have lost for me, and on the
assurance[29] of my faith: sets her heart on riches, and urges another suit[30]
upon me, to my misery. I cannot bear this, for to bear it is to be untrue to
you. I would rather share your struggles than look on. I want no better
home than you can give me. I know that you will aspire[31] and labour with
a higher courage if I am wholly yours, and let it be so when you will!'

I was blest indeed, that day, and a new world opened to me. We were
married in a very little while, and I took my wife to our happy home. 240
That was the beginning of the residence I have spoken of; the Castle we
have ever since inhabited together, dates from that time. All our children
have been born in it. Our first child – now married – was a little girl,
whom we called Christiana. Her son is so like Little Frank, that I hardly
know which is which.

The current impression as to my partner's dealings with me is also quite
erroneous. He did not begin to treat me coldly, as a poor simpleton, when
my uncle and I so fatally quarrelled; nor did he afterwards gradually
possess himself of our business and edge me out. On the contrary, he 250
behaved to me with the utmost good faith and honour.

Matters between us took this turn:— On the day of my separation
from my uncle, and even before the arrival at our counting-house of my
trunks (which he sent after me, *not* carriage paid), I went down to our
room of business, on our little wharf,[32] overlooking the river; and there I
told John Spatter what had happened. John did not say, in reply, that
rich old relatives were palpable facts, and that love and sentiment were
moonshine and fiction. He addressed me thus:

[29] *on the assurance of* – because you trust in

[30] *urges another suit* – tries to persuade me to marry someone else

[31] *aspire* – be ambitious

[32] *wharf* – area by the river for loading ships

'Michael,' said John, 'we were at school together, and I generally had the knack of getting on better than you, and making a higher reputation.'

'You had, John,' I returned.

'Although,' said John, 'I borrowed your books and lost them; borrowed your pocket-money, and never repaid it; got you to buy my damaged knives at a higher price than I had given for them new; and to own[33] to the windows that I had broken.'

'All not worth mentioning, John Spatter,' said I, 'but certainly true.'

'When you were first established in this infant business, which promises to thrive so well,' pursued John, 'I came to you, in my search, for almost any employment, and you made me your clerk.'

'Still not worth mentioning, my dear John Spatter,' said I; 'still, equally true.'

'And finding that I had a good head for business, and that I was really useful *to* the business, you did not like to retain me in that capacity, and thought it an act of justice soon to make me your partner.'

'Still less worth mentioning than any of those other little circumstances you have recalled, John Spatter,' said I; 'for I was, and am, sensible of your merits and my deficiencies.'

'Now, my good friend,' said John, drawing my arm through his, as he had had a habit of doing at school; while two vessels outside the windows of our counting-house – which were shaped like the stern windows of a ship – went lightly down the river with the tide, as John and I might then be sailing away in company, and in trust and confidence, on our voyage of life; 'let there, under these friendly circumstances, be a right understanding between us. You are too easy, Michael. You are nobody's enemy but your own. If I were to give you that damaging character among our connexion,[34] with a shrug, and a shake of the head, and a sigh; and if I were further to abuse the trust you place in me—'

'But you will never abuse it at all, John,' I observed.

'Never!' said he; 'but I am putting a case – I say, and if I were further to abuse that trust by keeping this piece of our common affairs in the dark, and this other piece in the light, and again this other piece in the twilight, and so on, I should strengthen my strength, and weaken your weakness, day by day, until at last I found myself on the high road to fortune, and you left behind on some bare common, a hopeless number of miles out of the way.'

'Exactly so,' said I.

'To prevent this, Michael,' said John Spatter, 'or the remotest chance

[33] *own* – own up to

[34] *connexion* – (old-fashioned spelling) connections: people they know and with whom they do business

of this, there must be perfect openness between us. Nothing must be concealed, and we must have but one interest.' 300

'My dear John Spatter,' I assured him, 'that is precisely what I mean.'

'And when you are too easy,' pursued John, his face glowing with friendship, 'you must allow me to prevent that imperfection in your nature from being taken advantage of, by any one; you must not expect me to humour it—'

'My dear John Spatter,' I interrupted, 'I *don't* expect you to humour it. I want to correct it.'

'And I, too,' said John.

'Exactly so!' cried I. 'We both have the same end in view; and, honourably seeking it, and fully trusting one another, and having but one 310 interest, ours will be a prosperous and happy partnership.'

'I am sure of it!' returned John Spatter. And we shook hands most affectionately.

I took John home to my Castle, and we had a very happy day. Our partnership throve[35] well. My friend and partner supplied what I wanted, as I had foreseen that he would; and by improving both the business and myself, amply acknowledged any little rise in life to which I had helped him.

I am not (said the poor relation, looking at the fire as he slowly rubbed his 320 hands) very rich, for I never cared to be that; but I have enough, and am above all moderate wants and anxieties. My Castle is not a splendid place, but it is very comfortable, and it has a warm and cheerful air, and is quite a picture of Home.

Our eldest girl, who is very like her mother, married John Spatter's eldest son. Our two families are closely united in other ties of attachment. It is very pleasant of an evening, when we are all assembled together – which frequently happens – and when John and I talk over old times, and the one interest there has always been between us.

I really do not know, in my Castle, what loneliness is. Some of our 330 children or grandchildren are always about it, and the young voices of my descendants are delightful – O, how delightful! – to me to hear. My dearest and most devoted wife, ever faithful, ever loving, ever helpful and sustaining and consoling, is the priceless blessing of my house; from whom all its other blessings spring. We are rather a musical family, and when Christiana sees me, at any time, a little weary or depressed, she steals to the piano and sings a gentle air[36] she used to sing when we were first betrothed. So weak a man am I, that I cannot bear to hear it from any

---

[35] *throve* – was successful

[36] *air* – song

340 other source. They played it once, at the Theatre, when I was there with Little Frank; and the child said wondering, 'Cousin Michael, whose hot tears are these that have fallen on my hand!'

Such is my Castle, and such are the real particulars of my life therein preserved. I often take Little Frank home there. He is very welcome to my grandchildren, and they play together. At this time of the year – the Christmas and New Year time – I am seldom out of my Castle. For, the associations of the season seem to hold me there, and the precepts[37] of the season seem to teach me that it is well to be there.

'And the Castle is—' observed a grave, kind voice among the company.

350 'Yes. My Castle,' said the poor relation, shaking his head as he still looked at the fire, 'is in the Air. John our esteemed host suggests its situation accurately. My Castle is in the Air! I have done. Will you be so good as to pass the story ?'

[37] *precepts* – commands; the rules

# The Secret Life of Walter Mitty

*James Thurber*

'We're going through!' The Commander's voice was like thin ice breaking. He wore his full-dress uniform, with the heavily braided white cap pulled down rakishly[1] over one cold grey eye. 'We can't make it, sir. It's spoiling for a hurricane, if you ask me.' 'I'm not asking you, Lieutenant Berg,' said the Commander. 'Throw on the power lights! Rev her up to 8,500! We're going through!' The pounding of the cylinders increased: ta-pocketa-pocketa-pocketa-*pocketa-pocketa*. The Commander stared at the ice forming on the pilot window. He walked over and twisted a row of complicated dials. 'Switch on No. 8 auxiliary!' he shouted. 'Switch on No. 8 auxiliary!' repeated Lieutenant Berg. 'Full strength in No. 3 turret!' shouted the Commander. 'Full strength in No. 3 turret!' The crew, bending to their various tasks in the huge, hurtling eight-engined Navy hydroplane[2] looked at each other and grinned. 'The Old Man'll get us through,' they said to one another. 'The Old Man ain't afraid of Hell!' . . .

'Not so fast! You're driving too fast!' said Mrs Mitty. 'What are you driving so fast for?'

'Hmm?' said Walter Mitty. He looked at his wife, in the seat beside him, with shocked astonishment. She seemed grossly unfamiliar, like a strange woman who had yelled at him in a crowd. 'You were up to fifty-five,' she said. 'You know I don't like to go more than forty. You were up to fifty-five.' Walter Mitty drove on toward Waterbury in silence, the roaring of the SN202 through the worst storm in twenty years of Navy flying fading in the remote, intimate airways of his mind. 'You're tensed up again,' said Mrs Mitty. 'It's one of your days. I wish you'd let Dr Renshaw look you over.'

Walter Mitty stopped the car in front of the building where his wife went to have her hair done. 'Remember to get those overshoes while I'm having my hair done,' she said. 'I don't need overshoes,' said Mitty. She put her mirror back into her bag. 'We've been all through that,' she said, getting out of the car. 'You're not a young man any longer.' He raced the engine a little. 'Why don't you wear your gloves? Have you lost your gloves?' Walter Mitty reached in a pocket and brought out the gloves. He put them on, but after she had turned and gone into the building and he

[1] *rakishly* – like a rake, a confident and immoral society man
[2] *hydroplane* – a boat that raises itself on underwater wings to race along the water's surface. Mitty mistakenly uses the word to mean a Navy plane

25

had driven on to a red light, he took them off again. 'Pick it up, brother!' snapped a cop as the light changed, and Mitty hastily pulled on his gloves and lurched ahead. He drove around the streets aimlessly for a time, and then he drove past the hospital on his way to the parking lot.

40     ... 'It's the millionaire banker, Wellington McMillan,' said the pretty nurse. 'Yes?' said Walter Mitty, removing his gloves slowly. 'Who has the case?' 'Dr Renshaw and Dr Benbow, but there are two specialists here, Dr Remington from New York and Mr Pritchard-Mitford from London. He flew over.' A door opened down a long, cool corridor and Dr Renshaw came out. He looked distraught and haggard. 'Hello, Mitty,' he said. 'We're having the devil's own time with McMillan, the millionaire banker and close personal friend of Roosevelt. Obstreosis of the ductal tract. Tertiary.[3] Wish you'd take a look at him.' 'Glad to,' said Mitty.

In the operating room there were whispered introductions: 'Dr Remington, Dr Mitty. Mr Pritchard-Mitford, Dr Mitty.' ' I've read your
50 book on streptothricosis,' said Pritchard-Mitford, shaking hands. 'A brilliant performance, sir.' 'Thank you,' said Walter Mitty. 'Didn't know you were in the States, Mitty,' grumbled Remington. 'Coals to Newcastle,[4] bringing Mitford and me up here for a tertiary.' 'You are very kind,' said Mitty. A huge, complicated machine, connected to the operating table with many tubes and wires, began at this moment to go pocketa-pocketa-pocketa. 'The new anaesthetizer is giving way!' shouted an interne.[5] 'There is no one in the East who knows how to fix it!' 'Quiet, man!' said Mitty, in a low, cool voice. He sprang to the machine, which was now going pocketa-pocketa-queep-pocketa-queep. He began
60 fingering delicately a row of glistening dials. 'Give me a fountain pen!' he snapped. Someone handed him a fountain pen. He pulled a faulty piston out of the machine and inserted the pen in its place. 'That will hold for ten minutes,' he said. 'Get on with the operation.' A nurse hurried over and whispered to Renshaw, and Mitty saw the man turn pale. 'Coreopsis has set in,' said Renshaw nervously. 'If you would take over, Mitty?' Mitty looked at him and at the craven[6] figure of Benbow, who drank, and at the grave, uncertain faces of the two great specialists. 'If you wish,' he said. They slipped a white gown on him; he adjusted a mask and drew on thin gloves; nurses handed him shining ...

70     'Back it up, Mac! Look out for that Buick!'[7] Walter Mitty jammed on

---

[3] *Obstreosis of the ductal tract. Tertiary* – An invented medical condition, a mixture of made up words and real ones. Many of Mitty's day-dreams contain these inventions

[4] *Coals to Newcastle* – (a saying) Remington feels that he and Pritchard-Mitford are unnecessary as Mitty is present

[5] *interne* – (American) an assistant surgeon

[6] *craven* – cowardly

[7] *Buick* – an American car

the brakes. 'Wrong lane, Mac,' said the parking-lot attendant, looking at Mitty closely. 'Gee. Yeh,' muttered Mitty. He began cautiously to back out of the lane marked 'Exit Only'. 'Leave her sit there,' said the attendant. 'I'll put her away.' Mitty got out of the car. 'Hey, better leave the key.' 'Oh,' said Mitty, handing the man the ignition key. The attendant vaulted into the car, backed it up with insolent skill, and put it where it belonged.

They're so damn cocky, thought Walter Mitty, walking along Main Street; they think they know everything. Once he had tried to take his chains[8] off, outside New Milford, and he had got them wound around the axles. A man had had to come out in a wrecking car and unwind them, a young, grinning garageman. Since then Mrs Mitty always made him drive to a garage to have the chains taken off. The next time, he thought, I'll wear my right arm in a sling; they won't grin at me then. I'll have my right arm in a sling and they'll see I couldn't possibly take the chains off myself. He kicked at the slush on the sidewalk. 'Overshoes,' he said to himself, and he began looking for a shoe store.

When he came out into the street again, with the overshoes in a box under his arm, Walter Mitty began to wonder what the other thing was his wife had told him to get. She had told him twice, before they set out from their house for Waterbury. In a way he hated these weekly trips to town – he was always getting something wrong. Kleenex, he thought, Squibb's, razor blades? No. Toothpaste, toothbrush, bicarbonate, carborundum, initiative and referendum?[9] He gave it up. But she would remember it. 'Where's the what's-its-name?' she would ask. 'Don't tell me you forgot the what's-its-name.' A newsboy went by shouting something about the Waterbury trial.

. . . 'Perhaps this will refresh your memory.' The District Attorney suddenly thrust a heavy automatic at the quiet figure on the witness stand. 'Have you ever seen this before?' Walter Mitty took the gun and examined it expertly. 'This is my Webley-Vickers 50.80,'[10] he said calmly. An excited buzz ran around the courtroom. The judge rapped for order. 'You are a crack shot with any sort of firearms, I believe?' said the District Attorney, insinuatingly.[11] 'Objection!' shouted Mitty's attorney. 'We have shown that the defendant could not have fired the shot. We have shown that he wore his right arm in a sling on the night of the fourteenth of July.' Walter Mitty raised his hand briefly and the bickering attorneys were stilled. 'With any known make of gun,' he said evenly, 'I

---

[8] *chains* – chains to put on tyres to help them run on snow-covered roads

[9] *carborundum, initiative and referendum* – nonsense or irrelevant words that spring into Mitty's mind as he tries to remember what he has to buy

[10] *Webley-Vickers 50.80* – another invention, this time a gun

[11] *insinuatingly* – cunningly, wheedlingly

could have killed Gregory Fitzhurst at three hundred feet *with my left*
110 *hand.*' Pandemonium broke loose in the courtroom. A woman's scream
rose above the bedlam and suddenly a lovely, dark-haired girl was in
Walter Mitty's arms. The District Attorney struck at her savagely.
Without rising from his chair, Mitty let the man have it on the point of
the chin. 'You miserable cur!'[12] . . .

'Puppy biscuit,' said Walter Mitty. He stopped walking and the build-
ings of Waterbury rose up out of the misty courtroom and surrounded
him again. A woman who was passing laughed. 'He said "Puppy
biscuit",' she said to her companion. 'That man said "Puppy biscuit" to
himself.' Walter Mitty hurried on. He went into an A. & P.,[13] not the first
120 one he came to but a smaller one farther up the street. 'I want some
biscuit for small, young dogs,' he said to the clerk. 'Any special brand,
sir?' The greatest pistol shot in the world thought a moment. 'It says
"Puppies Bark for It" on the box,' said Walter Mitty.

His wife would be through at the hairdresser's in fifteen minutes, Mitty
saw in looking at his watch, unless they had trouble drying it; sometimes
they had trouble drying it. She didn't like to get to the hotel first; she
would want him to be there waiting for her as usual. He found a big
leather chair in the lobby, facing a window, and he put the overshoes and
130 the puppy biscuit on the floor beside it. He picked up an old copy of
*Liberty* and sank down into the chair. 'Can Germany Conquer the World
Through the Air?' Walter Mitty looked at the pictures of bombing planes
and of ruined streets.

. . . 'The cannonading has got the wind up in young Raleigh, sir,' said
the sergeant. Captain Mitty looked up at him through tousled[14] hair. 'Get
him to bed,' he said wearily. 'With the others. I'll fly alone.' 'But you
can't, sir,' said the sergeant anxiously. 'It takes two men to handle that
bomber and the Archies are pounding hell out of the air. Von Richtman's
circus[15] is between here and Saulier.' 'Somebody's got to get that ammu-
140 nition dump,' said Mitty. 'I'm going over. Spot of brandy?' He poured a
drink for the sergeant and one for himself. War thundered and whined
around the dugout and battered at the door. There was a rending of wood
and splinters flew through the room. 'A bit of a near thing,' said Captain
Mitty carelessly. 'The box barrage is closing in,' said the sergeant. 'We
only live once, Sergeant,' said Mitty, with his faint, fleeting smile. 'Or do
we?' He poured another brandy and tossed it off. 'I never see a man could
hold his brandy like you, sir,' said the sergeant. 'Begging your pardon,

[12] *cur* – a low-bred bad-tempered dog
[13] *A. & P.* – a general groceries shop
50 [14] *tousled* – uncombed, messy hair
[15] *circus* – (slang) a term referring to the enemy's air force

28

sir.' Captain Mitty stood up and strapped on his huge Webley-Vickers automatic. 'It's forty kilometres through hell, sir,' said the sergeant. Mitty finished one last brandy. 'After all,' he said softly, 'what isn't?' 150 The pounding of the cannon increased; there was the rat-tat-tatting of machine guns, and from somewhere came the menacing pocketa-pocketa-pocketa of the new flamethrowers. Walter Mitty walked to the door of the dugout humming 'Auprès de Ma Blonde'. He turned and waved to the sergeant. 'Cheerio! ' he said . . .

Something struck his shoulder. 'I've been looking all over this hotel for you,' said Mrs Mitty. 'Why do you have to hide in this old chair? How did you expect me to find you?' 'Things close in,' said Walter Mitty, vaguely. 'What?' Mrs Mitty said. 'Did you get the what's-its-name? The puppy biscuit? What's in that box?' 'Overshoes,' said Mitty. 'Couldn't 160 you have put them on in the store?' 'I was thinking,' said Walter Mitty. 'Does it ever occur to you that I am sometimes thinking?' She looked at him. 'I'm going to take your temperature when I get you home,' she said.

They went out through the revolving doors that made a faintly derisive[16] whistling sound when you pushed them. It was two blocks to the parking lot. At the drugstore on the corner she said, 'Wait here for me. I forgot something. I won't be a minute.' She was more than a minute. Walter Mitty lighted a cigarette. It began to rain, rain with sleet in it. He stood up against the wall of the drugstore, smoking . . . He put his shoulders back and his heels together. 'To hell with the handkerchief,' 170 said Walter Mitty scornfully. He took one last drag on his cigarette and snapped it away. Then, with that faint, fleeting smile playing about his lips, he faced the firing squad; erect and motionless, proud and disdainful,[17] Walter Mitty the Undefeated, inscrutable[18] to the last.

[16] *derisive* – mocking
[17] *disdainful* – proud and uncaring
[18] *inscrutable* – mysterious

29

# Hero Worship

# The Sexton's Hero

*Elizabeth Gaskell*

The afternoon sun shed down his glorious rays on the grassy churchyard, making the shadow, cast by the old yew-tree under which we sat, seem deeper and deeper by contrast. The everlasting hum of myriads of summer insects made luxurious lullaby.

Of the view that lay beneath our gaze, I cannot speak adequately. The foreground was the grey-stone wall of the vicarage garden; rich in the colouring made by innumerable lichens, ferns, ivy of most tender green and most delicate tracery, and the vivid scarlet of the crane's-bill, which found a home in every nook and crevice – and at the summit of that old
10    wall flaunted some unpruned tendrils of the vine, and long flower-laden branches of the climbing rose-tree, trained against the inner side. Beyond, lay meadow green and mountain grey, and the blue dazzle of Morecambe Bay, as it sparkled between us and the more distant view.

For a while we were silent, living in sight and murmuring sound. Then Jeremy took up our conversation where, suddenly feeling weariness, as we saw that deep green shadowy resting-place, we had ceased speaking a quarter of an hour before.

It is one of the luxuries of holiday-time that thoughts are not rudely shaken from us by outward violence of hurry and busy impatience, but
20    fall maturely from our lips in the sunny leisure of our days. The stock[1] may be bad, but the fruit is ripe.

'How would you then define a hero?' I asked.

There was a long pause, and I had almost forgotten my question in watching a cloud-shadow floating over the faraway hills, when Jeremy made answer—

'My idea of a hero is one who acts up to the highest idea of duty he has been able to form,[2] no matter at what sacrifice. I think that by this defini-tion, we may include all phases of character, even to the heroes of old, whose sole[3] (and to us, low) idea of duty consisted in personal prowess.'[4]
30    'Then you would even admit the military heroes? ' asked I.

[1] *stock* – the parent plant
[2] *form* – imagine
[3] *sole* – only
[4] *prowess* – acts of daring and bravery

30

'I would; with a certain kind of pity for the circumstances which had given them no higher ideas of duty. Still, if they sacrificed self to do what they sincerely believed to be right, I do not think I could deny them the title of hero.'

'A poor, unchristian heroism, whose manifestation consists in injury to others!' I said.

We were both startled by a third voice.

'If I might make so bold, sir' – and then the speaker stopped.

It was the Sexton,[5] whom, when we first arrived, we had noticed, as an accessory to the scene, but whom we had forgotten, as much as though he were as inanimate[6] as one of the moss-covered headstones.

'If I might be so bold,' said he again, waiting leave[7] to speak. Jeremy bowed in deference[8] to his white, uncovered head. And, so encouraged, he went on.

'What that gentleman' (alluding to my last speech) 'has just now said, brings to my mind one who is dead and gone this many a year ago. I, may be, have not rightly understood your meaning, gentlemen, but as far as I could gather it, I think you'd both have given in to thinking poor Gilbert Dawson a hero. At any rate,' said he, heaving a long, quivering sigh, 'I have reason to think him so.'

'Will you take a seat, sir, and tell us about him?' said Jeremy, standing up until the old man was seated. I confess I felt impatient at the interruption.

'It will be forty-five year come Martinmas,'[9] said the Sexton, sitting down on a grassy mound at our feet, 'since I finished my 'prenticeship, and settled down at Lindal. You can see Lindal, sir, at evenings and mornings across the bay; a little to the right of Grange; at least, I used to see it, many a time, and oft, afore my sight grew so dark: and I have spent many a quarter of an hour a-gazing at it far away, and thinking of the days I lived there, till the tears came so thick to my eyes, I could gaze no longer. I shall never look upon it again, either far-off or near; but you may see it, both ways, and a terrible bonny spot it is. In my young days, when I went to settle there, it was full of as wild a set of young fellows as ever were clapped eyes on: all for fighting, poaching, quarrelling, and such-like work. I were startled[10] myself when I first found what a set I

---

[5] *sexton* – the person in charge of grave digging, bell-ringing, and other caretaking duties in a church

[6] *inanimate* – without life

[7] *leave* – permission

[8] *deference* – respect

[9] *Martinmas* – the feast of St Martin, 11th November

[10] *I were startled* – (dialect) I was startled. The sexton speaks in a Cumbrian dialect of the time.

were among, but soon I began to fall into their ways, and I ended by being as rough a chap as any on 'em. I'd been there a matter of two year, and were reckoned by most the cock of the village, when Gilbert Dawson, as I was speaking of, came to Lindal. He were about as strap-
70 ping a chap as I was (I used to be six feet high, though now I'm so shrunk and doubled up), and, as we were like in the same trade (both used to prepare osiers[11] and wood for the Liverpool coopers,[12] who get a deal of stuff from the copses[13] round the bay, sir), we were thrown together, and took mightily to each other. I put my best leg foremost to be equal with Gilbert, for I'd had some schooling, though since I'd been at Lindal I'd lost a good part of what I'd learnt; and I kept my rough ways out of sight for a time, I felt so ashamed of his getting to know them. But that did not last long. I began to think he fancied a girl I dearly loved, but who had always held off from me. Eh! but she was a pretty one in those days!
80 There's none like her, now. I think I see her going along the road with her dancing tread, and shaking back her long yellow curls, to give me or any other young fellow a saucy word; no wonder Gilbert was taken with her, for all[14] he was grave, and she so merry and light. But I began to think she liked him again;[15] and then my blood was all afire. I got to hate him for everything he did. Aforetime I had stood by, admiring to see him, how he leapt, and what a quoiter[16] and cricketer he was. And now I ground my teeth with hatred whene'er he did a thing which caught Letty's eye. I could read it in her look that she liked him, for all she held herself just as high with him as with all the rest. Lord God forgive me!
90 how I hated that man.'

He spoke as if the hatred were a thing of yesterday, so clear within his memory were shown the actions and feelings of his youth. And then he dropped his voice, and said—

'Well! I began to look out to pick a quarrel with him, for my blood was up to fight him. If I beat him (and I were a rare[17] boxer in those days), I thought Letty would cool towards him. So one evening at quoits (I'm sure I don't know how or why, but large doings grow out of small words) I fell out with him, and challenged him to fight. I could see he were very wroth[18] by his colour coming and going – and, as I said before, he were a

[11] *osiers* – a type of willow tree
[12] *coopers* – barrel makers
[13] *copses* – thickets of small trees
[14] *for all* – (dialect) despite the fact that
[15] *again* – (dialect) in return
[16] *quoiter* – someone who plays quoits, a game in which you try to throw a ring over a spike stuck in the ground
[17] *rare* – (dialect) very good
[18] *wroth* – very angry

fine active young fellow. But all at once he drew in, and said he would    100
not fight. Such a yell as the Lindal lads, who were watching us, set up! I
hear it yet. I could na'[19] help but feel sorry for him, to be so scorned,[20]
and I thought he'd not rightly taken my meaning, and I'd give him
another chance: so I said it again, and dared him, as plain as words could
speak, to fight out the quarrel. He told me then, he had no quarrel
against me; that he might have said something to put me up; he did not
know that he had, but that if he had, he asked pardon; but that he would
not fight no-how.

'I was so full of scorn at his cowardliness, that I was vexed I'd given
him the second chance, and I joined in the yell that was set up, twice as    110
bad as before. He stood it out, his teeth set, and looking very white, and
when we were silent for want of breath, he said out loud, but in a hoarse
voice, quite different from his own—

'"I cannot fight, because I think it is wrong to quarrel, and use
violence."

'Then he turned to go away; I were so beside myself with scorn and
hate, that I called out—

'"Tell truth, lad, at least; if thou dare not fight, dunnot go and tell a lie
about it. Mother's moppet[21] is afraid of a black eye, pretty dear. It
shannot be hurt, but it munnot tell lies."    120

'Well, they laughed, but I could not laugh. It seemed such a thing for a
stout young chap to be a coward and afraid!

'Before the sun had set, it was talked of all over Lindal how I had challenged Gilbert to fight, and how he'd denied me; and the folks stood at
their doors, and looked at him going up the hill to his home, as if he'd
been a monkey or a foreigner – but no one wished him good e'en. Such a
thing as refusing to fight had never been heard of afore at Lindal. Next
day, however, they had found voice. The men muttered the word
"coward" in his hearing, and kept aloof; the women tittered as he passed,
and the little impudent lads and lasses shouted out, "How long is it sin'    130
thou turned Quaker?"[22] "Good-bye, Jonathan Broad-brim,"[23] and such-
like jests.

'That evening I met him, with Letty by his side, coming up from the
shore. She was almost crying as I came upon them at the turn of the lane;
and looking up in his face, as if begging him something. And so she was,

---

[19] *could na'* – (dialect) could not

[20] *scorned* – teased

[21] *moppet* – (dialect) a baby

[22] *Quaker* – a member of the religious group, the Society of Friends, who believed in
peaceful principles and a plain style of dress

[23] *Jonathan Broad-Brim* – the villagers refer to Gilbert's Quaker associations.
Traditionally, Quakers wore a broad-brimmed hat.

she told me it after. For she did really like him, and could not abide[24] to hear him scorned by every one for being a coward; and she, coy[25] as she was, all but told him that very night that she loved him, and begged him not to disgrace himself, but fight me as I'd dared him to. When he still
140  stuck to it he could not, for that[26] it was wrong, she was so vexed and mad-like at the way she'd spoken, and the feelings she'd let out to coax him, that she said more stinging things about his being a coward than all the rest put together (according to what she told me, sir, afterwards), and ended by saying she'd never speak to him again, as long as she lived; she did once again, though – her blessing was the last human speech that reached his ear in his wild death-struggle.

'But much happened afore that time. From the day I met them walking, Letty turned towards me; I could see a part of it was to spite Gilbert, for she'd be twice as kind when he was near, or likely to hear of
150  it; but by-and-by she got to like me for my own sake, and it was all settled for our marriage. Gilbert kept aloof from every one, and fell into a sad, careless way. His very gait[27] was changed; his step used to be brisk and sounding, and now his foot lingered heavily on the ground. I used to try and daunt[28] him with my eye, but he would always meet my look in a steady, quiet way, for all so much about him was altered; the lads would not play with him; and, as soon as he found he was to be slighted[29] by them whenever he came to quoiting or cricket, he just left off coming.

'The old clerk was the only one he kept company with; or perhaps, rightly to speak, the only one who would keep company with him. They
160  got so thick[30] at last, that old Jonas would say, Gilbert had gospel on his side, and did no more than gospel told him to do; but we none of us gave much credit[31] to what he said, more by token[32] our vicar had a brother, a colonel in the army; and, as we threeped[33] it many a time to Jonas, would he set himself up to know the gospel better than the vicar? that would be putting the cart afore the horse, like the French radicals.[34] And, if the vicar had thought quarrelling and fighting wicked, and again[35] the Bible,

[24] *abide* – stand
[25] *coy* – modest and shy
[26] *for that* – (dialect) because
[27] *gait* – way of walking
[28] *daunt* – frighten, intimidate
[29] *slighted* – ignored
[30] *so thick* – such close friends
[31] *gave much credit* – believed
[32] *more by token* – (dialect) the more so because
[33] *threeped* – (dialect) argue aggressively about something
[34] *French radicals* – the French revolution overthrew the royal family and put the people in power. England was at war with France at this time
[35] *again* – against (dialect)

would he have made so much work about all the victories, that were as plenty as blackberries at that time of day, and kept the little bell of Lindal church for ever ringing; or would he have thought so much of "my brother the colonel," as he was always talking on? 170

'After I was married to Letty I left off hating Gilbert. I even kind of pitied him – he was so scorned and slighted; and, for all he'd a bold look about him, as if he were not ashamed, he seemed pining[36] and shrunk. It's a wearying thing to be kept at arm's length by one's kind; and so Gilbert found it, poor fellow. The little children took to him, though; they'd be round about him like a swarm of bees – them as was too young to know what a coward was, and only felt that he was ever ready to love and to help them, and was never loud or cross, however naughty they might be. After a while we had our little one, too; such a blessed darling she was, and dearly did we love her; Letty in especial, who seemed to get all the thought 180 I used to think sometimes she wanted, after she had her baby to care for.

'All my kin[37] lived on this side the bay, up above Kellet. Jane (that's her that lies buried near yon white rose-tree) was to be married, and nought would serve her but that Letty and I must come to the wedding; for all my sisters loved Letty, she had such winning ways with her. Letty did not like to leave her baby, nor yet did I want her to take it: so, after a talk, we fixed to leave it with Letty's mother for the afternoon. I could see her heart ached a bit, for she'd never left it till then, and she seemed to fear all manner of evil, even to the French coming and taking it away. Well! we borrowed a shandry,[38] and harnessed my old grey mare, as I 190 used in th' cart, and set off as grand as King George across the sands about three o'clock, for you see it were high-water about twelve, and we'd to go and come back same tide, as Letty could not leave her baby for long. It were a merry afternoon were that; last time I ever saw Letty laugh heartily; and, for that matter, last time I ever laughed downright hearty myself. The latest crossing-time fell about nine o'clock, and we were late at starting. Clocks were wrong; and we'd a piece of work chasing a pig father had given Letty to take home; we bagged him at last, and he screeched and screeched in the back part o' th' shandry, and we laughed and they laughed; and in the midst of all the merriment the sun set, and 200 that sobered us a bit, for then we knew what time it was. I whipped the old mare, but she was a deal beener[39] than she was in the morning, and would neither go quick up nor down the brows, and they're not a few 'twixt Kellet and the shore. On the sands it were worse. They were very

---

[36] *pining* – wasting away
[37] *kin* – relatives
[38] *shandry* – a horse-drawn cart
[39] *beener* – (dialect) more tired

heavy, for the fresh[40] had come down after the rains we'd had. Lord! how I did whip the poor mare, to make the most of the red light as yet lasted. You, may be, don't know the sands, gentlemen. From Bolton side, where we started from, it is better than six mile to Cart Lane, and two channels to cross, let alone holes and quicksands. At the second channel from us

210 the guide waits, all during crossing-time from sunrise to sunset; but for the three hours on each side high-water he's not there, in course.[41] He stays after sunset if he's forespoken, not else. So now you know where we were that awful night. For we'd crossed the first channel about two mile, and it were growing darker and darker above and around us, all but one red line of light above the hills, when we came to a hollow (for all the sands look so flat, there's many a hollow in them where you lose all sight of the shore). We were longer than we should ha' been in crossing the hollow, the sand was so quick;[42] and when we came up again, there, again the blackness, was the white line of the rushing tide coming up the

220 bay! It looked not a mile from us; and when the wind blows up the bay it comes swifter than a galloping horse. 'Lord help us!' said I; and then I were sorry I'd spoken, to frighten Letty; but the words were crushed out of my heart by the terror. I felt her shiver up by my side, and clutch my coat. And as if the pig (as had screeched himself hoarse some time ago) had found out the danger we were all in, he took to squealing again, enough to bewilder any man. I cursed him between my teeth for his noise; and yet it was God's answer to my prayer, blind sinner as I was. Ay! you may smile, sir, but God can work through many a scornful thing, if need be.

230 'By this time the mare was all in a lather, and trembling and panting, as if in mortal fright; for, though we were on the last bank afore the second channel, the water was gathering up her legs; and she so tired out. When we came close to the channel she stood still, and not all my flogging could get her to stir; she fairly groaned aloud, and shook in a terrible quaking way. Till now Letty had not spoken: only held my coat tightly. I heard her say something, and bent down my head.

'I think, John – I think – I shall never see baby again!'

'And then she sent up such a cry – so loud, and shrill, and pitiful! It fairly maddened me. I pulled out my knife to spur on the old mare, that it

240 might end one way or the other, for the water was stealing sullenly up to the very axle-tree, let alone the white waves that knew no mercy in their steady advance. That one quarter of an hour, sir, seemed as long as all my

[40] *the fresh* – fresh sands
[41] *in course* – as a rule
[42] *quick* – shifting, sinking

life since. Thoughts and fancies, and dreams, and memory ran into each other. The mist, the heavy mist, that was like a ghastly curtain, shutting us in for death, seemed to bring with it the scents of the flowers that grew around our own threshold; it might be, for it was falling on them like blessed dew, though to us it was a shroud. Letty told me at after, she heard her baby crying for her, above the gurgling of the rising waters, as plain as ever she heard anything; but the sea-birds were skirling,[43] and the pig shrieking; I never caught it; it was miles away, at any rate.          250

'Just as I'd gotten my knife out, another sound was close upon us, blending with the gurgle of the near waters, and the roar of the distant (not so distant though); we could hardly see, but we thought we saw something black against the deep lead colour of wave, and mist, and sky. It neared and neared: with slow, steady motion, it came across the channel right to where we were.

'Oh, God! it was Gilbert Dawson on his strong bay horse.

'Few words did we speak, and little time had we to say them in. I had no knowledge at that moment of past or future – only of one present thought – how to save Letty, and, if I could, myself. I only remembered          260 afterwards that Gilbert said he had been guided by an animal's shriek of terror; I only heard when all was over, that he had been uneasy about our return, because of the depth of fresh, and had borrowed a pillion,[44] and saddled his horse early in the evening, and ridden down to Cart Lane to watch for us. If all had gone well, we should ne'er have heard of it. As it was, old Jonas told it, the tears down-dropping from his withered cheeks.

'We fastened his horse to the shandry. We lifted Letty to the pillion. The waters rose every instant with sullen sound. They were all but in the shandry. Letty clung to the pillion handles, but drooped her head as if she had yet no hope of life. Swifter than thought (and yet he might have          270 had time for thought and for temptation, sir – if he had ridden off with Letty, he would have been saved, not me), Gilbert was in the shandry by my side.

' "Quick!" said he, clear and firm. "You must ride before her, and keep her up. The horse can swim. By God's mercy I will follow. I can cut the traces, and if the mare is not hampered with the shandry, she'll carry me safely through. At any rate, you are a husband and a father. No one cares for me."

'Do not hate me, gentlemen. I often wish that night was a dream. It has haunted my sleep ever since like a dream, and yet it was no dream. I took          280 his place on the saddle, and put Letty's arms around me, and felt her head rest on my shoulder. I trust in God I spoke some word of thanks;

[43]  *skirling* – (dialect) shrieking

[44]  *pillion* – a pad attached to a normal saddle to allow a second person to ride a horse

but I can't remember. I only recollect Letty raising her head, and calling out—

'"God bless you, Gilbert Dawson, for saving my baby from being an orphan this night." And then she fell against me, as if unconscious.

'I bore her through; or, rather, the strong horse swam bravely through the gathering waves. We were dripping wet when we reached the banks in-shore; but we could have but one thought – where was Gilbert? Thick
290   mists and heaving waters compassed us round. Where was he? We shouted. Letty, faint as she was, raised her voice and shouted clear and shrill. No answer came, the sea boomed on with ceaseless sullen beat. I rode to the guide's house. He was a-bed, and would not get up, though I offered him more than I was worth. Perhaps he knew it, the cursed old villain! At any rate, I'd have paid it if I'd toiled my life long. He said I might take his horn and welcome. I did, and blew such a blast through the still, black night, the echoes came back upon the heavy air; but no human voice or sound was heard – that wild blast could not awaken the dead!

'I took Letty home to her baby, over whom she wept the livelong
300   night. I rode back to the shore about Cart Lane; and to and fro, with weary march, did I pace along the brink of the waters, now and then shouting out into the silence a vain cry for Gilbert. The waters went back and left no trace. Two days afterwards he was washed ashore near Flukeborough. The shandry and poor old mare were found half-buried in a heap of sand by Arnside Knot. As far as we could guess, he had dropped his knife while trying to cut the traces, and so had lost all chance of life. Any rate, the knife was found in a cleft of the shaft.[45]

'His friends came over from Garstang to his funeral. I wanted to go chief mourner, but it was not my right, and I might not; though I've
310   never done mourning him to this day. When his sister packed up his things, I begged hard for something that had been his. She would give me none of his clothes (she was a right-down saving woman), as she had boys of her own, who might grow up into them. But she threw me his Bible, as she said they'd gotten one already, and his were but a poor used-up thing. It was his, and so I cared for it. It were a black leather one, with pockets at the sides, old-fashioned-wise;[46] and in one were a bunch of wild flowers, Letty said she could almost be sure were some she had once given him.

'There were many a text in the Gospel, marked broad with his
320   carpenter's pencil, which more than bore him out in his refusal to fight. Of a surety, sir, there's call enough for bravery in the service of God, and to show love to man, without quarrelling and fighting.

[45] *cleft of the shaft* – a fork in the wooden pole that attached the cart to the horse
[46] *old-fashioned-wise* – (dialect) in an old-fashioned style

'Thank you, gentlemen, for listening to me. Your words called up the thoughts of him, and my heart was full to speaking. But I must make up; I've to dig a grave for a little child, who is to be buried to-morrow morning, just when his playmates are trooping off to school.'

'But tell us of Letty; is she yet alive?' asked Jeremy.

The old man shook his head, and struggled against a choking sigh. After a minute's pause he said—

'She died in less than two year at after that night. She was never like the same again. She would sit thinking – on Gilbert, I guessed; but I could not blame her. We had a boy, and we named it Gilbert Dawson Knipe: he that's stoker on the London railway. Our girl was carried off in teething; and Letty just quietly drooped, and died in less than a six week. They were buried here; so I came to be near them, and away from Lindal, a place I could never abide after Letty was gone.'

He turned to his work; and we, having rested sufficiently, rose up, and came away.

330

# The Will

*Mary Lavin*

'I couldn't say what I thought while he was here!' said Kate, the eldest of the family, closing the door after the solicitor, who had just read their mother's will to the Conroy family. She ran over to her youngest sister and threw out her hands. 'I cannot tell you how shocked I am, Lally. We had no idea that she felt as bitter against you as all that. Had we?' She turned and appealed to the other members of the family who stood around the large red mahogany table, in their stiff black mourning clothes.

'I knew she felt bitter,' said Matthew, the eldest of the sons. 'We couldn't mention your name without raising a row!'

'She knocked over the lamp, once,' said Nonny, the youngest of the unmarried members. 'Of late years[1] she always kept a stick beside her on the counterpane[2] of the bed and she tapped with it on the floor when she wanted anything, and then one day someone said something about you, I forget what it is they said, but she caught up the stick and drove it through the air with all her force. The next thing we knew the lamp was reeling[3] off the table! The house would have been burned down about us if the lamp hadn't quenched with the draught of falling through the air!'

'Still, even after that we never thought that she'd leave your name out of the parchment[4] altogether. Did we?' Kate corroborated every remark by an appeal to the rest of the group. 'We thought she'd leave you something anyway, no matter how small it might be!'

'But I don't mind,' said Lally. 'Honestly I don't. I wish you didn't feel so bad about it, all of you.' She looked around from one to the other beseechingly.

'Why wouldn't we feel bad!' said Matthew. 'You're our own sister after all. She was your mother as well as ours, no matter what happened.'

'The only thing I regret,' said Lally, 'was that I didn't get here before she died.' The tears started into her eyes.

'I don't think it would have made any difference whether you got here in time or not before she went. The will was made years ago.'

'Oh, I didn't mean anything like that!' said Lally in dismay, and a red

---

[1] *of late years* – in recent years
[2] *counterpane* – a decorative bed cover that goes on top of the blankets
[3] *reeling* – going flying
[4] *parchment* – old-fashioned paper, originally of animal skin. It refers here to the will

blush struggled through the thickened cells of her skin. 'I only meant to say that I'd like to have seen her, no matter what, before she went.'

The tears streamed down her face then, and they ran freely, for her mind was far away thinking of the days before she left home at all. She made no attempt to dry her eyes. But the tears upset the others, who felt no inclination to cry. Having watched the old lady fade away in a long lingering illness, they had used up their emotional energy in anticipating grief. Their minds were filled now with practical arrangements.                    40

'Don't upset yourself, Lally,' said Kate. 'Perhaps it all turned out for the best. If she had seen you she might only have flown into one of her rages and died sitting up in the bed from a rush of blood to the forehead, instead of the nice natural death that she did get, lying straight out with her hands folded better than any undertaker could have folded them. Everything happened for the best.'

'I don't suppose she mentioned my name, did she? Near the end I mean.'

'No, the last time she spoke about you was so long ago I couldn't rightly say now when it was. It was one night that she was feeling bad.     50
She hadn't slept well the night before. I was tidying her room for her, plumping up her pillows and one thing and another, and she was looking out of the window. Suddenly she looked at me and asked me how old you were now. It gave me such a start to hear her mention your name after all those years that I couldn't remember what age you were, so I just said the first thing that came into my head.'

'What did she say?'

'She said nothing for a while, and then she began to ramble about something under her breath. I couldn't catch the meaning. She used to wander a bit in her mind, now and again, especially if she had lost her     60
sleep the night before.'

'Do you think it was me she was talking about under her breath?' said Lally, and her eyes and her open lips and even the half-gesture of her outstretched hands seemed to beg for an answer in the affirmative.

'Oh, I don't know what she was rambling about,' said Kate. 'I had my mind fixed on getting the bed straightened out so she could lie back at her ease. I wasn't listening to what she was saying. All I remember is that she was saying something about blue feathers. Blue feathers! Her mind was astray for the time being, I suppose.'

The tears glistened in Lally's eyes again.                              70

'I had two little blue feathers in my hat the morning I went into her room to tell her I was getting married. I had nothing new[5] to put on me. I

---

[5] *new* — it is a tradition at her wedding for the bride to wear 'something old, something new, something borrowed, and something blue'

was wearing my old green silk costume, and my old green hat, but I bought two little pale blue feathers and pinned them on the front of the hat. I think the feathers upset her more than going against her wishes with the marriage. She kept staring at them all the time I was in the room, and even when she ordered me to get out of her sight it was at the feathers in my hat she was staring and not at me.'

'Don't cry, Lally.' Kate felt uncomfortable. 'Don't cry. It's all over
80  long ago. Don't be going back to the past. What is to be, is to be. I always believe that.'

Matthew and Nonny believed that too. They told her not to cry. They said no good could be done by upsetting yourself.

'I never regretted it!' said Lally. 'We had a hard time at the beginning, but I never regretted it.'

Kate moved over and began to straighten the red plush curtains as if they had been the sole object of her change in position, but the movement brought her close to her thin brother Matthew where he stood fingering his chin uncertainly. Kate gave him a sharp nudge.
90  'Say what I told you,' she said, speaking rapidly in a low voice.

Matthew cleared his throat. 'You have no need for regret as far as we are concerned, Lally,' he said, and he looked back at Kate who nodded her head vigorously for him to continue. 'We didn't share our poor mother's feelings. Of course we couldn't help thinking that you could have done better for yourself but it's all past mending now, and we want you to know that we will do all in our power for you.' He looked again at his sister Kate who nodded her head still more vigorously indicating that the most important thing had still been left unsaid. 'We won't see you in want,' said Matthew.
100  When this much had been said, Kate felt that her brother's authority[6] had been deferred to[7] sufficiently, and she broke into the conversation again.

'We won't let it be said by anyone that we'd see you in want, Lally. We talked it all over. We can make an arrangement.' She looked across at Matthew again with a glance that seemed to toss the conversation to him as one might toss a ball.

'We were thinking,' said Matthew, 'that if each one of us was to part with a small sum the total would come to a considerable amount when it was all put together.'
110  But Lally put up her hands again.

'Oh no, no, no,' she said. 'I wouldn't want anything that didn't come to me by rights.'

[6] *brother's authority* – as the male of the household, by tradition Matthew is supposed to be the one who makes the decisions

[7] *deferred to* – given respect

'It would only be a small sum from each one,' said Nonny placatingly.[8] 'No one would feel any pinch.'

'No, no, no,' said Lally. 'I couldn't let you do that. It would be going against her wishes.'

'It's late in the day you let the thought of going against her wishes trouble you!' said Kate with an involuntary flash of impatience for which she hurried to atone[9] by the next remark. 'Why wouldn't you take it! It's yours as much as ours!'

'You might put it like that, anyhow,' said Matthew, 'as long as we're not speaking legally.'

'No, no, no,' said Lally for the third time. 'Don't you see? I'd hate taking it and knowing all the time that she didn't intend me to have it. And anyway, you have to think of yourselves.' She looked at Kate. 'You have your children to educate,' she said. 'You have this place to keep up, Matthew! And you have no one to look after you at all, Nonny. I won't take a penny from any of you.'

'What about your own children?' said Kate. 'Are you forgetting them?'

'Oh, they're all right,' said Lally. 'Things are different in the city. In the city there are plenty of free schools. And I'm doing very well. Every room in the house is full.'

There was silence after that for a few minutes, but glances passed between Kate and Nonny. Kate went over to the fire and picked up the poker. She drove it in among the blazing coals and rattled them up with such unusual violence that Matthew looked around at her where she knelt on the red carpet.

'Do you have to be prompted at every word?' said Kate when she got his attention.

Matthew cleared his throat again, and this time, at the sound, Lally turned towards him expectantly.

'There is another thing that we were talking about before you arrived,' he said, speaking quickly and nervously. 'It would be in the interests of the family, Lally, if you were to give up keeping lodgers.' He looked at her quickly to see how she took what he said, and then he stepped back a pace or two like an actor who had said his lines and made way for another person to say his.

While he was speaking Kate had remained kneeling at the grate with the poker in her hand, but when he stopped she made a move to rise quickly. Her stiff new mourning skirt got in her way, however, and the cold and damp at the graveside had brought about an unexpected return of rheumatism, and so as she went to rise up quickly she listed forward

---

[8] *placatingly* – trying to calm things down or make peace with
[9] *atone for* – to make up for something done wrong

with the jerky movement of a camel. It couldn't be certain whether Lally was laughing at Matthew's words, or at the camelish appearance of Kate. Kate, however, was the first to take offence. But she attributed[10] the laughing to Matthew's words.

'I don't see what there is to laugh at, Lally,' she said. 'It's not a very nice thing for us to feel that our sister is a common landlady in the city. Mother never forgave that! She might have forgiven your marriage in time, but she couldn't forgive you for lowering yourself to keeping lodgers.'

'We had to live somehow,' said Lally, but she spoke lightly, and as she spoke she was picking off the greenflies from the plant on the table.

'I can't say I blame Mother!' said Nonny, breaking into the discussion with a sudden venom. 'I don't see why you were so anxious to marry him when it meant keeping lodgers.'

'It was the other way round, Nonny,' said Lally. 'I was willing to keep lodgers because it meant I could marry him.'

'Easy now!' said Matthew. 'There's no need to quarrel. We must talk this thing over calmly. We'll come to some arrangement. But there's no need in doing everything the one day. Tomorrow is as good as today, and better. Lally must be tired after travelling all the way down and then going on to the funeral without five minutes rest. We'll talk it all over in the daylight tomorrow.'

Lally looked back and forth from one face to another as if she was picking the face that looked most lenient before she spoke again. At last she turned back to Matthew.

'I won't be here in the morning,' she said hurriedly, as if it was a matter of no consequence. 'I am going back tonight. I only came down for the burial. I can't stay any longer.'

'Why not?' demanded Kate, and then as if she knew the answer to the question and did not want to hear it upon her sister's lips, she continued to speak hurriedly. 'You've got to stay,' she said, stamping her foot. 'You've got to stay. That's all there is to say about the matter.'

'There is nothing to be gained by my staying, anyway,' said Lally. 'I wouldn't take the money, no matter what was said, tonight or tomorrow!'

Matthew looked at his other sisters. They nodded at him.

'There's nothing to be gained by being obstinate, Lally,' he said lamely.

'You may think you are behaving unselfishly,' said Kate, 'but let me tell you it's not a nice thing for my children to feel that their first cousins are going to free schools in the city and mixing with the lowest of the low, and running messages for your dirty lodgers. And as if that isn't bad

---

[10] *attributed the laughing to* – thought the laughing was caused by

enough, I suppose you'll be putting them behind the counter in some greengrocers, one of these days!'

Lally said nothing.

'If you kept an hotel, it wouldn't seem so bad,' said Matthew looking up suddenly with an animation that betrayed the fact that he was speaking for the first time upon his own initiative. 'If you kept an hotel we could make it a limited company.[11] We could all take shares. We could recommend it to the right kind of people. We could stay there ourselves whenever we were in the city.' His excitement grew with every word he uttered. He turned from Lally to Kate. 'That's not a bad idea. Is it?' He turned back to Lally again. 'You'll have to stay the night, now,' he said, enthusiastically, showing that he had not believed before that it was worth her while to comply with their wishes.

'I can't stay,' said Lally faintly.

'Of course you can.' Matthew dismissed her difficulties unheard. 'You'll have to stay,' he said. 'Your room is ready. Isn't it?'

'It's all ready,' said Nonny. 'I told them to light a fire in it and to put a hot jar[12] in the bed.' As an afterthought she explained further. 'We were going to fix up a room for you here, but with all the fuss we didn't have time to attend to it, and I thought that the simplest thing to do was to send out word to the Station Hotel that they were to fix up a nice room for you. They have the room all ready. I went out to see it. It's a big airy room with a nice big bed. It has two windows, and it looks out on the ball-alley.[13] You'll be more comfortable there than here. Of course, I could put a stretcher[14] into my room if you liked, but I think for your own sake you ought to leave things as I arranged them. You'll get a better night's rest. If you sleep here it may only remind you of things you'd rather forget.'

'I'm very grateful to you Nonny for all the trouble you took. I'm grateful to all of you. But I can't stay.'

'Why?' said someone then, voicing the look in every face.

'I have things to attend to!'

'What things?'

'Different things. You wouldn't understand.'

'They can wait.'

'No,' said Lally. 'I must go. There is a woman coming tonight to the room on the landing, and I'll have to be there to help her settle in her furniture.'

[11] *limited company* – a business owned by shareholders

[12] *hot jar* – hot water bottle

[13] *ball-alley* – a narrow enclosure for playing bowls

[14] *stretcher* – temporary bed

'Have you got her address?' said Matthew.

'Why?' said Lally.

'You could send her a telegram cancelling the arrangement.'

'Oh, but that would leave her in a hobble,'[15] said Lally.

'What do you care. You'll never see her again. When we start the hotel you'll be getting a different class of person altogether.'

'I'll never start an hotel,' said Lally. 'I won't make any change now. I'd hate to be making a lot of money and Robert gone where he couldn't
240   profit by it. It's too late now. I'm too old now.'

She looked down at her thin hands, with the broken finger-nails, and the fine web of lines deepened by dirt. And as she did so the others looked at her too. They all looked at her; at this sister that was younger than all of them, and a chill descended on them as they read their own decay in hers. They had been better preserved, that was all; hardship had hastened the disintegration of her looks, but the undeniable bending of the bone, the tightening of the skin, and the fading of the eye could not be guarded against. A chill fell on them. A grudge against her gnawed at them.

250   'I begin to see,' said Matthew, 'that Mother was right. I begin to see what she meant when she said that you were as obstinate as a tree.'

'Did she say that?' said Lally, and her face lit up for a moment with the sunlight of youth, as her mind opened wide in a wilful vision of tall trees, leafy, and glossy with light, against a sky as blue as the feathers in a young girl's hat.

Nonny stood up impatiently. 'What is the use of talking?' she said. 'No one can do anything for an obstinate person. They must be left to go their own way. But no one can say we didn't do our best.'

'I'm very grateful,' said Lally again.

260   'Oh, keep your thanks to yourself!' said Nonny. 'As Matthew said we didn't do it for your sake. It's not very nice to have people coming back from the city saying that they met you, and we knowing all the time the old clothes you were likely to be wearing, and your hair all tats and taws,[16] and your face dirty maybe, if all was told!'

'Do you ever look at yourself in a mirror?' said Matthew.

'What came over you that you let your teeth go so far?' said Kate. 'They're disgusting to look at.' She shivered.

'I'd be ashamed to be seen talking to you,' said Nonny.

Through the silent evening air there was a far sound of a train
270   shunting. Through the curtains the signal lights on the railway line could be seen changing from red to green. Even when the elderly maidservant

[15] *hobble* – an awkward situation

[16] *tats and taws* – messy

came in with the heavy brass lamp the green light shone through the pane, insistent as a thought.

'What time is it?' said Lally.

'You have plenty of time,' said Matthew; his words marked the general acceptance of the fact that she was going.

Tea was hurried in on a tray. A messenger was sent running upstairs to see if Lally's gloves were on the bed in Kate's room.

'Where did you leave them?' someone kept asking every few minutes and going away in the confusion without a satisfactory answer.    280

'Do you want to have a wash?' Nonny asked. 'It will freshen you for the journey. I left a jug of water on the landing.'

And once or twice, lowering his voice to a whisper, Matthew leaned across the table and asked her if she was absolutely certain that she was all right for the journey back. Had she a return ticket? Had she loose change for the porters?

But Lally didn't need anything, and when it came nearer to the time of the train, it appeared that she did not even want the car to take her to the station.

'But it's wet!' said Matthew.    290

'It's as dark as a pit outside,' said Kate.

And all of them, even the maidservant who was clearing away the tray, were agreed that it was bad enough for people to know she was going back the very night that her mother was lowered into the clay, without adding to the scandal by giving people a chance to say that her brother Matthew wouldn't drive her to the train in his car, and it pouring rain.

'They'll say we had a difference of opinion over the will,' said Nonny, who retained one characteristic at least of youth, its morbid sensitivity.

'What does it matter what they say?' said Lally, 'as long as we know it isn't true?'    300

'If everyone took that attitude it would be a queer world,' said Matthew.

'There's such a thing as keeping up appearances,' said Kate, and she threw a hard glance at Lally's coat. 'Is that coat black or is it blue?' she asked suddenly, catching the sleeve of it and pulling it nearer to the lamp.

'It's almost black,' said Lally. 'It's a very dark blue. I didn't have time to get proper mourning,[17] and the woman next door lent me this. She said you couldn't tell it from black.'

Nonny shrugged her shoulders and addressed herself to Matthew. 'She's too proud to accept things from her own, but she's not too proud    310 to accept things from strangers.'

A train whistle shrilled through the air.

---

[17] *mourning* – mourning clothes

'I must go,' said Lally.

She shook hands with them all. She looked up the stairway that the coffin had been carried down that morning. She put her hand on the door. While they were persuading her again to let them take her in the car, she opened the door and ran down the street.

They heard her footsteps on the pavement in the dark, as they had heard them often when she was a young girl running up the town on a message for their mother. And just as in those days, when she threw a coat over her head with the sleeves dangling, and ran out, the door was wide open upon the darkness. Matthew hesitated for a minute, and then he closed the door.

'Why didn't you insist?' said Kate.

'With people like Lally there is no use wasting your breath. They have their own ways of looking at things and nothing will change them. You might as well try to catch a falling leaf as try to find out what's at the back of Lally's mind.'

They stood in the cold hallway. Suddenly Kate began to cry awkwardly.

'Why are you crying now?' said Nonny. 'You were great at the cemetery. You kept us all from breaking down. Why are you crying now?' Her own voice had thinned and she dug her fingers into Matthew's sleeve.

'It's Lally!' said Kate. 'None of you remember her as well as I do. I made her a dress for her first dance. It was white muslin with blue bows all down the front. Her hair was like light.' Kate sobbed with thick hurtful sobs that shook her whole frame and shook Matthew's thin dried-up body when he put his arm around her.

Lally ran along the dark streets of the country town as she had run along them long ago as a young girl, and hardly remembered to slacken into a walking pace when she came to the patches of yellow lamplight that flooded out from shop windows and the open doors of houses near the Square. But the excitement of running now was caused by the beat of blood in her temple and the terrible throbbing of her heart. As a child it had been an excitement of the mind, for then it had seemed that the bright world ringed the town around, and that somewhere outside the darkness lay the mystery of life; one had only to run on, on past the old town gate, on under the dark railway bridge, on a little way out the twisty road, and you would reach the heart of that mystery. Some day she would go.

And one day she went. But there was no mystery now; anywhere. Life was just the same in the town, in the city, and in the twisty countryside. Life was the same in the darkness and the light. It was the same for the spinster and for the draggled mother of a family. You were yourself always, no matter where you went or what you did. You didn't change.

Her brothers and sisters were the same as they always were. She herself was the same as she always was, although her teeth were rotted, and a blue feather in her hat now would make her look like an old hag in a pantomime. Nothing you did made any real change in you. You might think beforehand that it would make a great change, but it wouldn't make any change. There was only one thing that could change you, and that was death. And no one knew what that change would be like.

No one knew what death was like, but people made terrible torturing guesses. Fragments of the old penny catechism[18] she had learned by rote[19] in school came back to her, distorted by a bad memory and a confused emotion. Pictures of flames and screaming souls writhing on gridirons,[20] rose before her mind as she ran down the street to the station. The whistle of the train when it screamed in the darkness gave a reality to her racing thoughts, and she paused and listened to it for a moment. Then turning rapidly around she ran a few paces in the way that she had come, and groped along the dark wall that lined the street at this point.

The wet black railings of a gate came in contact with her fingers. This was the gate leading into the residence of the Canon.[21] She banged the gate back against the piers[22] with the fierce determination with which she opened it. She ran up the wet gravelly drive to the priest's house.

In the dark she could not find the brass knocker and she beat against the panels of the door with her hard hands. The door was thrown open after a minute with a roughness that matched the rough knocking.

'What in the Name of God do you want?' said an elderly woman with an apron that blazed white in the darkness.

'I want to see the Canon!' said Lally.

'He's at his dinner,' said the woman, aggressively, and went to close the door.

'I must see him,' said Lally, and she stepped into the hall-way.

'I can't disturb him at his meals,' said the woman, but her anger had softened somewhat at seeing that Lally was a stranger to her. Two emotions cannot exist together and a strong curiosity possessed her at the moment. 'What name?' she said.

'Lally Conroy,' said Lally, the old associations being so strong that her maiden name came more naturally to her lips than the name she had carried for twenty-four years. The housekeeper went across the hall and opened a door on the left. She closed it after her, but the lock did not

[18] *catechism* – an instruction booklet about the Catholic faith, at one time learned off by heart by Catholic school children
[19] *by rote* – off by heart
[20] *gridirons* – grills for torturing people by roasting them alive
[21] *Canon* – a priest
[22] *piers* – stone pillars

catch and the door slid open again. Lally heard the conversation distinctly, but with indifference, as she sat down on the polished mahogany chair in the hall.

'There's a woman outside who insists on seeing you, Father.'

'Who is she?' said the priest, his voice muffled, as if by a serviette wiped across his mouth.

400 'She gave her name as Conroy,' said the woman, 'and she has a look of Matthew Conroy, but I never saw her before and she's dressed like a pauper.'

The priest's voice was slow and meditative. 'I heard that there was another sister,' he said, 'but there was a sad story about her, I forget what it was.' A chair scraped back. 'I'll see her,' he said. And his feet sounded on the polished floor as he crossed the room towards the hall.

Lally was sitting on the stiff chair with the wooden seat, shielding her face from the heat of the flames that dragged themselves like serpents along the logs in the fireplace.

'Father, I'm in a hurry. I'm going away on this train.'

410 The train had shrilled its whistle once again in the darkness outside.

'I'm sorry to disturb you. I only wanted to ask a question.' Her short phrases leaped uncontrollably as the leaping flames in the grate. 'I want to know if you will say a mass[23] for my mother first thing in the morning? My name is Lally Conroy. I'll send you the offering money the minute I get back to the city. I'll post it tonight. Will you do that, Father? Will you?' As if the interview was over she stood up and began to go towards the door, backwards, without waiting for an answer, repeating her urgent question, 'Will you? Will you do that, Father? First thing in the morning!'

420 The Canon took out a watch from under the cape of his shiny canonical robes.[24]

'You have six minutes, yet,' he said. 'Sit down. Sit down.'

'No, no, no,' said Lally. 'I mustn't miss the train.'

The whistle blew again and the sound seemed to race her thoughts to a gallop.

'I want three masses to be said,' she explained, 'but I want the first one to be said at once, tomorrow, first thing in the morning. You'll have the offering money as soon as I get back. I'll post it, tonight.'

The Canon looked at the shabby boots and the thick stockings, the

430 rubbed coat with the faded stitching on it.

'There is no need to worry about masses. She was a good woman,' he

---

[23] *a mass* – a religious service in which Catholics remember Christ; thought by some to have the power to help the dead find favour with God

[24] *canonical robes* – decorated clothes of a priest

said. 'And I understand that she left a large sum in her will for masses to be said for her after her death. Three hundred pounds I believe, or thereabouts; a very considerable sum, at any rate. There is no need for worry on that score.'

'It's not the same thing to leave money yourself for masses. It's the masses that other people have said for you that count.' Her excitement leaped like the leaping flames. 'I want a mass said for her with my money! With my money!'

The priest leaned forward with an unusual and ungovernable curiosity.     440

'Why?' he said.

'I'm afraid,' said Lally. 'I'm afraid she might suffer. I'm afraid for her soul.' The eyes that stared into the flaming heart of the fire were indeed filled with fear, and as a coal fell, revealing a gaping abyss of fire, those eyes filled with absolute horror. The reflection of the flames leaped in them. 'She was very bitter,' Lally Conroy sobbed for the first time since she had news of her mother's death. 'She was very bitter against me all the time, and she died without forgiving me. I'm afraid for her soul.' She looked up at the priest. 'You'll say them as soon as ever you can, Father?'     450

'I'll say them,' said the priest. 'But don't worry about the money. I'll offer them from myself.'

'That's not what I want,' said Lally, angrily. 'I want them to be paid for with my money. That is what will count most; that they are paid for out of my money.'

Humbly the priest in his stiff canonical robes, piped with red, accepted the dictates of the draggled woman in front of him.

'I will do as you wish,' he said. 'Is there anything else troubling you?'

'The train! The train!' said Lally, and she fumbled the catch of the door.     460

The priest took out his watch again.

'You have just time to catch it,' he said, 'if you hurry.' And he opened the door. Lally ran out into the dark again.

For a moment she felt peace at the thought of what she had done, and running down the wet gravelly drive with the cold rain beating on her flushed face, her mind was filled with practical thoughts about the journey home. But when she got into the hot and stuffy carriage of the train, where there was an odour of dust and of wet soot,[25] the tears began to stream down her face again, and she began to wonder if she had made herself clear to the Canon. She put her head out of the carriage window     470 as the train began to leave the platform and she called out to a porter who stood with a green flag in his hand.

[25] *wet soot* – soot from the engine. The train is a steam train.

'What time does this train arrive in the city?' she asked, but the porter could not hear her. He put his hand to his ear but just then the train rushed into the darkness under the railway bridge. Lally let the window up and sat back in the seat.

If the train got in before midnight, she thought, she would ring the night bell at the Franciscan Friary[26] and ask for a mass to be said there and then for her mother's soul. She had heard that masses were said
480   night and day in the Friary. She tried to remember where she had heard that, and who had told her, but her thoughts were in confusion. She leaned her head back against the cushions as the train roared into the night, and feverishly she added the prices she would get from the tenants in the top rooms and subtracted the amount that would be needed to buy food for herself and the children for the week. She would have a clear two pound ten.[27] She could have ten masses said at least for that. There might even be money over to light some holy lamps at the Convent of Perpetual Reparation.[28] She tried to comfort herself by these calculations, but as the dark train rushed through the darkness she sat more upright on the
490   red-carpeted seats that smelled of dust, and clenched her hands tightly as she thought of the torments of Purgatory.[29] Bright red sparks from the engine flew past the carriage window, and she began to pray with rapid unformed words that jostled themselves in her mind like sheafs[30] of burning sparks.

[26] *Franciscan Friary* – a community of Catholic monks

[27] *two pound ten* – two pounds and ten shillings in pre-decimal money

[28] *Convent of Perpetual Reparation* – a community of Catholics that is dedicated to asking for God's forgiveness 24 hours a day

[29] *Purgatory* – a place where souls are cleaned through suffering before they can enter heaven

[30] *sheafs* – bundles

# *Into the Unknown*

# The Superstitious Man's Story

*Thomas Hardy*

'William, as you may know, was a curious, silent man; you could feel when he came near 'ee;[1] and if he was in the house or anywhere behind your back without your seeing him, there seemed to be something clammy in the air, as if a cellar door was opened close by your elbow. Well, one Sunday, at a time that William was in very good health to all appearance, the bell that was ringing for church went very heavy all of a sudden; the sexton,[2] who told me o't,[3] said he'd not known the bell go so heavy in his hand for years – and he feared it meant a death in the parish. That was on the Sunday, as I say. During the week after, it chanced that William's wife was staying up late one night to finish her ironing, she    10 doing the washing for Mr and Mrs Hardcome. Her husband had finished his supper and gone to bed as usual some hour or two before. While she ironed she heard him coming downstairs; he stopped to put on his boots at the stair-foot, where he always left them, and then came on into the living-room where she was ironing, passing through it towards the door, this being the only way from the staircase to the outside of the house. No word was said on either side, William not being a man given to much speaking, and his wife being occupied with her work. He went out and closed the door behind him. As her husband had now and then gone out in this way at night before when unwell, or unable to sleep for want of a    20 pipe, she took no particular notice, and continued at her ironing. This she finished shortly after, and as he had not come in she waited a while for him, putting away the irons and things, and preparing the table for his breakfast in the morning. Still he did not return, and supposing him not far off, and wanting to get to bed herself, tired as she was, she left the door unbarred and went up the stairs, after writing on the back of the door with chalk: *Mind and do the door* (because he was a forgetful man).

'To her great surprise, and I might say alarm, on reaching the foot of the stairs his boots were standing there as they always stood when he had gone to rest; going up to their chamber she found him in bed sleeping as    30

[1] *'ee* – thee (old-fashioned version of 'you')
[2] *sexton* – the person in charge of grave-digging, bell-ringing, and other caretaking duties in a church
[3] *o't* – of it

sound as a rock. How he could have got back again without her seeing or
hearing him was beyond her comprehension. It could only have been by
passing behind her very quietly while she was bumping with the iron.
But this notion did not satisfy her: it was surely impossible that she
should not have seen him come in through a room so small. She could
not unravel the mystery, and felt very queer and uncomfortable about it.
However, she would not disturb him to question him then, and went to
bed herself.

'He rose and left for his work very early the next morning, before she
40  was awake, and she waited his return to breakfast with much anxiety for
an explanation, for thinking over the matter by daylight made it seem
only the more startling. When he came in to the meal he said, before she
could put her question, "What's the meaning of them words chalked on
the door ?"

'She told him, and asked him about his going out the night before.
William declared that he had never left the bedroom after entering it,
having in fact undressed, lain down, and fallen asleep directly, never
once waking till the clock struck five, and he rose up to go to his labour.

'Betty Privett was as certain in her own mind that he did go out as she
50  was of her own existence, and was little less certain that he did not return.
She felt too disturbed to argue with him, and let the subject drop as
though she must have been mistaken. When she was walking down
Longpuddle street later in the day she met Jim Weedle's daughter
Nancy, and said, "Well, Nancy, you do look sleepy to-day!"

'"Yes, Mrs Privett," says Nancy. "Now don't tell anybody, but I don't
mind letting you know what the reason o't is. Last night, being Old
Midsummer Eve,[4] some of us went to church porch, and didn't get home
till near one."

'"Did ye?" says Mrs Privett. "Old Midsummer yesterday, was it?
60  Faith I didn't think whe'r[5] 'twas Midsummer or Michaelmas;[6] I'd too
much work to do."

'"Yes. And we were frightened enough, I can tell 'ee, by what we saw."
'"What did ye see?"

'(You may not remember, sir, having gone off to foreign parts so
young, that on Midsummer Night it is believed hereabout that the faint
shapes of all the folk in the parish who are going to be at death's door
within the year can be seen entering the church. Those who get over
their illness come out again after a while; those that are doomed to die do
not return.)

[4] *Midsummer Eve* – the night before Midsummer day (21 June) was supposed to be
   magical
[5] *whe'r* – whether
[6] *Michaelmas* – the feast of St Michael (29 September)

'"What did you see ?" asked William's wife.                                    70

'"Well," says Nancy, backwardly – "we needn't tell what we saw, or who we saw."

'"You saw my husband," says Betty Privett, in a quiet way.

'"Well, since you put it so," says Nancy, hanging fire,[7] "we – thought we did see him; but it was darkish, and we was frightened, and of course it might not have been he."

'"Nancy, you needn't mind letting it out, though 'tis kept back in kindness. And he didn't come out of church again: I know it as well as you."

'Nancy did not answer yes or no to that, and no more was said. But    80 three days after, William Privett was mowing with John Chiles in Mr Hardcome's meadow, and in the heat of the day they sat down to eat their bit o' lunch under a tree, and empty their flagon.[8] Afterwards both of 'em fell asleep as they sat. John Chiles was the first to wake, and as he looked towards his fellow-mower he saw one of those great white miller's-souls as we call 'em – that is to say, a miller-moth – come from William's open mouth while he slept, and fly straight away. John thought it odd enough, as William had worked in a mill for several years when he was a boy. He then looked at the sun, and found by the place o't that they had slept a long while, and as William did not wake, John called to him and said it    90 was high time to begin work again. He took no notice, and then John went up and shook him, and found he was dead.

'Now on that very day old Philip Hookhorn was down at Longpuddle Spring dipping up a pitcher[9] of water; and as he turned away, who should he see coming down to the spring on the other side but William, looking very pale and odd. This surprised Philip Hookhorn very much, for years before that time William's little son – his only child – had been drowned in that spring while at play there, and this had so preyed upon William's mind that he'd never been seen near the spring afterwards, and had been known to go half a mile out of his way to avoid the place. On inquiry, it    100 was found that William in body could not have stood by the spring, being in the mead two miles off; and it also came out that the time at which he was seen at the spring was the very time when he died.'

---

[7] *hanging fire* – hesitating
[8] *flagon* – a large drinking vessel
[9] *pitcher* – a large vessel for liquids

# Night-Fears

*L.P. Hartley*

The coke[1]-brazier[2] was elegant enough but the night-watchman was not, consciously at any rate, sensitive to beauty of form.[3] No; he valued the brazier primarily for its warmth. He could not make up his mind whether he liked its light. Two days ago, when he first took on the job, he was inclined to suspect the light; it dazzled him, made a target of him, increased his helplessness; it emphasized the darkness. But tonight he was feeling reconciled[4] to it; and aided by its dark, clear rays, he explored his domain[5] – a long narrow rectangle, fenced off from the road by poles round and thick as flag-posts and lashed loosely at the ends. By day they
10 seemed simply an obstacle to be straddled over; but at night they were boundaries, defences almost. At their junctions, where the warning red lanterns dully gleamed, they bristled like a barricade. The night-watchman felt himself in charge of a fortress.

He took a turn up and down musing.[6] Now that the strangeness of the position had worn off he could think with less effort. The first night he had vaguely wished that the 'No Thoroughfare'[7] board had faced him instead of staring uselessly up the street: it would have given his thoughts a rallying-point.[8] Now he scarcely noticed its blankness. His thoughts were few but pleasant to dwell on, and in the solitude they had the inten-
20 sity of sensations.[9] He arranged them in cycles, the rotation coming at the end of ten paces or so when he turned to go back over his tracks. He enjoyed the thought that held his mind for the moment, but always with some agreeable impatience for the next. If he surmised[10] there would be a fresh development in it, he would deliberately refrain[11] from calling it up, leave it fermenting and ripening, as it were, in a luxury of expectation.

The night-watchman was a domesticated[12] man with a wife and two

[1] *coke* – a fuel, like coal
[2] *brazier* – a metal pan or basket for burning coke
[3] *form* – shape
[4] *reconciled* – come to terms with
[5] *domain* – lands, territory
[6] *musing* – thinking
[7] *No Thoroughfare* – no way through
[8] *rallying-point* – something to cheer you up
[9] *sensations* – physical feelings, touch
[10] *surmised* – thought
[11] *refrain* – stop himself
[12] *domesticated* – fond of his home life

children, both babies. One was beginning to talk. Since he took on his job wages had risen, and everything at home seemed gilt-edged.[13] It made a difference to his wife. When he got home she would say, as she had done on the preceding[14] mornings, 'Well, you do look a wreck. This night work doesn't suit you, I'm sure.' The night-watchman liked being addressed in that way and hearing his job described as night work; it showed an easy competent familiarity with a man's occupation. He would tell her with the air of one who had seen much, about the incidents of his vigil,[15] and what he hadn't seen he would invent, just for the pleasure of hearing her say: 'Well, I never! You do have some experiences, and no mistake.' He was very fond of his wife. Why, hadn't she promised to patch up the old blue-paper blinds, used once for the air-raids, but somewhat out of repair as a consequence of their being employed as a quarry for paper to wrap up parcels? He hadn't slept well, couldn't get accustomed to sleeping by day, the room was so light; but these blinds would be just the thing, and it would be nice to see them and feel that the war was over and there was no need for them, really.

The night-watchman yawned as for the twentieth time perhaps he came up sharp against the boundary of his walk. Loss of sleep, no doubt. He would sit in his shelter and rest a bit. As he turned and saw the narrowing gleams that transformed the separating poles into thin lines of fire, he noticed that nearly at the end, just opposite the brazier in fact and only a foot or two from the door of his hut, the left line was broken. Someone was sitting on the barrier, his back turned on the night-watchman's little compound. 'Strange I never heard him come,' thought the man, brought back with a jerk from his world of thoughts to the real world of darkness and the deserted street – well, no, not exactly deserted, for here was someone who might be inclined to talk for half an hour or so. The stranger paid no attention to the watchman's slowly advancing tread. A little disconcerting. He stopped. Drunk, I expect, he thought. This would be a real adventure to tell his wife. 'I told him I wasn't going to stand any rot from him. "Now my fine fellow, you go home to bed; that's the best place for you," I said.' He had heard drunk men addressed in that way, and wondered doubtfully whether he would be able to catch the tone; it was more important than the words, he reflected. At last, pulling himself together, he walked up to the brazier and coughed loudly, and feeling ill-at-ease, set about warming his hands with such energy he nearly burned them.

[13] *gilt-edged* – precious and safe
[14] *preceding* – previous
[15] *vigil* – watch

As the stranger took no notice, but continued to sit wrapped in thought, the night-watchman hazarded a remark to his bent back. 'A fine night,' he said rather loudly, though it was ridiculous to raise one's voice in an empty street. The stranger did not turn round.

'Yes,' he replied, 'but cold; it will be colder before morning.' The night-
70    watchman looked at his brazier, and it struck him that the coke was not lasting so well as on the previous nights. I'll put some more on, he thought, picking up a shovel; but instead of the little heap he had expected to see, there was nothing but dust and a few bits of grit – his night's supply had been somehow overlooked. 'Won't you turn round and warm your hands?' he said to the person sitting on the barrier. 'The fire isn't very good, but I can't make it up, for they forgot to give me any extra, unless somebody pinched it when my back was turned.' The night-watchman was talking for effect; he did not really believe that anyone had taken the coke. The stranger might have made a movement somewhere about the shoulders.
80    'Thank you,' he said, 'but I prefer to warm my back.'

Funny idea that, thought the watchman.

'Have you noticed,' proceeded the stranger, 'how easily men forget? This coke of yours, I mean; it looks as if they didn't care about you very much, leaving you in the cold like this.' It had certainly grown colder, but the man replied cheerfully: 'Oh, it wasn't that. They forgot it. Hurrying to get home, you know.' Still, they might have remembered, he thought. It was Bill Jackson's turn to fetch it – Old Bill, as the fellows call him. He doesn't like me very much. The chaps are a bit stand-offish.[16] They'll be all right when I know them better.
90    His visitor had not stirred. How I would like to push him off, the night-watchman thought, irritated and somehow troubled. The stranger's voice broke in upon his reflections.

'Don't you like this job?'

'Oh, not so bad,' said the man carelessly; 'good money, you know.'

'Good money,' repeated the stranger scornfully. 'How much do you get?'

The night-watchman named the sum.

'Are you married, and have you got any children?' the stranger persisted.
100    The night-watchman said 'Yes,' without enthusiasm.

'Well, that won't go very far when the children are a bit older,' declared the stranger. 'Have you any prospect of a rise?' The man said no, he had just had one.

'Prices going up, too,' the stranger commented.

[16] *stand-offish* – distant
[17] *hostility* – dislike

A change came over the night-watchman's outlook. The feeling of hostility[17] and unrest increased. He couldn't deny all this. He longed to say, 'What do you think you're getting at?' and rehearsed the phrase under his breath, but couldn't get himself to utter it aloud; his visitor had created his present state of mind and was lord of it. Another picture floated before him, less rosy than the first: an existence drab-coloured[18] with the dust of conflict, but relieved by the faithful support of his wife and children at home. After all, that's the life for a man, he thought; but he did not cherish[19] the idea, did not walk up and down hugging it, as he cherished and hugged the other.

'Do you find it easy to sleep in the daytime?' asked the stranger presently.

'Not very,' the night-watchman admitted.

'Ah,' said the stranger, 'dreadful thing, insomnia.'

'When you can't go to sleep, you mean,' interpreted the night-watchman, not without a secret pride.

'Yes,' came the answer. 'Makes a man ill, mad sometimes. People have done themselves in sooner than stand the torture.'

It was on the tip of the night-watchman's tongue to mention that panacea,[20] the blue blinds. But he thought it would sound foolish, and wondered whether they would prove such a sovereign remedy[21] after all.

'What about your children? You won't see much of them,' remarked the stranger, 'while you are on this job. Why they'll grow up without knowing you! Up when their papa's in bed and in bed when he's up! Not that you miss them much, I dare say. Still, if children don't get fond of their father while they're young, they never will.'

Why didn't the night-watchman take him up warmly, assuring him they were splendid kids; the eldest called him daddy, and the younger, his wife declared, already recognized him. She knew by its smile, she said. He couldn't have forgotten all that; half an hour ago it had been one of his chief thoughts. He was silent.

'I should try and find another job if I were you,' observed the stranger. 'Otherwise you won't be able to make both ends meet. What will your wife say then?'

The man considered; at least he thought he was facing the question, but his mind was somehow too deeply disturbed, and circled wearily and blindly in its misery. 'I was never brought up to a trade,' he said hesitatingly; 'father's fault.' It struck him that he had never confessed that before; had sworn not to give his father away. What am I coming to? he

110

120

130

140

[18] *drab-coloured* – dull brown

[19] *cherish* – treasure, value

[20] *panacea* – a cure for everything

[21] *sovereign remedy* – ultimate cure

thought. Then he made an effort. 'My wife's all right, she'll stick to me.'
He waited, positively dreading the stranger's next attack. Though the
fire was burning low, almost obscured under the coke ashes that always
seem more lifeless than any others, he felt drops of perspiration on his
forehead, and his clothes, he knew, were soaked. I shall get a chill, that'll
be the next thing, he thought; but it was involuntary:[22] such an idea
150   hadn't occurred to him since he was a child, supposedly delicate.

'Yes, your wife,' said the stranger at last, in tones so cold and clear that
they seemed to fill the universe; to admit of no contradiction; to be
graven with a fine unerring instrument out of the hard rock of truth
itself. 'You won't see much of her either. You leave her pretty much to
herself, don't you? Now with these women, you know, that's a *risk*.' The
last word rang like a challenge; but the night-watchman had taken the
offensive, shot his one little bolt, and the effort had left him more helpless than ever.

'When the eye doth not see,'[23] continued the stranger, 'the heart doth
160   not grieve; on the contrary, it makes merry.' He laughed, as the night-
watchman could see from the movement of his shoulders. 'I've known
cases very similar to yours. When the cat's away, you know! It's a pity
you're under contract to finish this job' (the night-watchman had not
mentioned a contract), 'but as you are, take my advice and get a friend to
keep an eye on your house. Of course, he won't be able to stay the night –
of course not; but tell him to keep his eyes open.'

The stranger seemed to have said his say, his head drooped a little
more; he might even be dropping off to sleep. Apparently he did not feel
the cold. But the night-watchman was breathing hard and could scarcely
170   stand. He tottered a little way down his territory, wondering absurdly
why the place looked so tidy; but what a travesty[24] of his former progress.
And what a confusion in his thoughts, and what a thumping in his
temples. Slowly from the writhing, tearing mass in his mind a resolve
shaped itself; like a cuckoo[25] it displaced all others. He loosened the red
handkerchief that was knotted round his neck, without remembering
whose fingers had tied it a few hours before, or that it had been promoted
(not without washing) to the status of a garment from the menial func-
tion of carrying his lunch. It had been an extravagance, that tin carrier,
much debated over, and justified finally by the rise in the night-
180   watchman's wages. He let the handkerchief drop as he fumbled for the
knife in his pocket, but the blade, which was stiff, he got out with little
difficulty. Wondering vaguely if he would be able to do it, whether the

[22]  *involuntary* – without wanting to
[23]  *when the eye doth not see . . .* – what you don't see can't hurt you
[24]  *travesty* – a ridiculous imitation
[25]  *cuckoo* – a bird that takes over other birds' nests, replacing their eggs with its own

right movement would come to him, why he hadn't practised it, he took a step towards the brazier. It was the one friendly object in the street. . . .

Later in the night the stranger, without putting his hands on the pole to steady himself, turned round for the first time and regarded the body of the night-watchman. He even stepped over into the little compound and, remembering perhaps the dead man's invitation, stretched out his hands over the still warm ashes in the brazier. Then he climbed back, and, crossing the street, entered a blind alley opposite, leaving a track of dark, irregular footprints; and since he did not return it is probable that he lived there.

190

# Rites of Passage

## Malachi's Cove

*Anthony Trollope*

On the northern coast of Cornwall, between Tintagel and Bossiney, down on the very margin of the sea, there lived not long since an old man who got his living by saving seaweed from the waves, and selling it for manure. The cliffs there are bold and fine, and the sea beats in upon them from the north with a grand violence. I doubt whether it be not the finest morsel of cliff scenery in England, though it is beaten by many portions of the west coast of Ireland, and perhaps also by spots in Wales and Scotland. Cliffs should be nearly precipitous, they should be broken in their outlines, and should barely admit here and there of an insecure passage from their summit to the sand at their feet. The sea should come, if not up to them, at least very near to them, and then, above all things, the water below them should be blue, and not of that dead leaden colour which is so familiar to us in England. At Tintagel all these requisites are there, except that bright blue colour which is so lovely. But the cliffs themselves are bold and well broken, and the margin of sand at high water is very narrow, – so narrow that at spring-tides there is barely a footing there.

Close upon this margin was the cottage or hovel of Malachi Trenglos, the old man of whom I have spoken. But Malachi, or old Glos, as he was commonly called by the people around him, had not built his house absolutely upon the sand. There was a fissure[1] in the rock so great that at the top it formed a narrow ravine,[2] and so complete from the summit to the base that it afforded an opening for a steep and rugged track from the top of the rock to the bottom. This fissure was so wide at the bottom that it had afforded space for Trenglos to fix his habitation on a foundation of rock, and here he had lived for many years. It was told of him that in the early days of his trade he had always carried the weed in a basket on his back to the top, but latterly he had been possessed of a donkey, which had been trained to go up and down the steep track with a single pannier over his loins,[3] for the rocks would not admit of panniers hanging by his side;

---

[1] *fissure* – a narrow opening in the cliff face
[2] *ravine* – a narrow steep sided valley
[3] *pannier over his loins* – a carrying basket on its back

and for this assistant he had built a shed adjoining his own, and almost as large as that in which he himself resided.

But, as years went on, old Glos procured other assistance than that of the donkey, or, as I should rather say, Providence supplied him with other help; and, indeed, had it not been so, the old man must have given up his cabin and his independence and gone into the workhouse[+] at Camelford. For rheumatism had afflicted him, old age had bowed him till he was nearly double, and by degrees he became unable to attend the donkey on its upward passage to the world above, or even to assist in rescuing the coveted weed from the waves.                                      40

At the time to which our story refers Trenglos had not been up the cliff for twelve months, and for the last six months he had done nothing towards the furtherance of his trade, except to take the money and keep it, if any of it was kept, and occasionally to shake down a bundle of fodder for the donkey. The real work of the business was done altogether by Mahala Trenglos, his granddaughter.

Mally Trenglos was known to all the farmers round the coast, and to all the small tradespeople in Camelford. She was a wild-looking, almost unearthly creature, with wild-flowing, black, uncombed hair, small in stature, with small hands and bright black eyes; but people said that she      50
was very strong, and the children around declared that she worked day and night and knew nothing of fatigue. As to her age there were many doubts. Some said she was ten, and others five-and-twenty, but the reader may be allowed to know that at this time she had in truth passed her twentieth birthday. The old people spoke well of Mally, because she was so good to her grandfather; and it was said of her that though she carried to him a little gin and tobacco almost daily, she bought nothing for herself; – and as to the gin, no one who looked at her would accuse her of meddling with that. But she had no friends and but few acquaintances among people of her own age. They said that she was fierce and ill-      60
natured, that she had not a good word for any one, and that she was, complete at all points, a thorough little vixen. The young men did not care for her; for, as regarded dress, all days were alike with her. She never made herself smart on Sundays. She was generally without stockings, and seemed to care not at all to exercise any of those feminine attractions which might have been hers had she studied to attain them. All days were the same to her in regard to dress; and, indeed, till lately, all days had, I fear, been the same to her in other respects. Old Malachi had never been seen inside a place of worship since he had taken to live under the cliff.

But within the last two years Mally had submitted herself to the      70

[+] *workhouse* – a building that provided work and accommodation for the unemployed poor of a parish

teaching of the clergyman at Tintagel, and had appeared at church on Sundays, if not absolutely with punctuality, at any rate so often that no one who knew the peculiarity of her residence was disposed to quarrel with her on that subject. But she made no difference in her dress on these occasions. She took her place on a low stone seat just inside the church door, clothed as usual in her thick red serge[5] petticoat and loose brown serge jacket, such being the apparel which she had found to be best adapted for her hard and perilous work among the waters. She had pleaded to the clergyman when he attacked her on the subject of church

80 attendance with vigour that she had got no church-going clothes. He had explained to her that she would be received there without distinction to her clothing. Mally had taken him at his word, and had gone, with a courage which certainly deserved admiration, though I doubt whether there was not mingled with it an obstinacy which was less admirable.

For people said that old Glos was rich, and that Mally might have proper clothes if she chose to buy them. Mr Polwarth, the clergyman, who, as the old man could not come to him, went down the rocks to the old man, did make some hint on the matter in Mally's absence. But old

90 Glos, who had been patient with him on other matters, turned upon him so angrily when he made an allusion to money, that Mr Polwarth found himself obliged to give that matter up, and Mally continued to sit upon the stone bench in her short serge petticoat, with her long hair streaming down her face. She did so far sacrifice to decency as on such occasions to tie up her black hair with an old shoestring. So tied it would remain through the Monday and Tuesday, but by Wednesday afternoon Mally's hair had generally managed to escape.

As to Mally's indefatigable industry[6] there could be no manner of doubt, for the quantity of seaweed which she and the donkey amassed

100 between them was very surprising. Old Glos, it was declared, had never collected half what Mally gathered together; but then the article was becoming cheaper, and it was necessary that the exertion should be greater. So Mally and the donkey toiled and toiled, and the seaweed came up in heaps which surprised those who looked at her little hands and light form. Was there not some one who helped her at nights, some fairy, or demon, or the like? Mally was so snappish in her answers to people that she had no right to be surprised if ill-natured things were said of her.

No one ever heard Mally Trenglos complain of her work, but about this time she was heard to make great and loud complaints of the treat-

110 ment she received from some of her neighbours. It was known that she

[5] *serge* – a cheap woollen cloth

[6] *indefatigable industry* – ability to work hard without getting tired

went with her plaints[7] to Mr Polwarth; and when he could not help her, or did not give her such instant help as she needed, she went – ah, so foolishly! to the office of a certain attorney at Camelford, who was not likely to prove himself a better friend than Mr Polwarth.

Now the nature of her injury was as follows. The place in which she collected her seaweed was a little cove; – the people had come to call it Malachi's Cove from the name of the old man who lived there; – which was so formed, that the margin of the sea therein could only be reached by the passage from the top down to Trenglos's hut. The breadth of the cove when the sea was out might perhaps be two hundred yards, and on each side the rocks ran out in such a way that both from north and south the domain[8] of Trenglos was guarded from intruders. And this locality had been well chosen for its intended purpose. 120

There was a rush of the sea into the cove, which carried there large, drifting masses of seaweed, leaving them among the rocks when the tide was out. During the equinoctial[9] winds of the spring and autumn the supply would never fail; and even when the sea was calm, the long, soft, salt-bedewed, trailing masses of the weed, could be gathered there when they could not be found elsewhere for miles along the coast. The task of getting the weed from the breakers was often difficult and dangerous, – so difficult that much of it was left to be carried away by the next incoming tide. 130

Mally doubtless did not gather half the crop that was there at her feet. What was taken by the returning waves she did not regret; but when interlopers[10] came upon her cove, and gathered her wealth, – her grandfather's wealth, beneath her eyes, then her heart was broken. It was this interloping, this intrusion, that drove poor Mally to the Camelford attorney. But, alas, though the Camelford attorney took Mally's money, he could do nothing for her, and her heart was broken!

She had an idea, in which no doubt her grandfather shared, that the path to the cove was, at any rate, their property. When she was told that the cove, and sea running into the cove, were not the freeholds[11] of her grandfather, she understood that the statement might be true. But what then as to the use of the path? Who had made the path what it was? Had she not painfully, wearily, with exceeding toil, carried up bits of rock with her own little hands, that her grandfather's donkey might have footing for his feet? Had she not scraped together crumbs of earth along 140

[7] *plaints* – complaints
[8] *domain* – the lands
[9] *equinoctial* – the times of year when day and night are about the same length, during autumn and spring
[10] *interlopers* – intruders
[11] *freeholds* – property

65

the face of the cliff that she might make easier to the animal the track of that rugged way? And now, when she saw big farmer's lads coming down 150 with other donkeys, – and, indeed, there was one who came with a pony; no boy, but a young man, old enough to know better than rob a poor old man and a young girl, – she reviled the whole human race, and swore that the Camelford attorney was a fool.

Any attempt to explain to her that there was still weed enough for her was worse than useless. Was it not all hers and his, or, at any rate, was not the sole way to it his and hers? And was not her trade stopped and impeded? Had she not been forced to back her laden donkey down, twenty yards she said, but it had, in truth, been five, because Farmer Gunliffe's son had been in the way with his thieving pony? Farmer 160 Gunliffe had wanted to buy her weed at his own price, and because she had refused he had set on his thieving son to destroy her in this wicked way.

'I'll hamstring[12] the beast the next time as he's down here!' said Mally to old Glos, while the angry fire literally streamed from her eyes.

Farmer Gunliffe's small homestead, – he held about fifty acres of land, was close by the village of Tintagel, and not a mile from the cliff. The sea-wrack, as they call it, was pretty well the only manure within his reach, and no doubt he thought it hard that he should be kept from using it by Mally Trenglos and her obstinacy.

170 'There's heaps of other coves, Barty,' said Mally to Barty Gunliffe, the farmer's son.

'But none so nigh,[13] Mally, nor yet none that fills 'emselves as this place.'

Then he explained to her that he would not take the weed that came up close to hand. He was bigger than she was, and stronger, and would get it from the outer rocks, with which she never meddled. Then, with scorn in her eye, she swore that she could get it where he durst[14] not venture,[15] and repeated her threat of hamstringing the pony. Barty laughed at her wrath,[16] jeered her because of her wild hair, and called her a mermaid.

180 'I'll mermaid you!' she cried. 'Mermaid, indeed! I wouldn't be a man to come and rob a poor girl and an old cripple. But you're no man, Barty Gunliffe! You're not half a man.'

Nevertheless, Bartholomew Gunliffe was a very fine young fellow as far as the eye went. He was about five feet eight inches high, with strong arms and legs, with light curly brown hair and blue eyes. His father was

---

12  *hamstring* – cripple
13  *nigh* – (dialect) near
14  *durst* – (dialect) dared
15  *venture* – dare to go
16  *wrath* – (old fashioned) anger

but in a small way as a farmer, but, nevertheless, Barty Gunliffe was well thought of among the girls around. Everybody liked Barty, – excepting only Mally Trenglos, and she hated him like poison.

Barty, when he was asked why so good-natured a lad as he persecuted a poor girl and an old man, threw himself upon the justice of the thing. It wouldn't do at all, according to his view, that any single person should take upon himself to own that which God Almighty sent as the common property of all. He would do Mally no harm, and so he had told her. But Mally was a vixen, – a wicked little vixen; and she must be taught to have a civil tongue in her head. When once Mally would speak him civil as he went for weed, he would get his father to pay the old man some sort of toll for the use of the path.

'Speak him civil?' said Mally. 'Never; not while I have a tongue in my mouth!' And I fear old Glos encouraged her rather than otherwise in her view of the matter.

But her grandfather did not encourage her to hamstring the pony. Hamstringing a pony would be a serious thing, and old Glos thought it might be very awkward for both of them if Mally were put into prison. He suggested, therefore, that all manner of impediments[17] should be put in the way of the pony's feet, surmising that the well-trained donkey might be able to work in spite of them. And Barty Gunliffe, on his next descent, did find the passage very awkward when he came near to Malachi's hut, but he made his way down, and poor Mally saw the lumps of rock at which she had laboured so hard pushed on one side or rolled out of the way with a steady persistency of injury towards herself that almost drove her frantic.

'Well, Barty, you're a nice boy,' said old Glos, sitting in the doorway of the hut, as he watched the intruder.

'I ain't a doing no harm to none as doesn't harm me,' said Barty. 'The sea's free to all, Malachi.'

'And the sky's free to all, but I musn't get up on the top of your big barn to look at it,' said Mally, who was standing among the rocks with a long hook in her hand. The long hook was the tool with which she worked in dragging the weed from the waves. 'But you ain't got no justice, nor yet no sperrit,[18] or you wouldn't come here to vex[19] an old man like he.'

'I didn't want to vex him, nor yet to vex you, Mally. You let me be for a while, and we'll be friends yet.'

'Friends!' exclaimed Mally. 'Who'd have the likes of you for a friend?

---

[17] *impediments* – obstacles
[18] *sperrit* – (dialect) spirit
[19] *vex* – annoy

What are you moving them stones for? Them stones belongs to grand-father.' And in her wrath she made a movement as though she were going to fly at him.

'Let him be, Mally,' said the old man; 'let him be. He'll get his punish-ment. He'll come to be drowned some day if he comes down here when
230   the wind is in shore.'

'That he may be drowned then!' said Mally, in her anger. 'If he was in the big hole there among the rocks, and the sea running in at half-tide, I wouldn't lift a hand to help him out.'

'Yes, you would, Mally; you'd fish me up with your hook like a big stick of seaweed.'

She turned from him with scorn as he said this, and went into the hut. It was time for her to get ready for her work, and one of the great injuries done her lay in this, – that such a one as Barty Gunliffe should come and look at her during her toil among the breakers.
240   It was an afternoon in April, and the hour was something after four o'clock. There had been a heavy wind from the north-west all the morning, with gusts of rain, and the sea-gulls had been in and out of the cove all the day, which was a sure sign to Mally that the incoming tide would cover the rocks with weed.

The quick waves were now returning with wonderful celerity[20] over the low reefs, and the time had come at which the treasure must be seized, if it was to be garnered[21] on that day. By seven o'clock it would be growing dark, at nine it would be high water, and before daylight the crop would be carried out again if not collected. All this Mally under-
250   stood very well, and some of this Barty was beginning to understand also.

As Mally came down with her bare feet, bearing her long hook in her hand, she saw Barty's pony standing patiently on the sand, and in her heart she longed to attack the brute. Barty at this moment, with a common three-pronged fork in his hand, was standing down on a large rock, gazing forth towards the waters. He had declared that he would gather the weed only at places which were inaccessible to Mally, and he was looking out that he might settle where he would begin.

'Let 'un[22] be, let 'un be,' shouted the old man to Mally, as he saw her take a step towards the beast, which she hated almost as much as she
260   hated the man.

Hearing her grandfather's voice through the wind, she desisted from her purpose, if any purpose she had had, and went forth to her work. As she passed down the cove, and scrambled in among the rocks, she saw

[20] *celerity* – speed
[21] *garnered* – gathered
[22] *'un* – (dialect) him, it, or her

Barty still standing on his perch; out beyond, the white-curling waves were cresting and breaking themselves with violence, and the wind was howling among the caverns and abutments[23] of the cliff.

Every now and then there came a squall of rain, and though there was sufficient light, the heavens were black with clouds. A scene more beautiful might hardly be found by those who love the glories of the coast. The light for such objects was perfect. Nothing could exceed the grandeur of the colours, – the blue of the open sea, the white of the breaking waves, the yellow sands, or the streaks of red and brown which gave such richness to the cliff. 270

But neither Mally nor Barty were thinking of such things as these. Indeed they were hardly thinking of their trade after its ordinary forms. Barty was meditating how he might best accomplish his purpose of working beyond the reach of Mally's feminine powers, and Mally was resolving that wherever Barty went she would go farther.

And, in many respects, Mally had the advantage. She knew every rock in the spot, and was sure of those which gave a good foothold, and sure also of those which did not. And then her activity had been made perfect by practice for the purpose to which it was to be devoted. Barty, no doubt, was stronger than she, and quite as active. But Barty could not jump among the waves from one stone to another as she could do, nor was he as yet able to get aid in his work from the very force of the water as she could get it. She had been hunting seaweed in that cove since she had been an urchin[24] of six years old, and she knew every hole and corner and every spot of vantage.[25] The waves were her friends, and she could use them. She could measure their strength, and knew when and where it would cease. 290

Mally was great down in the salt pools of her own cove, – great, and very fearless. As she watched Barty make his way forward from rock to rock, she told herself, gleefully, that he was going astray. The curl of the wind as it blew into the cove would not carry the weed up to the northern buttresses of the cove; and then there was the great hole just there, – the great hole of which she had spoken when she wished him evil.

And now she went to work, hooking up the dishevelled hairs of the ocean, and landing many a cargo on the extreme margin of the sand, from whence she would be able in the evening to drag it back before the invading waters would return to reclaim the spoil. 300

And on his side also Barty made his heap up against the northern buttresses of which I have spoken. Barty's heap became big and still

---

[23] *abutments* – parts of the cliff that jut out to sea, the same as buttresses

[24] *urchin* – a roguish, poor child

[25] *vantage* – better position

bigger, so that he knew, let the pony work as he might, he could not take it all up that evening. But still it was not as large as Mally's heap. Mally's hook was better than his fork, and Mally's skill was better than his strength. And when he failed in some haul Mally would jeer him with a wild, weird laughter, and shriek to him through the wind that he was not half a man. At first he answered her with laughing words, but before long, as she boasted of her success and pointed to his failure, he became 310 angry, and then he answered her no more. He became angry with himself, in that he missed so much of the plunder before him.

The broken sea was full of the long straggling growth which the waves had torn up from the bottom of the ocean, but the masses were carried past him, away from him, – nay, once or twice over him; and then Mally's weird voice would sound in his ear, jeering him. The gloom among the rocks was now becoming thicker and thicker, the tide was beating in with increased strength, and the gusts of wind came with quicker and greater violence. But still he worked on. While Mally worked he would work, and he would work for some time after she was 320 driven in. He would not be beaten by a girl.

The great hole was now full of water, but of water which seemed to be boiling as though in a pot. And the pot was full of floating masses, – large treasures of seaweed which were thrown to and fro upon its surface, but lying there so thick that one would seem almost able to rest upon it without sinking.

Mally knew well how useless it was to attempt to rescue aught from the fury of that boiling caldron. The hole went in under the rocks, and the side of it towards the shore lay high, slippery, and steep. The hole, even at low water, was never empty; and Mally believed that there was no 330 bottom to it. Fish thrown in there could escape out to the ocean, miles away, – so Mally in her softer moods would tell the visitors to the cove. She knew the hole well. Poulnadioul she was accustomed to call it; which was supposed, when translated, to mean that this was the hole of the Evil One. Never did Mally attempt to make her own of weed which had found its way into that pot.

But Barty Gunliffe knew no better, and she watched him as he endeavoured to steady himself on the treacherously slippery edge of the pool. He fixed himself there and made a haul, with some small success. How he managed it she hardly knew, but she stood still for a while watching him 340 anxiously, and then she saw him slip. He slipped, and recovered himself; – slipped again, and again recovered himself.

'Barty, you fool!' she screamed, 'if you get yourself pitched in there, you'll never come out no more.'

Whether she simply wished to frighten him, or whether her heart relented and she had thought of his danger with dismay, who shall say?

70

She could not have told herself. She hated him as much as ever, – but she could hardly have wished to see him drowned before her eyes.

'You go on, and don't mind me,' said he, speaking in a hoarse, angry tone.

'Mind you! – who minds you?' retorted the girl. And then she again prepared herself for her work.

But as she went down over the rocks with her long hook balanced in her hands, she suddenly heard a splash, and, turning quickly round, saw the body of her enemy tumbling amidst the eddying waves in the pool. The tide had now come up so far that every succeeding[26] wave washed into it and over it from the side nearest to the sea, and then ran down again back from the rocks, as the rolling wave receded, with a noise like the fall of a cataract.[27] And then, when the surplus water had retreated for a moment, the surface of the pool would be partly calm, though the fretting bubbles would still boil up and down, and there was ever a simmer on the surface, as though, in truth, the caldron were heated. But this time of comparative rest was but a moment, for the succeeding breaker would come up almost as soon as the foam of the preceding one had gone, and then again the waters would be dashed upon the rocks, and the sides would echo with the roar of the angry wave.

Instantly Mally hurried across to the edge of the pool, crouching down upon her hands and knees for security as she did so. As a wave receded, Barty's head and face was carried round near to her, and she could see that his forehead was covered with blood. Whether he were alive or dead she did not know. She had seen nothing but his blood, and the light-coloured hair of his head lying amidst the foam. Then his body was drawn along by the suction of the retreating wave; but the mass of water that escaped was not on this occasion large enough to carry the man out with it.

Instantly Mally was at work with her hook, and getting it fixed into his coat, dragged him towards the spot on which she was kneeling. During the half minute of repose she got him so close that she could touch his shoulder. Straining herself down, laying herself over the long bending handle of the hook, she strove to grasp him with her right hand. But she could not do it; she could only touch him.

Then came the next breaker, forcing itself on with a roar, looking to Mally as though it must certainly knock her from her resting-place, and destroy them both. But she had nothing for it but to kneel, and hold by her hook.

What prayer passed through her mind at that moment for herself or for him, or for that old man who was sitting unconsciously up at the cabin,

[26] *succeeding* – following
[27] *cataract* – waterfall

who can say? The great wave came and rushed over her as she lay almost prostrate, and when the water was gone from her eyes, and the tumult of the foam, and the violence of the roaring breaker had passed by her, she found herself at her length upon the rock, while his body had been lifted
390 up, free from her hook, and was lying upon the slippery ledge, half in the water and half out of it. As she looked at him, in that instant, she could see that his eyes were open and that he was struggling with his hands.

'Hold by the hook, Barty,' she cried, pushing the stick of it before him, while she seized the collar of his coat in her hands.

Had he been her brother, her lover, her father she could not have clung to him with more of the energy of despair. He did contrive to hold by the stick which she had given him, and when the succeeding wave had passed by, he was still on the ledge. In the next moment she was seated a yard or two above the hole, in comparative safety, while Barty lay upon the rocks
400 with his still bleeding head resting upon her lap.

What could she do now? She could not carry him; and in fifteen minutes the sea would be up where she was sitting. He was quite insensible, and very pale, and the blood was coming slowly, – very slowly, – from the wound on his forehead. Ever so gently she put her hand upon his hair to move it back from his face; and then she bent over his mouth to see if he breathed, and as she looked at him she knew that he was beautiful.

What would she not give that he might live? Nothing now was so precious to her as his life, – as this life which she had so far rescued from the waters. But what could she do? Her grandfather could scarcely get
410 himself down over the rocks, if indeed he could succeed in doing so much as that. Could she drag the wounded man backwards, if it were only a few feet, so that he might lie above the reach of the waves till further assistance could be procured?

She set herself to work and she moved him, almost lifting him. As she did so she wondered at her own strength, but she was very strong at that moment. Slowly, tenderly, falling on the rocks herself so that he might fall on her, she got him back to the margin of the sand, to a spot which the waters would not reach for the next two hours.

Here her grandfather met them, having seen at last what had happened
420 from the door.

'Dada,' she said, 'he fell into the pool yonder, and was battered against the rocks. See there at his forehead.'

'Mally, I'm thinking that he's dead already,' said old Glos, peering down over the body.

'No, dada; he is not dead; but mayhap[28] he's dying. But I'll go at once up to the farm.'

[28] *mayhap* – perhaps

72

'Mally,' said the old man, 'look at his head. They'll say we murdered him.'

'Who'll say so? Who'll lie like that? Didn't I pull him out of the hole?'

'What matters that? His father'll say we killed him.'                    430

It was manifest to Mally that whatever any one might say hereafter, her present course was plain before her. She must run up the path to Gunliffe's farm and get necessary assistance. If the world were as bad as her grandfather said, it would be so bad that she would not care to live longer in it. But be that as it might, there was no doubt as to what she must do now.

So away she went as fast as her naked feet could carry her up the cliff. When at the top she looked round to see if any person might be within ken,[29] but she saw no one. So she ran with all her speed along the head-land of the corn-field which led in the direction of old Gunliffe's house,    440
and as she drew near to the homestead she saw that Barty's mother was leaning on the gate. As she approached she attempted to call, but her breath failed her for any purpose of loud speech, so she ran on till she was able to grasp Mrs Gunliffe by the arm.

'Where's himself?' she said, holding her hand upon her beating heart that she might husband[30] her breath.

'Who is it you mean?' said Mrs Gunliffe, who participated in the family feud against Trenglos and his granddaughter. 'What does the girl clutch me for in that way?'

'He's dying then, that's all.'                                           450

'Who is dying? Is it old Malachi? If the old man's bad, we'll send some one down.'

'It ain't dada; it's Barty! Where's himself? where's the master?' But by this time Mrs Gunliffe was in an agony of despair, and was calling out for assistance lustily. Happily Gunliffe, the father, was at hand, and with him a man from the neighbouring village.

'Will you not send for the doctor?' said Mally. 'Oh, man, you should send for the doctor!'

Whether any orders were given for the doctor she did not know, but in a very few minutes she was hurrying across the field again towards the    460
path to the cove, and Gunliffe with the other man and his wife were following her.

As Mally went along she recovered her voice, for their step was not so quick as hers, and that which to them was a hurried movement, allowed her to get her breath again. And as she went she tried to explain to the father what had happened, saying but little, however, of her own doings

[29] *ken* – sight
[30] *husband* – save

in the matter. The wife hung behind listening, exclaiming every now and again that her boy was killed, and then asking wild questions as to his being yet alive. The father, as he went, said little. He was known as a
470 silent, sober man, well spoken of for diligence and general conduct, but supposed to be stern and very hard when angered.

As they drew near to the top of the path the other man whispered something to him, and then he turned round upon Mally and stopped her.

'If he has come by his death between you, your blood shall be taken for his,' said he.

Then the wife shrieked out that her child had been murdered, and Mally, looking round into the faces of the three, saw that her grand-father's words had come true. They suspected her of having taken the
480 life, in saving which she had nearly lost her own.

She looked round at them with awe in her face, and then, without saying a word, preceded them down the path. What had she to answer when such a charge as that was made against her? If they chose to say that she pushed him into the pool and hit him with her hook as he lay amidst the waters, how could she show that it was not so?

Poor Mally knew little of the law of evidence, and it seemed to her that she was in their hands. But as she went down the steep track with a hurried step, – a step so quick that they could not keep up with her, – her heart was very full, – very full and very high. She had striven[31] for the
490 man's life as though he had been her brother. The blood was yet not dry on her own legs and arms, where she had torn them in his service. At one moment she had felt sure that she would die with him in that pool. And now they said that she had murdered him! It may be that he was not dead, and what would he say if ever he should speak again? Then she thought of that moment when his eyes had opened, and he had seemed to see her. She had no fear for herself, for her heart was very high. But it was full also, – full of scorn, disdain,[32] and wrath.

When she had reached the bottom, she stood close to the door of the hut waiting for them, so that they might precede her to the other group,
500 which was there in front of them, at a little distance on the sand.

'He is there, and dada is with him. Go and look at him,' said Mally.

The father and mother ran on stumbling over the stones, but Mally remained behind by the door of the hut.

Barty Gunliffe was lying on the sand where Mally had left him, and old Malachi Trenglos was standing over him, resting himself with diffi-culty upon a stick.

---

[31] *striven* – struggled

[32] *scorn, disdain* – contempt

'Not a move he's moved since she left him,' said he; 'not a move. I put his head on the old rug as you see, and I tried 'un with a drop of gin, but he wouldn't take it, – he wouldn't take it.'

'Oh, my boy! my boy!' said the mother, throwing herself beside her son upon the sand. 510

'Haud[33] your tongue, woman,' said the father, kneeling down slowly by the lad's head, 'whimpering that way will do 'un no good.'

Then having gazed for a minute or two upon the pale face beneath him, he looked up sternly into that of Malachi Trenglos.

The old man hardly knew how to bear this terrible inquisition.

'He would come,' said Malachi; 'he brought it all upon hisself.'

'Who was it struck him?' said the father.

'Sure he struck hisself, as he fell among the breakers.'

'Liar!' said the father, looking up at the old man. 520

'They have murdered him! – they have murdered him!' shrieked the mother.

'Haud your peace, woman!' said the husband again. 'They shall give us blood for blood.'

Mally, leaning against the corner of the hovel, heard it all, but did not stir. They might say what they liked. They might make it out to be murder. They might drag her and her grandfather to Camelford gaol, and then to Bodmin, and the gallows; but they could not take from her the conscious feeling that was her own. She had done her best to save him, – her very best. And she had saved him! 530

She remembered her threat to him before they had gone down on the rocks together, and her evil wish. Those words had been very wicked; but since that she had risked her life to save his. They might say what they pleased of her, and do what they pleased. She knew what she knew.

Then the father raised his son's head and shoulders in his arms, and called on the others to assist him in carrying Barty towards the path. They raised him between them carefully and tenderly, and lifted their burden on towards the spot at which Mally was standing. She never moved, but watched them at their work; and the old man followed them, hobbling after them with his crutch. 540

When they had reached the end of the hut she looked upon Barty's face, and saw that it was very pale. There was no longer blood upon the forehead, but the great gash was to be seen there plainly, with its jagged cut, and the skin livid and blue round the orifice. His light brown hair was hanging back, as she had made it to hang when she had gathered it with her hand after the big wave had passed over them. Ah, how beautiful he was in Mally's eyes with that pale face, and the sad scar upon his

---

[33] *haud* – (dialect) hold

brow! She turned her face away, that they might not see her tears; but she did not move, nor did she speak.

550 But now, when they had passed the end of the hut, shuffling along with their burden, she heard a sound which stirred her. She roused herself quickly from her leaning posture, and stretched forth her head as though to listen; then she moved to follow them. Yes, they had stopped at the bottom of the path, and had again laid the body on the rocks. She heard that sound again, as of a long, long sigh, and then, regardless of any of them, she ran to the wounded man's head.

'He is not dead,' she said. 'There; he is not dead.'

As she spoke Barty's eyes opened, and he looked about him.

'Barty, my boy, speak to me,' said the mother.

560 Barty turned his face upon his mother, smiled, and then stared about him wildly.

'How is it with thee, lad?' said his father. Then Barty turned his face again to the latter voice, and as he did so his eyes fell upon Mally.

'Mally!' he said, 'Mally!'

It could have wanted nothing further to any of those present to teach them that, according to Barty's own view of the case, Mally had not been his enemy; and, in truth, Mally herself wanted no further triumph. That word had vindicated[34] her, and she withdrew back to the hut.

'Dada,' she said, 'Barty is not dead, and I'm thinking they won't say 570 anything more about our hurting him.'

Old Glos shook his head. He was glad the lad hadn't met his death there; he didn't want the young man's blood, but he knew what folk would say. The poorer he was the more sure the world would be to trample on him. Mally said what she could to comfort him, being full of comfort herself.

She would have crept up to the farm if she dared, to ask how Barty was. But her courage failed her when she thought of that, so she went to work again, dragging back the weed she had saved to the spot at which on the morrow she would load the donkey. As she did this she saw Barty's 580 pony still standing patiently under the rock; so she got a lock of fodder and threw it down before the beast.

It had become dark down in the cove, but she was still dragging back the seaweed, when she saw the glimmer of a lantern coming down the pathway. It was a most unusual sight, for lanterns were not common down in Malachi's Cove. Down came the lantern rather slowly, – much more slowly than she was in the habit of descending, and then through the gloom she saw the figure of a man standing at the bottom of the path. She went up to him, and saw that it was Mr Gunliffe, the father.

---

[34] *vindicated* – cleared her from suspicion

'Is that Mally?' said Gunliffe.

'Yes, it is Mally; and how is Barty, Mr Gunliffe?' 590

'You must come to 'un yourself, now at once,' said the farmer. 'He won't sleep a wink till he's seed you. You must not say but you'll come.'

'Sure I'll come if I'm wanted,' said Mally.

Gunliffe waited a moment, thinking that Mally might have to prepare herself, but Mally needed no preparation. She was dripping with salt water from the weed which she had been dragging, and her elfin locks were streaming wildly from her head; but, such as she was, she was ready.

'Dada's in bed,' she said, 'and I can go now if you please.'

Then Gunliffe turned round and followed her up the path, wondering 600 at the life which this girl led so far away from all her sex. It was now dark night, and he had found her working at the very edge of the rolling waves by herself, in the darkness, while the only human being who might seem to be her protector had already gone to his bed.

When they were at the top of the cliff Gunliffe took her by her hand, and led her along. She did not comprehend this, but she made no attempt to take her hand from his. Something he said about falling on the cliffs, but it was muttered so lowly that Mally hardly understood him. But in truth the man knew that she had saved his boy's life, and that he had injured her instead of thanking her. He was now taking her to his 610 heart, and as words were wanting to him, he was showing his love after this silent fashion. He held her by the hand as though she were a child, and Mally tripped along at his side asking him no questions.

When they were at the farm-yard gate he stopped there for a moment.

'Mally, my girl,' he said, 'he'll not be content till he sees thee, but thou must not stay long wi' him, lass. Doctor says he's weak like, and wants sleep badly.'

Mally merely nodded her head, and then they entered the house. Mally had never been within it before, and looked about with wondering eyes at the furniture of the big kitchen. Did any idea of her future destiny 620 flash upon her then, I wonder? But she did not pause here a moment, but was led up to the bedroom above stairs, where Barty was lying on his mother's bed.

'Is it Mally herself?' said the voice of the weak youth.

'It's Mally herself,' said the mother, 'so now you can say what you please.'

'Mally,' said he, 'Mally, it's along of[35] you that I'm alive this moment.'

'I'll not forget it on her,' said the father, with his eyes turned away from her. 'I'll never forget it on her.'

---

[35] *along of* – (dialect) because of

630 'We hadn't a one but only him,' said the mother, with her apron up to her face.

'Mally, you'll be friends with me now?' said Barty.

To have been made lady of the manor of the cove for ever, Mally couldn't have spoken a word now. It was not only that the words and presence of the people there cowed her and made her speechless, but the big bed, and the looking-glass, and the unheard-of wonders of the chamber, made her feel her own insignificance. But she crept up to Barty's side, and put her hand upon his.

'I'll come and get the weed, Mally; but it shall all be for you,' said
640 Barty.

'Indeed, you won't then, Barty dear,' said the mother; 'you'll never go near the awsome place again. What would we do if you were took from us?'

'He mustn't go near the hole if he does,' said Mally, speaking at last in a solemn voice, and imparting the knowledge which she had kept to herself while Barty was her enemy; ''specially not if the wind's any way from the nor'rard.'

'She'd better go down now,' said the father.

Barty kissed the hand which he held, and Mally, looking at him as he
650 did so, thought that he was like an angel.

'You'll come and see us to-morrow, Mally?' said he.

To this she made no answer, but followed Mrs Gunliffe out of the room. When they were down in the kitchen the mother had tea for her, and thick milk, and a hot cake, – all the delicacies which the farm could afford. I don't know that Mally cared much for the eating and drinking that night, but she began to think that the Gunliffes were good people, – very good people. It was better thus, at any rate, than being accused of murder and carried off to Camelford prison.

'I'll never forget it on her – never,' the father had said.

660 Those words stuck to her from that moment, and seemed to sound in her ears all the night. How glad she was that Barty had come down to the cove, – oh, yes, how glad! There was no question of his dying now, and as for the blow on his forehead, what harm was that to a lad like him?

'But father shall go with you,' said Mrs Gunliffe, when Mally prepared to start for the cove by herself. Mally, however, would not hear of this. She could find her way to the cove whether it was light or dark.

'Mally, thou art my child now, and I shall think of thee so,' said the mother, as the girl went off by herself.

Mally thought of this, too, as she walked home. How could she become
670 Mrs Gunliffe's child; ah, how?

I need not, I think, tell the tale any further. That Mally did become Mrs Gunliffe's child, and how she became so the reader will understand;

and in process of time the big kitchen and all the wonders of the farm-house were her own. The people said that Barty Gunliffe had married a mermaid out of the sea; but when it was said in Mally's hearing I doubt whether she liked it; and when Barty himself would call her a mermaid she would frown at him, and throw about her black hair, and pretend to cuff him with her little hand.

Old Glos was brought up to the top of the cliff, and lived his few remaining days under the roof of Mr Gunliffe's house; and as for the cove and the right of seaweed, from that time forth all that has been supposed to attach itself to Gunliffe's farm, and I do not know that any of the neighbours are prepared to dispute the right.

680

# Eveline

## *James Joyce*

She sat at the window watching the evening invade the avenue. Her head was leaned against the window curtains and in her nostrils was the odour of dusty cretonne.[1] She was tired.

Few people passed. The man out of the last house passed on his way home; she heard his footsteps clacking along the concrete pavement and afterwards crunching on the cinder path before the new red houses. One time there used to be a field in which they used to play every evening with other people's children. Then a man from Belfast bought the field and built houses in it – not like their little brown houses, but bright brick
10 houses with shining roofs. The children of the avenue used to play together in that field – the Devines, the Waters, the Dunns, little Keogh the cripple, she and her brothers and sisters. Ernest, however, never played: he was too grown up. Her father used often to hunt them in out of the field with his blackthorn stick; but usually little Keogh used to keep *nix*[2] and call out when he saw her father coming. Still they seemed to have been rather happy then. Her father was not so bad then; and besides, her mother was alive. That was a long time ago; she and her brothers and sisters were all grown up; her mother was dead. Tizzie Dunn was dead, too, and the Waters had gone back to England.
20 Everything changes. Now she was going to go away like the others, to leave her home.

Home! She looked round the room, reviewing all its familiar objects which she had dusted once a week for so many years, wondering where on earth all the dust came from. Perhaps she would never see again those familiar objects from which she had never dreamed of being divided. And yet during all those years she had never found out the name of the priest whose yellowing photograph hung on the wall above the broken harmonium[3] beside the coloured print of the promises made to Blessed Margaret Mary Alacoque.[4] He had been a school friend of her father.
30 Whenever he showed the photograph to a visitor her father used to pass it with a casual word:

[1] *cretonne* – a cheap cotton cloth used for curtains
[2] nix – (slang) look out
[3] *harmonium* – a musical instrument
[4] *Blessed Margaret Mary Alacoque* – a French seventeenth-century nun who claimed to be married to Christ in a vision. Famous for her self-sacrifice: she only drank water that had been used to wash clothes; she drank pus instead of tea. Now a saint.

– He is in Melbourne now.

She had consented to go away, to leave her home. Was that wise? She tried to weigh each side of the question. In her home anyway she had shelter and food; she had those whom she had known all her life about her. Of course she had to work hard, both in the house and at business. What would they say of her in the Stores when they found out that she had run away with a fellow? Say she was a fool, perhaps; and her place would be filled up by advertisement. Miss Gavan would be glad. She had always had an edge on her, especially whenever there were people listening.

– Miss Hill, don't you see these ladies are waiting?

– Look lively, Miss Hill, please.

She would not cry many tears at leaving the Stores.

But in her new home, in a distant unknown country, it would not be like that. Then she would be married – she, Eveline. People would treat her with respect then. She would not be treated as her mother had been. Even now, though she was over nineteen, she sometimes felt herself in danger of her father's violence. She knew it was that that had given her the palpitations.[5] When they were growing up he had never gone for her, like he used to go for Harry and Ernest, because she was a girl; but latterly[6] he had begun to threaten her and say what he would do to her only for her dead mother's sake. And now she had nobody to protect her. Ernest was dead and Harry, who was in the church decorating business, was nearly always down somewhere in the country. Besides, the invariable squabble for money on Saturday nights had begun to weary her unspeakably. She always gave her entire wages – seven shillings – and Harry always sent up what he could but the trouble was to get any money from her father. He said she used to squander[7] the money, that she had no head,[8] that he wasn't going to give his hard-earned money to throw about the streets, and much more, for he was usually fairly bad[9] of a Saturday night. In the end he would give her the money and ask her had she any intention of buying Sunday's dinner. Then she had to rush out as quickly as she could and do her marketing,[10] holding her black leather purse tightly in her hand as she elbowed her way through the crowds and returning home late under her load of provisions. She had hard work to keep the house together and to see that the two young children who had been left to her charge went to school regularly and got their meals regu-

[5] *palpitations* – an unsteady heart

[6] *latterly* – recently

[7] *squander* – waste

[8] *no head* – no head for business

[9] *fairly bad* – (slang) drunk

[10] *marketing* – shopping in the market

larly. It was hard work – a hard life – but now that she was about to leave
70    it she did not find it a wholly undesirable life.

She was about to explore another life with Frank. Frank was very kind,
manly, open-hearted. She was to go away with him by the night-boat to
be his wife and to live with him in Buenos Ayres[11] where he had a home
waiting for her. How well she remembered the first time she had seen
him; he was lodging in a house on the main road where she used to visit.
It seemed a few weeks ago. He was standing at the gate, his peaked cap
pushed back on his head and his hair tumbled forward over a face of
bronze. Then they had come to know each other. He used to meet her
outside the Stores every evening and see her home. He took her to see
80    *The Bohemian Girl*[12] and she felt elated[13] as she sat in an unaccustomed
part of the theatre with him. He was awfully fond of music and sang a
little. People knew that they were courting[14] and, when he sang about the
lass that loves a sailor, she always felt pleasantly confused. He used to call
her Poppens[15] out of fun. First of all it had been an excitement for her to
have a fellow and then she had begun to like him. He had tales of distant
countries. He had started as a deck boy at a pound a month on a ship of
the Allan Line[16] going out to Canada. He told her the names of the ships
he had been on and the names of the different services. He had sailed
through the Straits of Magellan[17] and he told her stories of the terrible
90    Patagonians.[18] He had fallen on his feet[19] in Buenos Ayres, he said, and
had come over to the old country[20] just for a holiday. Of course, her
father had found out the affair and had forbidden her to have anything to
say to him.

– I know these sailor chaps, he said.

One day he had quarrelled with Frank and she had to meet her lover
secretly.

The evening deepened in the avenue. The white of two letters in her
lap grew indistinct. One was to Harry; the other was to her father. Ernest
had been her favourite but she liked Harry too. Her father was becoming
100    old lately, she noticed; he would miss her. Sometimes he could be very

[11] *Buenos Ayres* – Buenos Aires, the capital of Argentina (literally: Good Airs)
[12] The Bohemian Girl – a play about a girl who thinks about running away from home
[13] *elated* – in very high spirits
[14] *courting* – to go out with someone in the lead up to marriage
[15] *Poppens* – a loving nickname for Eveline. It is also the real life nickname of Joyce's
sister, Margaret, who promised their mother that she would look after the family
house after her death
[16] *Allan Line* – a shipping company
[17] *Straits of Magellan* – dangerous channel to the south of Argentina
[18] *Patagonians* – there were legends about people from this area of Argentina
50    [19] *fallen on his feet* – he had been very lucky (saying)
[20] *the old country* – (slang) Ireland

nice. Not long before, when she had been laid up[21] for a day, he had read her out a ghost story and made toast for her at the fire. Another day, when their mother was alive, they had all gone for a picnic to the Hill of Howth. She remembered her father putting on her mother's bonnet to make the children laugh.

Her time was running out but she continued to sit by the window leaning her head against the window curtain, inhaling the odour of dusty cretonne. Down far in the avenue she could hear a street organ playing. She knew the air.[22] Strange that it should come that very night to remind her of the promise to her mother, her promise to keep the home together as long as she could. She remembered the last night of her mother's illness; she was again in the close dark room at the other side of the hall and outside she heard the melancholy air of Italy. The organ-player had been ordered to go away and given sixpence. She remembered her father strutting back into the sickroom saying:

– Damned Italians! coming over here!

As she mused,[23] the pitiful vision of her mother's life laid its spell on the very quick[24] of her being – that life of commonplace sacrifices closing in final craziness. She trembled as she heard again her mother's voice saying constantly with foolish insistence:

– Derevaun Seraun![25] Derevaun Seraun!

She stood up in a sudden impulse of terror. Escape! She must escape! Frank would save her. He would give her life, perhaps love, too. But she wanted to live. Why should she be unhappy? She had a right to happiness. Frank would take her in his arms, fold her in his arms. He would save her.

She stood among the swaying crowd in the station at the North Wall. He held her hand and she knew that he was speaking to her, saying something about the passage over and over again. The station was full of soldiers with brown baggages. Through the wide doors of the sheds she caught a glimpse of the black mass of the boat, lying in beside the quay wall, with illumined portholes. She answered nothing. She felt her cheek pale and cold and, out of a maze of distress, she prayed to God to direct her, to show her what was her duty. The boat blew a long mournful whistle into the mist. If she went, to-morrow she would be on the sea with Frank, steaming towards Buenos Ayres. Their passage had been

[21] *laid up* – (slang) ill in bed
[22] *air* – song
[23] *mused* – thought
[24] *the very quick* – the heart
[25] *Derevaun Seraun* – the last words of Eveline's mother, which have no definite meaning. The people at her bedside may have misheard her last words.

booked. Could she still draw back after all he had done for her? Her distress woke a nausea in her body and she kept moving her lips in silent fervent prayer.

A bell clanged upon her heart. She felt him seize her hand:

– Come!

All the seas of the world tumbled about her heart. He was drawing her into them: he would drown her. She gripped with both hands at the iron railing.

– Come!

No! No! No! It was impossible. Her hands clutched the iron in frenzy. Amid the seas she sent a cry of anguish!

– Eveline! Evvy!

He rushed beyond the barrier and called to her to follow. He was shouted at to go on but he still called to her. She set her white face to him, passive, like a helpless animal. Her eyes gave him no sign of love or farewell or recognition.

# Winners and Losers

# The Bottle Imp

*Robert Louis Stevenson*

There was a man of the Island of Hawaii,[1] whom I shall call Keawe; for
the truth is, he still lives, and his name must be kept secret; but the place
of his birth was not far from Honaunau, where the bones of Keawe the
Great lie hidden in a cave. This man was poor, brave, and active; he
could read and write like a schoolmaster; he was a first-rate mariner[2]
besides, sailed for some time in the island steamers, and steered a whaleboat on the Hamakua coast. At length it came in Keawe's mind to have a
sight of the great world and foreign cities, and he shipped on a vessel
bound to San Francisco.

This is a fine town, with a fine harbour, and rich people uncountable;    10
and, in particular, there is one hill which is covered with palaces. Upon
this hill Keawe was one day taking a walk with his pocket full of money,
viewing the great houses upon either hand with pleasure. 'What fine
houses these are!' he was thinking, 'and how happy must those people be
who dwell in them, and take no care for the morrow!' The thought was in
his mind when he came abreast[3] of a house that was smaller than some
others, but all finished and beautified like a toy; the steps of that house
shone like silver, and the borders of the garden bloomed like garlands,
and the windows were bright like diamonds; and Keawe stopped and
wondered at the excellence of all he saw. So stopping, he was aware of a    20
man that looked forth upon him through a window so clear that Keawe
could see him as you see a fish in a pool upon the reef. The man was
elderly, with a bald head and a black beard; and his face was heavy with
sorrow, and he bitterly sighed. And the truth of it is, that as Keawe
looked in upon the man, and the man looked out upon Keawe, each
envied the other.

All of a sudden, the man smiled and nodded, and beckoned Keawe to
enter, and met him at the door of the house.

'This is a fine house of mine,' said the man, and bitterly sighed.
'Would you not care to view the chambers?'    30

[1] *Hawaii* – Stevenson's story is set in the American islands of Hawaii which are in the
Pacific Ocean, like Samoa where Stevenson spent his final years
[2] *mariner* – sailor
[3] *abreast of* – opposite to

So he led Keawe all over it, from the cellar to the roof, and there was nothing there that was not perfect of its kind, and Keawe was astonished.

'Truly,' said Keawe, 'this is a beautiful house; if I lived in the like of it, I should be laughing all day long. How comes it, then, that you should be sighing?'

'There is no reason,' said the man, 'why you should not have a house in all points similar to this, and finer, if you wish. You have some money, I suppose?'

'I have fifty dollars,' said Keawe; 'but a house like this will cost more
40 than fifty dollars.'

The man made a computation. 'I am sorry you have no more,' said he, 'for it may raise you trouble in the future; but it shall be yours at fifty dollars.'

'The house?' asked Keawe.

'No, not the house,' replied the man; 'but the bottle. For, I must tell you, although I appear to you so rich and fortunate, all my fortune, and this house itself and its garden, came out of a bottle not much bigger than a pint. This is it.'

And he opened a lockfast place, and took out a round-bellied bottle
50 with a long neck; the glass of it was white like milk, with changing rainbow colours in the grain. Withinsides something obscurely moved, like a shadow and a fire.

'This is the bottle,' said the man; and, when Keawe laughed, 'You do not believe me?' he added. 'Try, then, for yourself. See if you can break it.'

So Keawe took the bottle up and dashed it on the floor till he was weary; but it jumped on the floor like a child's ball, and was not injured.

'This is a strange thing,' said Keawe. 'For by the touch of it, as well as by the look, the bottle should be of glass.'

60 'Of glass it is,' replied the man, sighing more heavily than ever; 'but the glass of it was tempered[4] in the flames of hell. An imp lives in it, and that is the shadow we behold[5] there moving; or so I suppose. If any man buy this bottle the imp is at his command; all that he desires – love, fame, money, houses like this house, ay, or a city like this city – all are his at the word uttered. Napoleon had this bottle, and by it he grew to be the king of the world; but he sold it at the last, and fell. Captain Cook had this bottle, and by it he found his way to so many islands; but he, too, sold it, and was slain upon Hawaii. For, once it is sold, the power goes and the protection; and unless a man remain content with what he has, ill will
70 befall him.'

[4] *tempered* – hardened through heat treatment
[5] *behold* – see

'And yet you talk of selling it yourself?' Keawe said.

'I have all I wish, and I am growing elderly,' replied the man. 'There is one thing the imp cannot do – he cannot prolong life; and, it would not be fair to conceal from you, there is a drawback to the bottle; for if a man die before he sells it, he must burn in hell for ever.'

'To be sure, that is a drawback and no mistake,' cried Keawe. 'I would not meddle with the thing. I can do without a house, thank God; but there is one thing I could not be doing with one particle, and that is to be damned.'

'Dear me, you must not run away with things,' returned the man. 'All     80
you have to do is to use the power of the imp in moderation, and then sell it to someone else, as I do to you, and finish your life in comfort.'

'Well, I observe two things,' said Keawe. 'All the time you keep sighing like a maid in love, that is one; and, for the other, you sell this bottle very cheap.'

'I have told you already why I sigh,' said the man. 'It is because I fear my health is breaking up; and, as you said yourself, to die and go to the devil is a pity for anyone. As for why I sell so cheap, I must explain to you there is a peculiarity about the bottle. Long ago, when the devil brought it first upon earth, it was extremely expensive, and was sold first of all to     90
Prester John[6] for many millions of dollars; but it cannot be sold at all, unless sold at a loss. If you sell it for as much as you paid for it, back it comes to you again like a homing pigeon. It follows that the price has kept falling in these centuries, and the bottle is now remarkably cheap. I bought it myself from one of my great neighbours on this hill, and the price I paid was only ninety dollars. I could sell it for as high as eighty-nine dollars and ninety-nine cents, but not a penny dearer, or back the thing must come to me. Now, about this there are two bothers. First, when you offer a bottle so singular for eighty odd dollars, people suppose you to be jesting. And second – but there is no hurry about that – and I need not go     100
into it. Only remember it must be coined money that you sell it for.'

'How am I to know that this is all true?' asked Keawe.

'Some of it you can try at once,' replied the man. 'Give me your fifty dollars, take the bottle, and wish your fifty dollars back into your pocket. If that does not happen, I pledge you my honour I will cry off the bargain and restore your money.'

'You are not deceiving me?' said Keawe.

The man bound himself with a great oath.

'Well, I will risk that much,' said Keawe, 'for that can do no harm.' And he paid over his money to the man, and the man handed him the bottle.     110

[6] *Prester John* – John the Priest, a legendary king who had an enormous eastern empire in the Middle Ages

'Imp of the bottle,' said Keawe, 'I want my fifty dollars back.' And sure enough he had scarce said the word before his pocket was heavy as ever.

'To be sure this is a wonderful bottle,' said Keawe.

'And now, good morning to you, my fine fellow, and the devil go with you for me!' said the man.

'Hold on,' said Keawe, 'I don't want any more of this fun. Here take your bottle back.'

'You have bought it for less than I paid for it,' replied the man rubbing his hands. 'It is yours now; and, for my part, I am only concerned to see the back of you.' And with that he rang for his Chinese servant, and had Keawe shown out of the house.

Now, when Keawe was in the street, with the bottle under his arm, he began to think. 'If all is true about this bottle, I may have made a losing bargain,' thinks he. 'But perhaps the man was only fooling me.' The first thing he did was to count his money; the sum was exact – forty-nine dollars American money, and one Chili piece.[7] 'That looks like the truth,' said Keawe. 'Now I will try another part.'

The streets in that part of the city were as clean as a ship's decks, and though it was noon, there were no passengers. Keawe set the bottle in the gutter and walked away. Twice he looked back, and there was the milky, round-bellied bottle where he left it. A third time he looked back, and turned a corner; but he had scarce done so, when something knocked upon his elbow, and behold! it was the long neck sticking up; and as for the round belly, it was jammed into the pocket of his pilot-coat.[8]

'And that looks like the truth,' said Keawe.

The next thing he did was to buy a cork-screw in a shop, and go apart into a secret place in the fields. And there he tried to draw the cork, but as often as he put the screw in, out it came again, and the cork as whole as ever.

'This is some new sort of cork,' said Keawe, and all at once he began to shake and sweat, for he was afraid of that bottle.

On his way back to the port-side, he saw a shop where a man sold shells and clubs from the wild islands, old heathen deities,[9] old coined money, pictures from China and Japan, and all manner of things that sailors bring in their sea-chests. And here he had an idea. So he went in and offered the bottle for a hundred dollars. The man of the shop laughed at him at the first, and offered him five; but, indeed, it was a curious bottle – such glass was never blown in any human glass-works, so prettily the colours shone under the milky white, and so strangely the shadow

---

[7] *Chili* – Chilean; from Chile
[8] *pilot-coat* – a coarse woollen sailor's overcoat
[9] *heathen deities* – non-Christian gods

hovered in the midst; so, after he had disputed awhile after the manner of his kind, the shopman gave Keawe sixty silver dollars for the thing, and set it on a shelf in the midst of his window.

'Now,' said Keawe, 'I have sold that for sixty which I bought for fifty – or, to say truth, a little less, because one of my dollars was from Chili. Now I shall know the truth upon another point.'

So he went back on board his ship, and, when he opened his chest, there was the bottle, and had come more quickly than himself. Now Keawe had a mate on board whose name was Lopaka.

'What ails[10] you?' said Lopaka, 'that you stare in your chest?'

They were alone in the ship's forecastle,[11] and Keawe bound him to secrecy, and told all.

'This is a very strange affair,' said Lopaka; 'and I fear you will be in trouble about this bottle. But there is one point very clear – that you are sure of the trouble, and you had better have the profit in the bargain. Make up your mind what you want with it; give the order, and if it is done as you desire, I will buy the bottle myself; for I have an idea of my own to get a schooner,[12] and go trading through the islands.'

'That is not my idea,' said Keawe; 'but to have a beautiful house and garden on the Kona Coast, where I was born, the sun shining in at the door, flowers in the garden, glass in the windows, pictures on the walls, and toys and fine carpets on the tables, for all the world like the house I was in this day – only a storey higher, and with balconies all about like the King's palace; and to live there without care and make merry with my friends and relatives.'

'Well,' said Lopaka, 'let us carry it back with us to Hawaii, and if all comes true, as you suppose, I will buy the bottle, as I said, and ask a schooner.'

Upon that they were agreed, and it was not long before the ship returned to Honolulu, carrying Keawe and Lopaka, and the bottle. They were scarce come ashore when they met a friend upon the beach, who began at once to condole[13] with Keawe.

'I do not know what I am to be condoled about,' said Keawe.

'Is it possible you have not heard,' said the friend, 'your uncle that good old man – is dead, and your cousin – that beautiful boy – was drowned at sea?'

Keawe was filled with sorrow, and, beginning to weep and to lament he forgot about the bottle. But Lopaka was thinking to himself, and

---

[10] *ails* – troubles
[11] *forecastle* – the sailors' quarters at the front of a ship
[12] *schooner* – a large sailing boat
[13] *condole* – express sympathy with

presently, when Keawe's grief was a little abated, 'I have been thinking,' said Lopaka. 'Had not your uncle lands in Hawaii, in the district of Kaü?'

190 'No,' said Keawe, 'not in Kaü; they are on the mountain-side – a little way south of Hookena.'

'These lands will now be yours?' asked Lopaka.

'And so they will,' says Keawe, and began again to lament for his relatives.

'No,' said Lopaka, 'do not lament at present. I have a thought in my mind. How if this should be the doing of the bottle? For here is the place ready for your house.'

'If this be so,' cried Keawe, 'it is a very ill way to serve me by killing my relatives. But it may be, indeed; for it was in just such a station that I saw
200 the house with my mind's eye.'

'The house, however, is not yet built,' said Lopaka.

'No, nor like to be!' said Keawe; 'for though my uncle has some coffee and ava and bananas, it will not be more than will keep me in comfort; and the rest of that land is the black lava.'

'Let us go to the lawyer,' said Lopaka; 'I have still this idea in my mind.'

Now, when they came to the lawyer's, it appeared Keawe's uncle had grown monstrous rich in the last days, and there was a fund of money.

'And here is the money for the house!' cried Lopaka.

210 'If you are thinking of a new house,' said the lawyer, 'here is the card of a new architect, of whom they tell me great things.'

'Better and better!' cried Lopaka. 'Here is all made plain for us. Let us continue to obey orders.'

So they went to the architect, and he had drawings of houses on his table.

'You want something out of the way,' said the architect. 'How do you like this?' and he handed a drawing to Keawe.

Now, when Keawe set eyes on the drawing, he cried out aloud, for it was the picture of his thought exactly drawn.

220 'I am in for this house,' thought he. 'Little as I like the way it comes to me, I am in for it now, and I may as well take the good along with the evil.'

So he told the architect all that he wished, and how he would have that house furnished, and about the pictures on the wall and the knick-knacks on the tables; and he asked the man plainly for how much he would undertake the whole affair.

The architect put many questions, and took his pen and made a computation; and when he had done he named the very sum that Keawe had inherited.

230 Lopaka and Keawe looked at one another and nodded.

'It is quite clear,' thought Keawe, 'that I am to have this house, whether or no. It comes from the devil, and I fear I will get little good by that; and of one thing I am sure, I will make no more wishes as long as I have this bottle. But with the house I am saddled, and I may as well take the good along with the evil.'

So he made his terms with the architect, and they signed a paper; and Keawe and Lopaka took ship again and sailed to Australia; for it was concluded between them they should not interfere at all, but leave the architect and the bottle imp to build and to adorn that house at their own pleasure.                                                                          240

The voyage was a good voyage, only all the time Keawe was holding in his breath, for he had sworn he would utter no more wishes, and take no more favours from the devil. The time was up when they got back. The architect told them that the house was ready, and Keawe and Lopaka took a passage in the *Hall*,[14] and went down Kona way to view the house, and see if all had been done fitly according to the thought that was in Keawe's mind.

Now, the house stood on the mountain-side, visible to ships. Above, the forest ran up into the clouds of rain; below, the black lava fell in cliffs, where the kings of old lay buried. A garden bloomed about that house with       250
every hue of flowers; and there was an orchard of papaia on the one hand and an orchard of breadfruit on the other, and right in front, toward the sea, a ship's mast had been rigged up and bore a flag. As for the house, it was three storeys high, with great chambers and broad balconies on each. The windows were of glass, so excellent that it was as clear as water and as bright as day. All manner of furniture adorned the chambers. Pictures hung upon the wall in golden frames: pictures of ships, and men fighting, and of the most beautiful women, and of singular places; nowhere in the world are there pictures of so bright a colour as those Keawe found hanging in his house. As for the knick-knacks, they were extraordinary       260
fine; chiming clocks and musical boxes, little men with nodding heads, books filled with pictures, weapons of price from all quarters of the world, and the most elegant puzzles to entertain the leisure of a solitary man. And as no one would care to live in such chambers, only to walk through and view them, the balconies were made so broad that a whole town might have lived upon them in delight; and Keawe knew not which to prefer, whether the back porch, where you got the land breeze, and looked upon the orchards and the flowers, or the front balcony, where you could drink the wind of the sea, and look down the steep wall of the mountain and see the *Hall* going by once a week or so between Hookena and the hills of Pele,       270
or the schooners plying up the coast for wood and ava and bananas.

[14] *the* Hall – the name of a steamer

When they had viewed all, Keawe and Lopaka sat on the porch.

'Well,' asked Lopaka, 'is it all as you designed?'

'Words cannot utter it,' said Keawe. 'It is better than I dreamed, and I am sick with satisfaction.'

'There is but one thing to consider,' said Lopaka; 'all this may be quite natural, and the bottle imp have nothing whatever to say to it. If I were to buy the bottle, and got no schooner after all, I should have put my hand in the fire for nothing. I gave you my word, I know; but yet I think you would not grudge me one more proof.'

'I have sworn I would take no more favours,' said Keawe. 'I have gone already deep enough.'

'This is no favour I am thinking of,' replied Lopaka. 'It is only to see the imp himself. There is nothing to be gained by that, and so nothing to be ashamed of; and yet, if I once saw him, I should be sure of the whole matter. So indulge me so far, and let me see the imp; and, after that, here is the money in my hand, and I will buy it.'

'There is only one thing I am afraid of,' said Keawe. 'The imp may be very ugly to view; and if you once set eyes upon him you might be very undesirous of the bottle.'

'I am a man of my word,' said Lopaka. 'And here is the money betwixt us.'

'Very well,' replied Keawe. 'I have a curiosity myself. So come, let us have one look at you, Mr Imp.'

Now as soon as that was said, the imp looked out of the bottle, and in again, swift as a lizard; and there sat Keawe and Lopaka turned to stone. The night had quite come, before either found a thought to say or voice to say it with; and then Lopaka pushed the money over and took the bottle.

'I am a man of my word,' said he, 'and had need to be so, or I would not touch this bottle with my foot. Well, I shall get my schooner and a dollar or two for my pocket; and then I will be rid of this devil as fast as I can. For to tell you the plain truth, the look of him has cast me down.'

'Lopaka,' said Keawe, 'do not you think any worse of me than you can help; I know it is night, and the roads bad, and the pass by the tombs an ill place to go by so late, but I declare since I have seen that little face, I cannot eat or sleep or pray till it is gone from me. I will give you a lantern, and a basket to put the bottle in, and any picture or fine thing in all my house that takes your fancy; – and be gone at once, and go sleep at Hookena with Nahinu.'[15]

'Keawe,' said Lopaka, 'many a man would take this ill; above all, when

---

[15] *Nahinu* – David Nahinu, a real-life friend of Stevenson, owned a large house. Keawe suggests Lopaka stays there

I am doing you a turn so friendly, as to keep my word and buy the bottle; and for that matter, the night and the dark, and the way by the tombs, must be all tenfold more dangerous to a man with such a sin upon his conscience, and such a bottle under his arm. But for my part, I am so extremely terrified myself, I have not the heart to blame you. Here I go then; and I pray God you may be happy in your house, and I fortunate with my schooner, and both get to heaven in the end in spite of the devil and his bottle.'

So Lopaka went down the mountain; and Keawe stood in his front   320 balcony, and listened to the clink of the horse's shoes, and watched the lantern go shining down the path, and along the cliff of caves where the old dead are buried; and all the time he trembled and clasped his hands, and prayed for his friend, and gave glory to God that he himself was escaped out of that trouble.

But the next day came very brightly, and that new house of his was so delightful to behold that he forgot his terrors. One day followed another, and Keawe dwelt there in perpetual joy. He had his place on the back porch; it was there he ate and lived, and read the stories in the Honolulu newspapers; but when anyone came by they would go in and view the   330 chambers and the pictures. And the fame of the house went far and wide; it was called *Ka-Hale Nui* – the Great House – in all Kona; and sometimes the Bright House, for Keawe kept a Chinaman, who was all day dusting and furbishing; and the glass, and the gilt,[16] and the fine stuffs, and the pictures, shone as bright as the morning. As for Keawe himself, he could not walk in the chambers without singing, his heart was so enlarged; and when ships sailed by upon the sea, he would fly his colours on the mast.

So time went by, until one day Keawe went upon a visit as far as Kailua to certain of his friends. There he was well feasted; and left as soon as he could the next morning, and rode hard, for he was impatient to behold   340 his beautiful house; and, besides, the night then coming on was the night in which the dead of old days go abroad in the sides of Kona; and having already meddled with the devil, he was the more chary[17] of meeting with the dead. A little beyond Honaunau, looking far ahead, he was aware of a woman bathing in the edge of the sea; and she seemed a well-grown girl, but he thought no more of it. Then he saw her white shift[18] flutter as she put it on, and then her red holoku;[19] and by the time he came abreast of her she was done with her toilet, and had come up from the sea, and stood by the track-side in her red holoku, and she was all freshened with

[16] *gilt* – gilded, covered with gold
[17] *chary* – cautious
[18] *shift* – a vest for a woman; a camisole
[19] *holoku* – a woman's garment

350 the bath, and her eyes shone and were kind. Now Keawe no sooner beheld her than he drew rein.

'I thought I knew everyone in this country,' said he. 'How comes it that I do not know you?'

'I am Kokua, daughter of Kiano,' said the girl, 'and I have just returned from Oahu. Who are you?'

'I will tell you who I am in a little,' said Keawe, dismounting from his horse, 'but not now. For I have a thought in my mind, and if you knew who I was, you might have heard of me, and would not give me a true answer. But tell me, first of all, one thing: Are you married?'

360 At this Kokua laughed out aloud. 'It is you who ask questions,' she said. 'Are you married yourself?'

'Indeed, Kokua, I am not,' replied Keawe, 'and never thought to be until this hour. But here is the plain truth. I have met you here at the roadside, and I saw your eyes, which are like the stars, and my heart went to you as swift as a bird. And so now, if you want none of me, say so, and I will go on to my own place; but if you think me no worse than any other young man, say so, too, and I will turn aside to your father's for the night, and tomorrow I will talk with the good man.'

Kokua said never a word, but she looked at the sea and laughed.

370 'Kokua,' said Keawe, 'if you say nothing, I will take that for the good answer; so let us be stepping to your father's door.'

She went on ahead of him, still without speech; only sometimes she glanced back and glanced away again, and she kept the strings of her hat in her mouth.

Now, when they had come to the door, Kiano came out on his verandah, and cried out and welcomed Keawe by name. At that the girl looked over, for the fame of the great house had come to her ears; and, to be sure, it was a great temptation. All that evening they were very merry together; and the girl was as bold as brass under the eyes of her parents,
380 and made a mock of Keawe, for she had a quick wit. The next day he had a word with Kiano, and found the girl alone.

'Kokua,' said he, 'you made a mock of me all the evening; and it is still time to bid me go. I would not tell you who I was, because I have so fine a house, and I feared you would think too much of that house and too little of the man that loves you. Now you know all, and if you wish to have seen the last of me, say so at once.'

'No,' said Kokua; but this time she did not laugh, nor did Keawe ask for more.

This was the wooing of Keawe; things had gone quickly; but so an
390 arrow goes, and the ball of a rifle swifter still, and yet both may strike the target. Things had gone fast, but they had gone far also, and the thought of Keawe rang in the maiden's head; she heard his voice in the breach of

the surf upon the lava, and for this young man that she had seen but twice she would have left father and mother and her native islands. As for Keawe himself, his horse flew up the path of the mountain under the cliff of tombs, and the sound of the hoofs, and the sound of Keawe singing to himself for pleasure, echoed in the caverns of the dead. He came to the Bright House, and still he was singing. He sat and ate in the broad balcony, and the Chinaman wondered at his master, to hear how he sang between the mouthfuls. The sun went down into the sea, and the night came; and Keawe walked the balconies by lamplight, high on the mountains, and the voice of his singing startled men on ships.

'Here am I now upon my high place,' he said to himself. 'Life may be no better; this is the mountain top; and all shelves[20] about me toward the worse. For the first time I will light up the chambers, and bathe in my fine bath with the hot water and the cold, and sleep alone in the bed of my bridal chamber.'

So the Chinaman had word, and he must rise from sleep and light the furnaces; and as he wrought[21] below, besides the boilers, he heard his master singing and rejoicing above him in the lighted chambers. When the water began to be hot the Chinaman cried to his master; and Keawe went into the bathroom; and the Chinaman heard him sing as he filled the marble basin; and heard him sing, and the singing broken, as he undressed; until of a sudden, the song ceased. The Chinaman listened, and listened; he called up the house to Keawe to ask if all were well, and Keawe answered him 'Yes,' and bade him go to bed; but there was no more singing in the Bright House; and all night long, the Chinaman heard his master's feet go round and round the balconies without repose.

Now the truth of it was this: as Keawe undressed for his bath, he spied upon his flesh a patch like a patch of lichen[22] on a rock, and it was then that he stopped singing. For he knew the likeness of that patch, and knew that he was fallen in the Chinese Evil.[23]

Now, it is a sad thing for any man to fall into this sickness. And it would be a sad thing for anyone to leave a house so beautiful and so commodious, and depart from all his friends to the north coast of Molokai between the mighty cliff and the sea-breakers. But what was that to the case of the man Keawe, he who had met his love but yesterday, and won her but that morning, and now saw all his hopes break, in a moment, like a piece of glass?

Awhile he sat upon the edge of the bath; then sprang, with a cry, and

[20] *shelves* – goes downwards
[21] *wrought* – worked
[22] *lichen* – moss
[23] *Chinese Evil* – leprosy

ran outside; and to and fro, to and fro, along the balcony, like one despairing.

'Very willingly could I leave Hawaii, the home of my fathers,' Keawe was thinking. 'Very lightly could I leave my house, the high-placed, the many-windowed, here upon the mountains. Very bravely could I go to Molokai, to Kalaupapa by the cliffs, to live with the smitten[24] and to sleep there, far from my fathers. But what wrong have I done, what sin lies upon my soul, that I should have encountered Kokua coming cool from the sea-water in the evening? Kokua, the soul ensnarer! Kokua, the light
440 of my life! Her may I never wed, her may I look upon no longer, her may I no more handle with my loving hand; and it is for this, it is for you, O Kokua! that I pour my lamentations!'

Now you are to observe what sort of a man Keawe was, for he might have dwelt there in the Bright House for years, and no one been the wiser of his sickness; but he reckoned nothing of that, if he must lose Kokua. And again, he might have wed Kokua even as he was; and so many would have done, because they have the souls of pigs; but Keawe loved the maid manfully, and he would do her no hurt and bring her in no danger.

A little beyond the midst of the night, there came in his mind the
450 recollection of that bottle. He went round to the back porch, and called to memory the day when the devil had looked forth; and at the thought ice ran in his veins.

'A dreadful thing is the bottle,' thought Keawe, 'and dreadful is the imp, and it is a dreadful thing to risk the flames of hell. But what other hope have I to cure my sickness or to wed Kokua? What!' he thought, 'would I beard[25] the devil once, only to get me a house, and not face him again to win Kokua?'

Thereupon he called to mind it was the next day the *Hall* went by on her return to Honolulu. 'There must I go first,' he thought, 'and see
460 Lopaka. For the best hope that I have now is to find that same bottle I was so pleased to be rid of.'

Never a wink could he sleep; the food stuck in his throat; but he sent a letter to Kiano, and about the time when the steamer would be coming, rode down beside the cliff of the tombs. It rained; his horse went heavily; he looked up at the black mouths of the caves, and he envied the dead that slept there and were done with trouble; and called to mind how he had galloped by the day before, and was astonished. So he came down to Hookena, and there was all the country gathered for the steamer as usual. In the shed before the store they sat and jested and passed the news; but
470 there was no matter of speech in Keawe's bosom, and he sat in their

[24] *smitten* – infected
[25] *beard* – challenge

96

midst and looked without on the rain falling on the houses, and the surf beating among the rocks, and the sighs arose in his throat.

'Keawe of the Bright House is out of spirits,' said one to another. Indeed, and so he was, and little wonder.

Then the *Hall* came, and the whaleboat carried him on board. The after-part of the ship was full of Haoles[26] who had been to visit the volcano, as their custom is; and the midst was crowded with Kanakas,[27] and the forepart with wild bulls from Hilo and horses from Kaü; but Keawe sat apart from all in his sorrow, and watched for the house of Kiano. There it sat, low upon the shore in the black rocks, and shaded by 480 the cocoa palms, and there by the door was a red holoku, no greater than a fly, and going to and fro with a fly's busyness.

'Ah, queen of my heart,' he cried, 'I'll venture my dear soul to win you!'

Soon after, darkness fell, and the cabins were lit up, and the Haoles sat and played at the cards and drank whisky as their custom is; but Keawe walked the deck all night; and all the next day, as they steamed under the lee of Maui or of Molohi, he was still pacing to and fro like a wild animal in a menagerie.[28]

Towards evening they passed Diamond Head, and came to the pier 490 of Honolulu. Keawe stepped out among the crowd and began to ask for Lopaka. It seemed he had become the owner of a schooner – none better in the islands – and was gone upon an adventure as far as Pola-Pola or Kahiki; so there was no help to be looked for from Lopaka. Keawe called to mind a friend of his, a lawyer in the town (I must not tell his name), and inquired of him. They said he was grown suddenly rich, and had a fine new house upon Waikiki shore; and this put a thought in Keawe's head, and he called a hack[29] and drove to the lawyer's house.

The house was all brand new, and the trees in the garden no greater 500 than walking-sticks, and the lawyer, when he came, had the air of a man well pleased.

'What can I do to serve you?' said the lawyer.

'You are a friend of Lopaka's,' replied Keawe, 'and Lopaka purchased from me a certain piece of goods that I thought you might enable me to trace.'

The lawyer's face became very dark. 'I do not profess to misunder-stand you, Mr Keawe,' said he, 'though this is an ugly business to be stir-

---

[26] *Haoles* – white people
[27] *Kanakas* – people from Kanaka
[29] *menagerie* – zoo
[29] *hack* – a horse-drawn taxi

ring in. You may be sure I know nothing, but yet I have a guess, and if
510  you would apply in a certain quarter I think you might have news.'

And he named the name of a man, which, again, I had better not
repeat. So it was for days, and Keawe went from one to another, finding
everywhere new clothes and carriages, and fine new houses and men
everywhere in great contentment, although, to be sure, when he hinted at
his business their faces would cloud over.

'No doubt I am upon the track,' thought Keawe. 'These new clothes
and carriages are all the gifts of the little imp, and these glad faces are the
faces of men who have taken their profit and got rid of the accursed thing
in safety. When I see pale cheeks and hear sighing, I shall know that I am
520  near the bottle.'

So it befell at last that he was recommended to a Haole in Beritania
Street. When he came to the door, about the hour of the evening meal,
there were the usual marks of the new house, and the young garden, and
the electric light shining in the windows; but when the owner came, a
shock of hope and fear ran through Keawe; for here was a young man,
white as a corpse, and black about the eyes, the hair shedding from his
head, and such a look in his countenance as a man may have when he is
waiting for the gallows.

'Here it is, to be sure,' thought Keawe, and so with this man he noways
530  veiled his errand. 'I am come to buy the bottle,' said he.

At the word, the young Haole of Beritania Street reeled against the
wall.

'The bottle!' he gasped. 'To buy the bottle!' Then be seemed to choke,
and seizing Keawe by the arm carried him into a room and poured out
wine in two glasses.

'Here is my respects,' said Keawe, who had been much about with
Haoles in his time. 'Yes,' he added, 'I am come to buy the bottle. What is
the price by now?'

At that word the young man let his glass slip through his fingers, and
540  looked upon Keawe like a ghost.

'The price,' says he; 'the price! You do not know the price?'

'It is for that I am asking you,' returned Keawe. 'But why are you so
much concerned? Is there anything wrong about the price?'

'It has dropped a great deal in value since your time, Mr Keawe,' said
the young man, stammering.

'Well, well, I shall have the less to pay for it,' says Keawe. 'How much
did it cost you?'

The young man was as white as a sheet. 'Two cents,' said he.

'What?' cried Keawe, 'two cents? Why, then, you can only sell it for
550  one. And he who buys it—' The words died upon Keawe's tongue; he
who bought it could never sell it again, the bottle and the bottle imp must

abide with him until be died, and when he died must carry him to the red end of hell.

The young man of Beritania Street fell upon his knees. 'For God's sake buy it!' he cried. 'You can have all my fortune in the bargain. I was mad when I bought it at that price. I had embezzled money at my store; I was lost else; I must have gone to jail.'

'Poor creature,' said Keawe, 'you would risk your soul upon so desperate an adventure, and to avoid the proper punishment of your own disgrace; and you think I could hesitate with love in front of me. Give me   560 the bottle, and the change which I make sure you have all ready. Here is a five-cent piece.'

It was as Keawe supposed; the young man had the change ready in a drawer; the bottle changed hands, and Keawe's fingers were no sooner clasped upon the stalk than he had breathed his wish to be a clean man. And, sure enough, when he got home to his room, and stripped himself before a glass, his flesh was whole like an infant's. And here was the strange thing: he had no sooner seen this miracle, than his mind was changed within him, and be cared naught for the Chinese Evil, and little enough for Kokua; and had but the one thought, that here he was bound   570 to the bottle imp for time and for eternity, and had no better hope but to be a cinder for ever in the flames of hell. Away ahead of him he saw them blaze with his mind's eye, and his soul shrank, and darkness fell upon the light.

When Keawe came to himself a little, he was aware it was the night when the band played at the hotel. Thither he went, because he feared to be alone; and there, among happy faces, walked to and fro, and heard the tunes go up and down, and saw Berger[30] beat the measure, and all the while he heard the flames crackle, and saw the red fire burning in the bottomless pit. Of a sudden the band played *Hiki-ao-ao*; that was a song   580 that he had sung with Kokua, and at the strain courage returned to him.

'It is done now,' he thought, 'and once more let me take the good along with the evil.'

So it befell that he returned to Hawaii by the first steamer, and as soon as it could be managed he was wedded to Kokua, and carried her up the mountain side to the Bright House.

Now it was so with these two, that when they were together, Keawe's heart was stilled; but so soon as he was alone he fell into a brooding horror, and heard the flames crackle, and saw the red fire burn in the bottomless pit. The girl, indeed, had come to him wholly; her heart leapt   590 in her side at sight of him, her hand clung to his; and she was so fashioned from the hair upon her head to the nails upon her toes that

[30] *Berger* – the Berger Royal Hawaiian Band played popular Hawaiian songs

none could see her without joy. She was pleasant in her nature. She had the good word always. Full of song she was, and went to and fro in the Bright House, the brightest thing in its three storeys, carolling like the birds. And Keawe beheld and heard her with delight, and then must shrink upon one side, and weep and groan to think upon the price that he had paid for her; and then he must dry his eyes, and wash his face, and go and sit with her on the broad balconies joining in her songs, and, with a sick spirit, answering her smiles.

There came a day when her feet began to be heavy and her songs more rare; and now it was not Keawe only that would weep apart, but each would sunder from the other and sit in opposite balconies with the whole width of the Bright House betwixt. Keawe was so sunk in his despair, he scarce observed the change, and was only glad he had more hours to sit alone and brood upon his destiny, and was not so frequently condemned to pull a smiling face on a sick heart. But one day, coming softly through the house, he heard the sound of a child sobbing, and there was Kokua rolling her face upon the balcony floor, and weeping like the lost.

'You do well to weep in this house, Kokua,' he said. 'And yet I would give the head off my body that you (at least) might have been happy.'

'Happy!' she cried. 'Keawe, when you lived alone in your Bright House, you were the word of the island for a happy man; laughter and song were in your mouth, and your face was as bright as the sunrise. Then you wedded poor Kokua; and the good God knows what is amiss in her – but from that day you have not smiled. Oh!' she cried, 'what ails me? I thought I was pretty, and I knew I loved him. What ails me that I throw this cloud upon my husband?'

'Poor Kokua,' said Keawe. He sat down by her side, and sought to take her hand; but that she plucked away. 'Poor Kokua,' he said, again. 'My poor child – my pretty. And I thought all this while to spare you! Well, you shall know all. Then, at least, you will pity poor Keawe; then you will understand how much he loved you in the past – that he dared hell for your possession – and how much he loves you still (the poor condemned one), that he can yet call up a smile when he beholds you.'

With that, he told her all, even from the beginning.

'You have done this for me?' she cried. 'Ah, well then what do I care!' – and she clasped and wept upon him.

'Ah, child!' said Keawe, 'and yet, when I consider of the fire of hell, I care a good deal!'

'Never tell me,' said she; 'no man can be lost because he loved Kokua, and no other fault. I tell you, Keawe, I shall save you with these hands, or perish in your company. What! you loved me, and gave your soul, and you think I will not die to save you in return?'

'Ah, my dear! you might die a hundred times, and what difference would that make?' he cried, 'except to leave me lonely till the time comes of my damnation?'

'You know nothing,' said she. 'I was educated in a school in Honolulu; I am no common girl. And I tell you, I shall save my lover. What is this you say about a cent? But all the world is not American. In England they have a piece they call a farthing, which is about half a cent. Ah sorrow!' she cried, 'that makes it scarcely better, for the buyer must be lost, and we shall find none so brave as my Keawe! But, then, there is France; they have a small coin there which they call a centime, and these go five to the cent or thereabout. We could not do better. Come, Keawe, let us go to the French islands; let us go to Tahiti, as fast as ships can bear us. There we have four centimes, three centimes, two centimes, one centime; four possible sales to come and go on; and two of us to push the bargain. Come, my Keawe! kiss me, and banish care. Kokua will defend you.'

'Gift of God!' he cried. 'I cannot think that God will punish me for desiring aught so good! Be it as you will, then; take me where you please: I put my life and my salvation in your hands.'

Early the next day Kokua was about her preparations. She took Keawe's chest that he went with sailoring; and first she put the bottle in a corner; and then packed it with the richest of their clothes and the bravest of the knick-knacks in the house. 'For,' said she, 'we must seem to be rich folks, or who will believe in the bottle?' All the time of her preparation she was as gay as a bird; only when she looked upon Keawe, the tears would spring in her eye, and she must run and kiss him. As for Keawe, a weight was off his soul; now that he had his secret shared, and some hope in front of him, he seemed like a new man, his feet went lightly on the earth, and his breath was good to him again. Yet was terror still at his elbow; and ever and again, as the wind blows out a taper, hope died in him, and he saw the flames toss and the red fire burn in hell.

It was given out in the country they were gone pleasuring to the States, which was thought a strange thing, and yet not so strange as the truth, if any could have guessed it. So they went to Honolulu in the *Hall*, and thence in the *Umatilla* to San Francisco with a crowd of Haoles, and at San Francisco took their passage by the mail brigantine,[31] the *Tropic Bird*, for Papeete,[32] the chief place of the French in the south islands. Thither they came, after a pleasant voyage, on a fair day of the Trade Wind, and saw the reef with the surf breaking, and Motuiti with its palms, and the schooner riding within-side, and the white houses of the town low down along the shore among green trees, and overhead the mountains and the clouds of Tahiti, the wise island.

---

[31] *brigantine* – a type of sailing boat
[32] *Papeete* – the capital city of the French colony of Tahiti

It was judged the most wise to hire a house, which they did accordingly, opposite the British Consul's, to make a great parade of money, and themselves conspicuous with carriages and horses. This it was very easy to do, so long as they had the bottle in their possession; for Kokua was more bold than Keawe, and, whenever she had a mind, called on the imp for twenty or a hundred dollars. At this rate they soon grew to be remarked in the town; and the strangers from Hawaii, their riding and their driving, the fine holokus and the rich lace of Kokua, became the matter of much talk.

They got on well after the first with the Tahitian language, which is indeed like to the Hawaiian, with a change of certain letters; and as soon as they had any freedom of speech, began to push the bottle. You are to consider it was not an easy subject to introduce; it was not easy to persuade people you were in earnest, when you offered to sell them for four centimes the spring of health and riches inexhaustible. It was necessary besides to explain the dangers of the bottle; and other people disbelieved the whole thing and laughed, or they thought the more of the darker part, became overcast with gravity, and drew away from Keawe and Kokua, as from persons who had dealings with the devil. So far from gaining ground, these two began to find they were avoided in the town; the children ran away from them screaming, a thing intolerable to Kokua; Catholics crossed themselves as they went by; and all persons began with one accord to disengage themselves from their advances.

Depression fell upon their spirits. They would sit at night in their new house, after a day's weariness, and not exchange one word, or the silence would be broken by Kokua bursting suddenly into sobs. Sometimes they would pray together; sometimes they would have the bottle out upon the floor, and sit all evening watching how the shadow hovered in the midst. At such times they would be afraid to go to rest. It was long ere slumber came to them, and, if either dozed off, it would be to wake and find the other silently weeping in the dark, or, perhaps, to wake alone, the other having fled from the house and the neighbourhood of that bottle, to pace under the bananas in the little garden, or to wander on the beach by moonlight.

One night it was so when Kokua awoke. Keawe was gone. She felt in the bed and his place was cold. Then fear fell upon her, and she sat up in bed. A little moonshine filtered through the shutters. The room was bright, and she could spy the bottle on the floor. Outside it blew high, the great trees of the avenue cried aloud, and the fallen leaves rattled in the verandah. In the midst of this Kokua was aware of another sound; whether of a beast or of a man she could scarce tell, but it was as sad as death, and cut her to the soul. Softly she arose, set the door ajar, and looked forth into the moonlit yard. There, under the bananas, lay Keawe, his mouth in the dust, and as he lay he moaned. 720

It was Kokua's first thought to run forward and console him; her second potently withheld her. Keawe had borne himself before his wife like a brave man; it became her little[33] in the hour of weakness to intrude upon his shame. With the thought she drew back into the house.

'Heaven!' she thought, 'how careless have I been – how weak! It is he, not I, that stands in this eternal peril; it was he, not I, that took the curse upon his soul. It is for my sake, and for the love of a creature of so little worth and such poor help, that he now beholds so close to him the flames of hell – ay, and smells the smoke of it, lying without there in the wind and moonlight. Am I so dull of spirit that never till now I have surmised 730 my duty, or have I seen it before and turned aside? But now, at least, I take up my soul in both the hands of my affection; now I say farewell to the white steps of heaven and the waiting faces of my friends. A love for a love, and let mine be equalled with Keawe's! A soul for a soul, and be it mine to perish!'

She was a deft woman with her hands, and was soon apparelled. She took in her hands the change – the precious centimes they kept ever at their side; for this coin is little used, and they had made provision at a Government office. When she was forth in the avenue clouds came on the wind, and the moon was blackened. The town slept, and she knew 740 not whither to turn till she heard one coughing in the shadow of the trees.

'Old man,' said Kokua, 'what do you here abroad in the cold night?'

The old man could scarce express himself for coughing, but she made out that he was old and poor, and a stranger in the island.

'Will you do me a service?' said Kokua. 'As one stranger to another, and as an old man to a young woman, will you help a daughter of Hawaii?'

'Ah,' said the old man. 'So you are the witch from the eight islands, and even my old soul you seek to entangle. But I have heard of you, and defy your wickedness.' 750

'Sit down here,' said Kokua, 'and let me tell you a tale.' And she told him the story of Keawe from the beginning to the end.

'And now,' said she, 'I am his wife, whom he bought with his soul's welfare. And what should I do? If I went to him myself and offered to buy it, he would refuse. But if you go, he will sell it eagerly; I will await you here; you will buy it for four centimes, and I will buy it again for three. And the Lord strengthen a poor girl!'

'If you meant falsely,' said the old man, 'I think God would strike you dead.'

---

[33] *became her little*– it was not fitting for her

760 'He would!' cried Kokua. 'Be sure he would. I could not be so treacherous – God would not suffer it.'

'Give me the four centimes and await me here,' said the old man.

Now, when Kokua stood alone in the street, her spirit died. The wind roared in the trees, and it seemed to her the rushing of the flames of hell; the shadows tossed in the light of the street lamp, and they seemed to her the snatching hands of evil ones. If she had had the strength, she must have run away, and if she had had the breath she must have screamed aloud; but, in truth, she could do neither, and stood and trembled in the avenue, like an affrighted child.

770 Then she saw the old man returning, and he had the bottle in his hand.

'I have done your bidding,' said he. 'I left your husband weeping like a child; tonight he will sleep easy.' And he held the bottle forth.

'Before you give it me,' Kokua panted, 'take the good with the evil – ask to be delivered from your cough.'

'I am an old man,' replied the other, 'and too near the gate of the grave to take a favour from the devil. But what is this? Why do you not take the bottle? Do you hesitate?'

'Not hesitate!' cried Kokua. 'I am only weak. Give me a moment. It is my hand resists, my flesh shrinks back from the accursed thing. One
780 moment only!'

The old man looked upon Kokua kindly. 'Poor child!' said he, 'you fear; your soul misgives you. Well, let me keep it. I am old, and can never more be happy in this world, and as for the next—'

'Give it me!' gasped Kokua. 'There is your money. Do you think I am so base as that? Give me the bottle.'

'God bless you, child,' said the old man.

Kokua concealed the bottle under her holoku, said farewell to the old man, and walked off along the avenue, she cared not whither. For all roads were now the same to her, and led equally to hell. Sometimes she
790 walked, and sometimes ran; sometimes she screamed out loud in the night, and sometimes lay by the wayside in the dust and wept. All that she had heard of hell came back to her; she saw the flames blaze, and she smelt the smoke, and her flesh withered on the coals.

Near day she came to her mind again, and returned to the house. It was even as the old man said – Keawe slumbered like a child. Kokua stood and gazed upon his face.

'Now, my husband,' said she, 'it is your turn to sleep. When you wake it will be your turn to sing and laugh. But for poor Kokua, alas! that meant no evil – for poor Kokua no more sleep, no more singing, no more
800 delight, whether in earth or heaven.'

With that she lay down in the bed by his side, and her misery was so extreme that she fell in a deep slumber instantly.

Late in the morning her husband woke her and gave her the good news. It seemed he was silly with delight, for he paid no heed to her distress, ill though she dissembled it. The words stuck in her mouth, it mattered not; Keawe did the speaking. She ate not a bite, but who was to observe it? for Keawe cleared the dish. Kokua saw and heard him, like some strange thing in a dream; there were times when she forgot or doubted, and put her hands to her brow; to know herself doomed and hear her husband babble, seemed so monstrous.

All the while Keawe was eating and talking, and planning the time of their return, and thanking her for saving him, and fondling her, and calling her the true helper after all. He laughed at the old man that was fool enough to buy that bottle.

'A worthy old man he seemed,' Keawe said. 'But no one can judge by appearances. For why did the old reprobate require the bottle?'

'My husband,' said Kokua, humbly, 'his purpose may have been good.'

Keawe laughed like an angry man.

'Fiddle-de-dee!' cried Keawe. 'An old rogue, I tell you; and an old ass to boot. For the bottle was hard enough to sell at four centimes; and at three it will be quite impossible. The margin is not broad enough, the thing begins to smell of scorching – brrr!' said he, and shuddered. 'It is true I bought it myself at a cent, when I knew not there were smaller coins. I was a fool for my pains; there will never be found another: and whoever has that bottle now will carry it to the pit.'

'O my husband!' said Kokua. 'Is it not a terrible thing to save oneself by the eternal ruin of another? It seems to me I could not laugh. I would be humbled. I would be filled with melancholy. I would pray for the poor holder.'

Then Keawe, because he felt the truth of what she said, grew the more angry. 'Heighty-teighty!' cried he. 'You may be filled with melancholy if you please. It is not the mind of a good wife. If you thought at all of me, you would sit shamed.'

Thereupon he went out, and Kokua was alone.

What chance had she to sell that bottle at two centimes? None, she perceived. And if she had any, here was her husband hurrying her away to a country where there was nothing lower than a cent. And here – on the morrow of her sacrifice – was her husband leaving her and blaming her.

She would not even try to profit by what time she had, but sat in the house, and now had the bottle out and viewed it with unutterable fear, and now, with loathing, hid it out of sight.

By-and-by, Keawe came back, and would have her take a drive.

'My husband, I am ill,' she said. 'I am out of heart. Excuse me, I can take no pleasure.'

Then was Keawe more wroth[34] than ever. With her, because he thought she was brooding over the case of the old man; and with himself, because he thought she was right, and was ashamed to be so happy.

'This is your truth,' cried he, 'and this your affection! Your husband is just saved from eternal ruin, which he encountered for the love of you – and you take no pleasure! Kokua, you have a disloyal heart.'

He went forth again furious, and wandered in the town all day. He met friends, and drank with them; they hired a carriage and drove into the country, and there drank again. All the time Keawe was ill at ease, because he was taking this pastime while his wife was sad, and because he knew in his heart that she was more right than he; and the knowledge made him drink the deeper.

Now there was an old brutal Haole drinking with him, one that had been a boatswain[35] of a whaler, a runaway, a digger in gold mines, a convict in prisons. He had a low mind and a foul mouth; he loved to drink and to see others drunken; and he pressed the glass upon Keawe. Soon there was no more money in the company.

'Here, you!' says the boatswain, 'you are rich, you have been always saying. You have a bottle or some foolishness.'

'Yes,' says Keawe, 'I am rich; I will go back and get some money from my wife, who keeps it.'

'That's a bad idea, mate,' said the boatswain. 'Never you trust a petticoat with dollars. They're all as false as water; you keep an eye on her.'

Now, this word struck in Keawe's mind; for he was muddled with what he had been drinking.

'I should not wonder but she was false, indeed,' thought he. 'Why else should she be so cast down at my release? But I will show her I am not the man to be fooled. I will catch her in the act.'

Accordingly, when they were back in town, Keawe bade the boatswain wait for him at the corner, by the old calaboose,[36] and went forward up the avenue alone to the door of his house. The night had come again; there was a light within, but never a sound; and Keawe crept about the corner, opened the back door softly, and looked in.

There was Kokua on the floor, the lamp at her side, before her was a milk-white bottle, with a round belly and a long neck; and as she viewed it, Kokua wrung her hands.

A long time Keawe stood and looked in the doorway. At first he was struck stupid; and then fear fell upon him that the bargain had been made amiss, and the bottle had come back to him as it came at San

[34] *wroth* – (old fashioned) angry
[35] *boatswain* – a ship's officer
[36] *calaboose* – a prison

Francisco; and at that his knees were loosened, and the fumes of the wine departed from his head like mists off a river in the morning. And then he had another thought; and it was a strange one, that made his cheeks to burn.

'I must make sure of this,' thought he.

So he closed the door, and went softly round the corner again, and then came noisily in, as though he were but now returned. And, lo! by the time he opened the front door no bottle was to be seen; and Kokua sat in a chair and started up like one awakened out of sleep.

'I have been drinking all day and making merry,' said Keawe. 'I have been with good companions, and now I only come back for money, and return to drink and carouse with them again.'

Both his face and voice were as stern as judgement, but Kokua was too troubled to observe.

'You do well to use your own, my husband,' said she, and her words trembled.

'O, I do well in all things,' said Keawe, and he went straight to the chest and took out money. But he looked besides in the corner where they kept the bottle, and there was no bottle there.

At that the chest heaved upon the floor like a sea-billow, and the house span about him like a wreath of smoke, for he saw he was lost now, and there was no escape. 'It is what I feared,' he thought. 'It is she who has bought it.'

And then he came to himself a little and rose up; but the sweat streamed on his face as thick as the rain and as cold as the well-water.

'Kokua,' said he, 'I said to you today what ill became me. Now I return to carouse with my jolly companions,' and at that he laughed a little quietly. 'I will take more pleasure in the cup if you forgive me.'

She clasped his knees in a moment; she kissed his knees with flowing tears.

'O,' she cried, 'I asked but a kind word!'

'Let us never one think hardly of the other,' said Keawe, and was gone out of the house.

Now, the money that Keawe had taken was only some of that store of centime pieces they had laid in at their arrival. It was very sure he had no mind to be drinking. His wife had given her soul for him, now he must give his for hers; no other thought was in the world with him.

At the corner, by the old calaboose, there was the boatswain waiting.

'My wife has the bottle,' said Keawe, 'and, unless you help me to recover it, there can be no more money and no more liquor tonight.'

'You do not mean to say you are serious about that bottle?' cried the boatswain.

'There is the lamp,' said Keawe. 'Do I look as if I was jesting?'

'That is so,' said the boatswain. 'You look as serious as a ghost.'

930 'Well, then,' said Keawe, 'here are two centimes; you must go to my wife in the house, and offer her these for the bottle, which (if I am not much mistaken) she will give you instantly. Bring it to me here, and I will buy it back from you for one; for that is the law with this bottle, that it still must be sold for a less sum. But whatever you do, never breathe a word to her that you have come from me.'

'Mate, I wonder are you making a fool of me?' asked the boatswain.

'It will do you no harm if I am,' returned Keawe.

'That is so, mate,' said the boatswain.

'And if you doubt me,' added Keawe, 'you can try. As soon as you are clear of the house, wish to have your pocket full of money, or a bottle of 940 the best rum, or what you please, and you will see the virtue of the thing.'

'Very well, Kanaka,' says the boatswain. 'I will try; but if you are having your fun out of me, I will take my fun out of you with a belaying pin.'[37]

So the whaler-man went off up the avenue; and Keawe stood and waited. It was near the same spot where Kokua had waited the night before; but Keawe was more resolved, and never faltered in his purpose; only his soul was bitter with despair.

It seemed a long time he had to wait before he heard a voice singing in 950 the darkness of the avenue. He knew the voice to be the boatswain's; but it was strange how drunken it appeared upon a sudden.

Next, the man himself came stumbling into the light of the lamp. He had the devil's bottle buttoned in his coat; another bottle was in his hand; and even as he came in view he raised it to his mouth and drank.

'You have it,' said Keawe. 'I see that.'

'Hands off!' cried the boatswain, jumping back. 'Take a step near me, and I'll smash your mouth. You thought you could make a cat's-paw[38] of me, did you?'

'What do you mean?' cried Keawe.

960 'Mean?' cried the boatswain. 'This is a pretty good bottle, this is; that's what I mean. How I got it for two centimes I can't make out; but I'm sure you shan't have it for one.'

'You mean you won't sell?' gasped Keawe.

'No, *sir!*' cried the boatswain. 'But I'll give you a drink of the rum, if you like.'

'I tell you,' said Keawe, 'the man who has that bottle goes to hell.'

'I reckon I'm going anyway,' returned the sailor; 'and this bottle's the

[37] *belaying-pin* – a wooden club used on sailing ships
50 [38] *cat's-paw* – (slang) fool

best thing to go with I've struck yet. 'No, sir!' he cried again, 'this is my bottle now, and you can go and fish for another.'

'Can this be true?' Keawe cried. 'For your own sake, I beseech you, sell it me!'

'I don't value any of your talk,' replied the boatswain. 'You thought I was a flat;[39] now you see I'm not; and there's an end. If you won't have a swallow of the rum, I'll have one myself. Here's your health, and good-night to you!'

So off he went down the avenue towards town, and there goes the bottle out of the story.

But Keawe ran to Kokua light as the wind; and great was their joy that night; and great, since then, has been the peace of all their days in the Bright House.

[39] *a flat* – a dull, stupid person

# The Rocking-horse Winner

## D.H. Lawrence

There was a woman who was beautiful, who started with all the advantages, yet she had no luck. She married for love, and the love turned to dust. She had bonny children, yet she felt they had been thrust upon her, and she could not love them. They looked at her coldly, as if they were finding fault with her. And hurriedly she felt she must cover up some fault in herself. Yet what it was that she must cover up she never knew. Nevertheless, when her children were present, she always felt the centre of her heart go hard. This troubled her, and in her manner, she was all the more gentle and anxious for her children, as if she loved them very
10   much. Only she herself knew that at the centre of her heart was a hard little place that could not feel love, no, not for anybody. Everybody else said of her. 'She is such a good mother. She adores her children.' Only she herself, and her children themselves, knew it was not so. They read it in each other's eyes.

There was a boy and two little girls. They lived in a pleasant house, with a garden, and they had discreet servants, and felt themselves superior to anyone in the neighbourhood.

Although they lived in style, they felt always an anxiety in the house. There was never enough money. The mother had a small income, and
20   the father had a small income, but not nearly enough for the social position[1] which they had to keep up. The father went into town to some office. But though he had good prospects, these prospects never materialized. There was always the grinding sense of the shortage of money, though the style was always kept up.

At last the mother said, 'I will see if *I* can't make something.' But she did not know where to begin. She racked her brains, and tried this thing and the other, but could not find anything successful. The failure made deep lines come into her face. Her children were growing up, they would have to go to school.[2] There must be more money, there must be more
30   money. The father, who was always very handsome and expensive in his tastes, seemed as if he never *would* be able to do anything worth doing. And the mother, who had a great belief in herself, did not succeed any better, and her tastes were just as expensive.

And so the house came to be haunted by the unspoken phrase: *There*

---

[1] *social position* – upper middle class
[2] *school* – an expensive private school

*must be more money! There must be more money!* The children could hear it all the time, though nobody said it aloud. They heard it at Christmas, when the expensive and splendid toys filled the nursery.[3] Behind the shining modern rocking-horse, behind the smart doll's-house, a voice would start whispering, 'There *must* be more money! There *must* be more money!' And the children would stop playing, to listen for a moment. 40 They would look into each other's eyes, to see if they had all heard. And each one saw in the eyes of the other two that they too had heard. 'There *must* be more money! There *must* be more money!'

It came whispering from the springs of the still-swaying rocking-horse, and even the horse, bending his wooden, champing head, heard it. The big doll, sitting so pink and smirking in her new pram, could hear it quite plainly, and seemed to be smirking all the more self-consciously because of it. The foolish puppy too, that took the place of the teddy-bear, he was looking so extraordinarily foolish for no other reason but that he heard the secret whisper all over the house. 'There *must* be more 50 money.'

Yet nobody ever said it aloud. The whisper was everywhere, and therefore no one spoke it. Just as no one ever says: 'We are breathing!' in spite of the fact that breath is coming and going all the time.

'Mother!' said the boy Paul one day. 'Why don't we keep a car of our own? Why do we always use uncle's or else a taxi?'

'Because we're the poor members of the family,' said the mother.

'But *why* are we, Mother?'

'Well – I suppose,' she said slowly and bitterly, 'it's because your father has no luck.' 60

The boy was silent for some time.

'Is luck money, Mother?' he asked, rather timidly.

'No, Paul! Not quite. It's what causes you to have money.'

'Oh!' said Paul vaguely. 'I thought when Uncle Oscar said *filthy lucker*, it meant money.'

'*Filthy lucre*[4] does mean money,' said the mother. 'But it's lucre, not luck.'

'Oh!' said the boy. 'Then what *is* luck, Mother?'

'It's what causes you to have money. If you're lucky you have money. That's why it's better to be born lucky than rich. If you're rich, you may 70 lose your money. But if you're lucky, you will always get more money.'

'Oh! Will you! And is Father not lucky?'

'Very unlucky, I should say,' she said, bitterly.

The boy watched her with unsure eyes.

---

[3] *nursery* – the children's play room
[4] *filthy lucre* – money gained dishonestly (from the Bible); any money (humorous)

'Why?' he asked.

'I don't know. Nobody ever knows why one person is lucky and another unlucky.'

'Don't they? Nobody at all? Does *nobody* know?'

'Perhaps God! But He never tells.'

80 'He ought to, then. And aren't you lucky either, Mother?'

'I can't be, if I married an unlucky husband.'

'But by yourself, aren't you?'

'I used to think I was, before I married. Now I think I am very unlucky indeed.'

'Why?'

'Well – never mind! Perhaps I'm not really,' she said.

The child looked at her, to see if she meant it. But he saw, by the lines of her mouth, that she was only trying to hide something from him.

'Well, anyhow,' he said stoutly. 'I'm a lucky person.'

90 'Why?' said his mother, with a sudden laugh.

He stared at her. He didn't even know why he had said it.

'God told me,' he asserted, brazening it out.[5]

'I hope He did, dear!' she said, again with a laugh, but rather bitter.

'He did, Mother!'

'Excellent!' said the mother, using one of her husband's exclamations.

The boy saw she did not believe him; or rather, that she paid no attention to his assertion. This angered him somewhere, and made him want to compel her attention.

He went off by himself, vaguely, in a childish way, seeking for the clue
100 to 'luck'. Absorbed, taking no heed[6] of other people, he went about with a sort of stealth, seeking inwardly for luck. He wanted luck, he wanted it, he wanted it. When the two girls were playing dolls, in the nursery, he would sit on his big rocking-horse, charging madly into space, with a frenzy that made the little girls peer at him uneasily. Wildly the horse careered, the waving dark hair of the boy tossed, his eyes had a strange glare in them. The little girls dared not speak to him.

When he had ridden to the end of his mad little journey, he climbed down and stood in front of his rocking-horse, staring fixedly into its lowered face. Its red mouth was slightly open, its big eye was wide and
110 glassy bright.

'Now!' he would silently command the snorting steed. 'Now take me where there is luck! Now take me!'

And he would slash the horse on the neck with the little whip he had asked Uncle Oscar for. He *knew* the horse could take him to where there

[5] *brazening it out* – bluffing cheekily

[6] *heed* – notice

was luck, if only he forced it. So he would mount again, and start on his furious ride, hoping at last to get there. He knew he could get there.

'You'll break your horse, Paul!' said the nurse.

'He's always riding like that! I wish he'd leave off,' said his elder sister Joan.

But he only glared down on them in silence. Nurse gave him up. She could make nothing of him. Anyhow he was growing beyond her.

One day his mother and his Uncle Oscar came in when he was on one of his furious rides. He did not speak to them.

'Hallo! you young jockey! Riding a winner?' said his uncle.

'Aren't you growing too big for a rocking-horse? You're not a very little boy any longer, you know,' said his mother.

But Paul only gave a blue glare from his big, rather close-set eyes.

He would speak to nobody when he was in full tilt. His mother watched him with an anxious expression on her face.

At last he suddenly stopped forcing his horse into the mechanical gallop, and slid down.

'Well, I got there!' he announced fiercely, his blue eyes still flaring, and his sturdy long legs straddling apart.

'Where did you get to?' asked his mother.

'Where I wanted to go to,' he flared back at her.

'That's right, son!' said Uncle Oscar. 'Don't you stop till you get there. What's the horse's name?'

'He doesn't have a name,' said the boy.

'Gets on without all right?' asked the uncle.

'Well, he has different names. He was called Sansovino last week.'

'Sansovino, eh? Won the Ascot. How did you know his name?'

'He always talks about horse-races with Bassett,' said Joan.

The uncle was delighted to find that his small nephew was posted with all the racing news. Bassett, the young gardener who had been wounded in the left foot in the war, and had got his present job through Oscar Cresswell, whose batman[7] he had been, was a perfect blade of the 'turf'. He lived in the racing events, and the small boy lived with him.

Oscar Cresswell got it all from Bassett.

'Master Paul comes and asks me, so I can't do more than tell him, sir,' said Bassett, his face terribly serious, as if he were speaking of religious matters.

'And does he ever put anything on a horse he fancies?'

'Well – I don't want to give him away – he's a young sport, a fine sport, sir. Would you mind asking him himself? He sort of takes a plea-

---

[7] *batman* – an officer's servant

sure in it, and perhaps he'd feel I was giving him away, sir, if you don't mind.'

Bassett was serious as a church.

160 The uncle went back to his nephew, and took him off for a ride in the car.

'Say, Paul, old man, do you ever put anything on a horse?' the uncle asked.

The boy watched the handsome man closely.

'Why, do you think I oughtn't to?' he parried.

'Not a bit of it! I thought perhaps you might give me a tip for the Lincoln.'[8]

The car sped on into the country, going down to Uncle Oscar's place in Hampshire.

'Honour bright?'[9] said the nephew.

170 'Honour bright, son!' said the uncle.

'Well, then, Daffodil.'

'Daffodil! I doubt it, sonny. What about Mirza?'

'I only know the winner,' said the boy. 'That's Daffodil!'

'Daffodil, eh?'

There was a pause. Daffodil was an obscure horse, comparatively.

'Uncle!'

'Yes, son?'

'You won't let it go any further, will you? I promised Bassett.'

'Bassett be damned, old man! What's he got to do with it?'

180 'We're partners! We've been partners from the first! Uncle, he lent me my first five shillings, which I lost. I promised him, honour bright, it was only between me and him: only you gave me that ten-shilling note I started winning with, so I thought you were lucky. You won't let it go any further, will you?'

The boy gazed at his uncle from those big, hot, blue eyes, set rather close together. The uncle stirred and laughed uneasily.

'Right you are, son! I'll keep your tip private. Daffodil, eh! How much are you putting on him?'

'All except twenty pounds,' said the boy. 'I keep that in reserve.'

190 The uncle thought it a good joke.

'You keep twenty pounds in reserve, do you, you young romancer? What are you betting, then?'

'I'm betting three hundred,' said the boy gravely. 'But it's between you and me, Uncle Oscar! Honour bright?'

[8] *the Lincoln* – one of several famous horse races that are mentioned in this story

[9] *honour bright* – an old-fashioned way of asking someone if they are sincere, or of saying that you are sincere and will not break your word

The uncle burst into a roar of laughter.

'It's between you and me all right, you young Nat Gould,'[10] he said, laughing. 'But where's your three hundred?'

'Bassett keeps it for me. We're partners.'

'You are, are you! And what is Bassett putting on Daffodil?'

'He won't go quite as high as I do, I expect. Perhaps he'll go a hundred and fifty.'

'What, pennies?' laughed the uncle.

'Pounds,' said the child, with a surprised look at his uncle. 'Bassett keeps a bigger reserve than I do.'

Between wonder and amusement, Uncle Oscar was silent. He pursued the matter no further, but he determined to take his nephew with him to the Lincoln races.

'Now, son,' he said. 'I'm putting twenty on Mirza, and I'll put five for you on any horse you fancy. What's your pick?'

'Daffodil, uncle!'

'No, not the fiver on Daffodil!'

'I should if it was my own fiver,' said the child.

'Good! Good! Right you are! A fiver for me and a fiver for you on Daffodil.'

The child had never been to a race-meeting before, and his eyes were blue fire. He pursed his mouth tight, and watched. A Frenchman just in front had put his money on Lancelot. Wild with excitement, he flared his arms up and down, yelling '*Lancelot! Lancelot!*' in his French accent.

Daffodil came in first, Lancelot second, Mirza third. The child, flushed and with eyes blazing, was curiously serene. His uncle brought him five five-pound notes: four to one.

'What am I to do with these?' he cried, waving them before the boy's eyes.

'I suppose we'll talk to Bassett,' said the boy. 'I expect I have fifteen hundred now: and twenty in reserve: and this twenty.'

His uncle studied him for some moments.

'Look here, son!' he said. 'You're not serious about Bassett and that fifteen hundred, are you?'

'Yes, I am. But it's between you and me, uncle! Honour bright!'

'Honour bright, all right, son! But I must talk to Bassett.'

'If you'd like to be a partner, uncle, with Bassett and me, we could all be partners. Only you'd have to promise, honour bright, uncle, not to let it go beyond us three. Bassett and I are lucky, and you must be lucky, because it was your ten shillings I started winning with . . .'

---

[10] *Nat Gould* – a famous horse race expert

Uncle Oscar took both Bassett and Paul into Richmond Park for an afternoon, and there they talked.

'It's like this, you see, sir,' Bassett said. 'Master Paul would get me talking about racing events, spinning yarns, you know, sir. And he was always keen on knowing if I'd made or if I'd lost. It's about a year since, now, that I put five shillings on Blush of Dawn for him: and we lost. Then the luck turned, with that ten shillings he had from you: that we put on Singhalese. And since that time, it's been pretty steady, all things considering. What do you say, Master Paul?'

'We're all right when we're *sure*,' said Paul. 'It's when we're not quite sure that we go down.'

'Oh, but we're careful then,' said Bassett.

'But when are you *sure*?' smiled Uncle Oscar.

'It's Master Paul, sir,' said Bassett, in a secret, religious voice. 'It's as if he had it from heaven. Like Daffodil, now, for the Lincoln. That was as sure as eggs.'

'Did you put anything on Daffodil?' asked Oscar Cresswell.

'Yes, sir. I made my bit.'

'And my nephew?'

Bassett was obstinately silent, looking at Paul.

'I made twelve hundred, didn't I, Bassett? I told uncle I was putting three hundred on Daffodil.'

'That's right,' said Bassett, nodding.

'But where's the money?' asked the uncle.

'I keep it safe locked up, sir. Master Paul, he can have it any minute he likes to ask for it.'

'What, fifteen hundred pounds?'

'And twenty! And *forty*, that is, with the twenty he made on the course.'

'It's amazing,' said the uncle.

'If Master Paul offers you to be partners, sir, I would, if I were you: if you'll excuse me,'[11] said Bassett.

Oscar Cresswell thought about it.

'I'll see the money,' he said.

They drove home again, and sure enough, Bassett came round to the garden-house with fifteen hundred pounds in notes. The twenty pounds reserve was left with Joe Glee, in the Turf Commission deposit.[12]

'You see, it's all right, uncle, when I'm *sure*! Then we go strong, for all we're worth. Don't we, Bassett?'

'We do that, Master Paul.'

---

[11] *if you'll excuse me* – Bassett apologizes for offering advice to his former officer
[12] *Turf Commission* – the bookmaker

'And when are you sure?' said the uncle, laughing.

'Oh well, sometimes I'm absolutely sure, like about Daffodil,' said the boy; 'and sometimes I have an idea; and sometimes I haven't an idea, have I, Bassett? Then we're careful, because we mostly go down.'

'You do, do you! And when you're sure, like about Daffodil, what makes you sure, sonny?'

'Oh, well, I don't know,' said the boy uneasily. 'I'm sure, you know, uncle; that's all.'

'It's as if he had it from heaven, sir,' Bassett reiterated.

'I should say so!' said the uncle.

But he became a partner. And when the Leger was coming on, Paul was 'sure' about Lively Spark, which was a quite inconsiderable horse. The boy insisted on putting a thousand on the horse, Bassett went for five hundred, and Oscar Cresswell two hundred. Lively Spark came in first and the betting had been ten to one against him. Paul had made ten thousand.

'You see', he said, 'I was absolutely sure of him.'

Even Oscar Cresswell had cleared two thousand.

'Look here, son,' he said, 'this sort of thing makes me nervous.'

'It needn't, uncle! Perhaps I shan't be sure again for a long time.'

'But what are you going to do with your money?' asked the uncle.

'Of course,' said the boy, 'I started it for Mother. She said she had no luck, because Father is unlucky, so I thought if I was lucky, it might stop whispering.'

'What might stop whispering?'

'Our house! I *hate* our house for whispering.'

'What does it whisper?'

'Why – why' – the boy fidgeted – 'why I don't know! But it's always short of money, you know, uncle.'

'I know it, son, I know it.'

'You know people send Mother writs,[13] don't you uncle?'

'I'm afraid I do,' said the uncle.

'And then the house whispers like people laughing at you behind your back. It's awful, that is! I thought if I was lucky—'

'You might stop it,' added the uncle.

The boy watched him with big blue eyes, that had an uncanny cold fire in them, and he said never a word.

'Well, then!' said the uncle. 'What are we doing?'

'I shouldn't like Mother to know I was lucky,' said the boy.

'Why not, son?'

'She'd stop me.'

---

[13] *writs* – a court order (to pay unpaid bills)

'I don't think she would.'

'Oh!' – and the boy writhed in an odd way – 'I *don't* want her to know, uncle.'

320 'All right, son! We'll manage it without her knowing.'

They managed it very easily. Paul, at the other's suggestion, handed over five thousand pounds to his uncle, who deposited it with the family lawyer, who was then to inform Paul's mother that a relative had put five thousand pounds into his hands, which sum was to be paid out a thousand pounds at a time, on the mother's birthday, for the next five years.

'So she'll have a birthday present of a thousand pounds for five successive years,' said Uncle Oscar.

'I hope it won't make it all the harder for her later.'

Paul's mother had her birthday in November. The house had been
330 'whispering' worse than ever lately, and even in spite of his luck, Paul could not bear up against it. He was very anxious to see the effect of the birthday letter, telling his mother about the thousand pounds.

When there were no visitors, Paul now took his meals with his parents, as he was beyond the nursery control. His mother went into town nearly every day. She had discovered that she had an odd knack of sketching furs and dress materials, so she worked secretly[14] in the studio of a friend who was the chief 'artist' for the leading drapers.[15] She drew the figures of ladies in furs and ladies in silk and sequins for the newspaper advertisements. This young woman artist earned several thousand pounds a
340 year, but Paul's mother only made several hundreds, and she was again dissatisfied. She so wanted to be first in something, and she did not succeed, even in making sketches for drapery advertisements.

She was down to breakfast on the morning of her birthday. Paul watched her face as she read her letters. He knew the lawyer's letter. As his mother read it, her face hardened and became more expressionless. Then a cold, determined look came on her mouth. She hid the letter under the pile of others, and said not a word about it.

'Didn't you have anything nice in the post for your birthday, Mother?' said Paul.

350 'Quite moderately nice,' she said, her voice cold and absent.

She went away to town without saying more.

But in the afternoon Uncle Oscar appeared. He said Paul's mother had had a long interview with the lawyer, asking if the whole five thousand could not be advanced at once, as she was in debt.

'What do you think, uncle?' said the boy.

'I leave it to you, son.'

---

[14] *worked secretly* – a woman of Paul's mother's class should not need to work
[15] *drapers* – a fabric retailer

'Oh, let her have it, then! We can get some more with the other,' said the boy.

'A bird in the hand is worth two in the bush, laddie!' said Uncle Oscar.

'But I'm sure to *know* for the Grand National; or the Lincolnshire; or else the Derby. I'm sure to know for *one* of them,' said Paul.

So Uncle Oscar signed the agreement, and Paul's mother touched the whole five thousand. Then something very curious happened. The voices in the house suddenly went mad, like a chorus of frogs on a spring evening. There were certain new furnishings, and Paul had a tutor. He was *really* going to Eton,[16] his father's school, in the following autumn. There were flowers in the winter, and a blossoming of the luxury Paul's mother had been used to. And yet the voices in the house, behind the sprays of mimosa and almond-blossom,[17] and from under the piles of iridescent[18] cushions, simply trilled and screamed in a sort of ecstasy: 'There *must* be more money! Oh-h-h! There *must* be more money! Oh, now, now-w! now-w-w there *must* be more money! – more than ever! More than ever!'

It frightened Paul terribly. He studied away at his Latin and Greek[19] with his tutors. But his intense hours were spent with Bassett. The Grand National had gone by; he had not 'known', and had lost a hundred pounds. Summer was at hand. He was in agony for the Lincoln. But even for the Lincoln he didn't 'know', and he lost fifty pounds. He became wild-eyed and strange, as if something were going to explode in him.

'Let it alone, son! Don't you bother about it!' urged Uncle Oscar. But it was as if the boy couldn't really hear what his uncle was saying.

'I've got to know for the Derby! I've got to know for the Derby!' the child reiterated, his big blue eyes blazing with a sort of madness.

His mother noticed how overwrought he was.

'You'd better go to the seaside. Wouldn't you like to go now to the seaside, instead of waiting? I think you'd better,' she said, looking down at him anxiously, her heart curiously heavy because of him.

But the child lifted his uncanny blue eyes.

'I couldn't possibly go before the Derby, Mother!' he said. 'I couldn't possibly!'

'Why not?' she said, her voice becoming heavy when she was opposed. 'Why not? You can still go from the seaside to see the Derby with your Uncle Oscar if that's what you wish. No need for you to wait here.

---

[16] *Eton* – an expensive private school
[17] *mimosa and almond blossom* – fragrant flowers
[18] *iridescent* – glittering with many colours
[19] *Latin and Greek* – subjects that Paul would need to study at Eton

Besides, I think you care too much about these races. It's a bad sign. My family has been a gambling family, and you won't know till you grow up how much damage it has done. But it has done damage. I shall have to send Bassett away and ask Uncle Oscar not to talk racing to you, unless you promise to be reasonable about it; go away to the seaside and forget
400   it. You're all nerves!'

'I'll do what you like, Mother, so long as you don't send me away till after the Derby,' the boy said.

'Send you away from where? Just from this house?'

'Yes,' he said, gazing at her.

'Why, you curious child, what makes you care about this house so much, suddenly? I never knew you loved it!'

He gazed at her without speaking. He had a secret within a secret, something he had not divulged, even to Bassett or to his Uncle Oscar.

But his mother, after standing undecided and a little bit sullen for
410   some moments, said:

'Very well, then! Don't go to the seaside till after the Derby, if you don't wish it. But promise me you won't let your nerves go to pieces! Promise you won't think so much about horse-racing and *events*, as you call them!'

'Oh no!' said the boy, casually. 'I won't think much about them, Mother. You needn't worry. I wouldn't worry, Mother, if I were you.'

'If you were me and I were you,' said his mother, 'I wonder what we *should* do!'

'But you know you needn't worry, Mother, don't you?' the boy
420   repeated.

'I should be awfully glad to know it,' she said wearily.

'Oh, well, you can, you know. I mean you ought to know you needn't worry!' he insisted.

'Ought I? Then I'll see about it,' she said.

Paul's secret of secrets was his wooden horse, that which had no name. Since he was emancipated[20] from a nurse and a nursery governess, he had had his rocking-horse removed to his own bedroom at the top of the house.

'Surely you're too big for a rocking-horse,' his mother had remon-
430   strated.

'Well, you see, Mother, till I can have a *real* horse, I like to have *some* sort of animal about,' had been his quaint answer.

'Do you feel he keeps you company?' she laughed.

'Oh yes! He's very good, he always keeps me company, when I'm there,' said Paul.

[20] *emancipated* – freed

So the horse, rather shabby, stood in an arrested prance[21] in the boy's bedroom.

The Derby was drawing near, and the boy grew more and more tense. He hardly heard what was spoken to him, he was very frail, and his eyes were really uncanny. His mother had sudden strange seizures of uneasiness about him. Sometimes, for half an hour, she would feel a sudden anxiety about him that was almost anguish. She wanted to rush to him at once, and know he was safe.

Two nights before the Derby, she was at a big party in town, when one of her rushes of anxiety about her boy, her first-born, gripped her heart till she could hardly speak. She fought with the feeling, might and main,[22] for she believed in common-sense. But it was too strong. She had to leave the dance and go downstairs to telephone to the country. The children's nursery governess was terribly surprised and startled at being rung up in the night.

'Are the children all right, Miss Wilmot?'

'Oh yes, they are quite all right.'

'Master Paul? Is he all right?'

'He went to bed as right as a trivet.[23] Shall I run up and look at him?'

'No!' said Paul's mother reluctantly. 'No! Don't trouble. It's all right. Don't sit up. We shall be home fairly soon.' She did not want her son's privacy intruded upon.

'Very good,' said the governess.

It was about one o'clock when Paul's mother and father drove up to their house. All was still. Paul's mother went to her room and slipped off her white fur cloak. She had told the maid not to wait up for her. She heard her husband downstairs, mixing a whisky-and-soda.

And then, because of the strange anxiety at her heart, she stole upstairs to her son's room. Noiselessly, she went along the upper corridor. Was there a faint noise? What was it?

She stood, with arrested muscles, outside his door, listening. There was a strange, heavy, and yet not loud noise. Her heart stood still. It was a soundless noise, yet rushing and powerful. Something huge, in violent, hushed motion. What was it? What in God's Name was it? She ought to know. She felt she *knew* the noise. She knew what it was.

Yet she could not place it. She couldn't say what it was. And on and on it went, like a madness.

Softly, frozen with anxiety and fear, she turned the door-handle.

The room was dark. Yet in the space near the window, she heard

---

[21] *arrested prance* – mid gallop

[22] *might and main* – with all her strength

[23] *as right as a trivet* – perfectly well (an old-fashioned saying)

and saw something plunging to and fro. She gazed in fear and amazement.

Then suddenly she switched on the light, and saw her son, in his green pyjamas, madly surging on his rocking-horse. The blaze of light suddenly lit him up, as he urged the wooden horse, and lit her up, as she
480   stood, blonde, in her dress of pale green and crystal, in the doorway.

'Paul!' she cried. 'Whatever are you doing?'

'It's Malabar!' he screamed, in a powerful, strange voice. 'It's Malabar!'

His eyes blazed at her for one strange and senseless second, as he ceased urging his wooden horse. Then he fell with a crash to the ground, and she, all her tormented motherhood flooding upon her, rushed to gather him up.

But he was unconscious, and unconscious he remained, with some brain-fever. He talked and tossed, and his mother sat stonily by his side.
490   'Malabar! It's Malabar! Bassett, Bassett, I *know*: it's Malabar!'

So the child cried, trying to get up and urge the rocking-horse that gave him his inspiration.

'What does he mean by Malabar?' asked the heart-frozen mother.

'I don't know,' said the father stonily.

'What does he mean by Malabar?' she asked her brother Oscar.

'It's one of the horses running for the Derby,' was the answer.

And, in spite of himself Oscar Cresswell spoke to Bassett, and himself put a thousand on Malabar: at fourteen to one.

The third day of the illness was critical: they were watching for a
500   change. The boy, with his rather long, curly hair, was tossing ceaselessly on the pillow. He neither slept nor regained consciousness, and his eyes were like blue stones. His mother sat, feeling her heart had gone, turned actually into a stone.

In the evening, Oscar Cresswell did not come, but Bassett sent a message, saying could he come up for one moment, just one moment? Paul's mother was very angry at the intrusion, but on second thoughts she agreed. The boy was the same. Perhaps Bassett might bring him to consciousness.

The gardener, a shortish fellow with a little brown moustache and
510   sharp little brown eyes, tiptoed into the room, touched his imaginary cap[24] to Paul's mother, and stole to the bedside, staring with glittering, smallish eyes at the tossing, dying child.

'Master Paul!' he whispered. 'Master Paul! Malabar came in first all right, a clean win. I did as you told me. You've made over seventy thou-

---

[24] *touched his imaginary cap* – Bassett does this to show respect to Paul's mother, who is of a higher social class than him

sand pounds, you have; you've got over eighty thousand. Malabar came in all right, Master Paul.'

'Malabar! Malabar! Did I say Malabar, Mother? Did I say Malabar! Do you think I'm lucky, Mother? I knew Malabar, didn't I? Over eighty thousand pounds! I call that lucky, don't you, Mother? Over eighty thousand pounds! I knew, didn't I know I knew? Malabar came in all right. If I ride my horse till I'm sure, then I tell you, Bassett, you can go as high as you like. Did you go for all you were worth, Bassett?'     520

'I went a thousand on it, Master Paul.'

'I never told you, Mother, that if I can ride my horse, and *get there*, then I'm absolutely sure – oh, absolutely! Mother, did I ever tell you? I *am* lucky!'

'No, you never did,' said the mother.

But the boy died in the night.

And even as he lay dead, his mother heard her brother's voice saying to her: 'My God, Hester, you're eighty-odd thousand to the good, and a poor devil of a son to the bad. But, poor devil, poor devil, he's best gone out of a life where he rides his rocking-horse to find a winner.'     530

# Activities

## Care in the Community
## *Old Mrs Chundle* and *A Visit of Charity*

### Understanding the Stories

Work on these questions in pairs or groups, but keep your own detailed notes of your answers. They will be useful for your coursework assignment later.

### Before reading

1 How are vulnerable people treated in our society? Whose responsibility is it to look after these vulnerable groups? Were they treated any differently 50 or 100 years ago?
2 Who benefits most from acts of charity, the person giving the charity or the person receiving it? Could you imagine someone not wanting to receive a charitable gift or act? What might be their reasons?
3 What are old people like? How does a stereotypical view of old people compare with an old person that you know?

### Social, historical, and cultural context

Thomas Hardy (1840–1928) wrote about country life in the south west of England towards the end of the Nineteenth century. The kind of stories that sold well to magazines were ones with a strong and entertaining story line, often with a touch of sentimentality, just like *Old Mrs Chundle*, (written between 1880 and 1890). At this time religion was an important part of life: people were expected to attend church on most Sundays. The parish priests, who took services and looked after the people's 'spiritual welfare', came from well-off and educated families outside the community. When new to a parish they were not familiar with local ways. These ministers were respected and sometimes even feared – after all, they represented the word of God as well as being socially superior. Hardy's curate is one such minister.

Eudora Welty (1909–) is an American novelist and short story writer, whose stories often reveal edgy and insecure individuals in ordinary middle-class settings. *A Visit of Charity* (1949) depicts just such a scene: there is a *Campfire Girl*, (a Girl Guide in Britain), and an *Old Ladies' Home*, which is paid for with taxes raised by the *city* (like a council-run home). Just like Girl Guides, Campfire Girls do 'good deeds' in the community in return for rewards. In this story, Marian hopes to earn points towards her reward by visiting some old ladies in a Home.

### Plot

**Old Mrs Chundle**
1 How does the curate meet Mrs Chundle?
2 What does the curate find out that makes him go back to see Mrs Chundle? What does he hope to achieve by seeing her again?
3 What is it that has been preventing Mrs Chundle from going to church?

4   After one failure, the curate successfully solves Mrs Chundle's problem. How does he do it?
5   The solution creates a problem for the curate. What is this? How does he intend to solve it?
6   What causes Mrs Chundle's death?

### A Visit of Charity
The following is a jumbled summary of the story. Put the events in order.
1   Marian arrives by bus and meets the nurse on reception.
2   The younger of the women grabs Marian's arm as she is leaving and pretends to beg for money.
3   The younger one snatches Marian's hat off her head.
4   Marian looks closely at the older woman, Addie, and realizes that she is crying.
5   The two old women argue about whether Addie is sick.
6   Marian runs out of the Home, collects her apple and runs for the bus.
7   Marian gets pushed into the room by the nurse and pulled further into the room by the younger woman.
8   Addie reveals her false teeth.
9   Marian jumps from her chair and makes to leave.
10  The nurse on reception takes Marian to a room where there are two old women.

### Characters

#### The curate
1   First make a note of all the facts you know about the curate: his age, his social class, his hobbies and interests, his appearance, how recently he has moved to the area. Add to this any comments Hardy makes on his character, e.g. *the kind-hearted curate.*
2   What do the following situations tell us about the curate? Look at: a) the way he addresses Mrs Chundle, and what he expects from her at the start (lines 1–75); b) his reasons for helping Mrs Chundle (lines 76–94); c) his reaction to the failure of his first plan (lines 147–172); d) the words he uses, especially during his sermon (lines 198–222); e) his reactions to the smells during the sermon (lines 186–231); f) the way he reacts to the rector (lines 241–252); g) how he deals with the problem caused by the sound tube (lines 253–256); h) his reaction to the death of Mrs Chundle (lines 270–303).
4   Why does the curate decide to help Mrs Chundle in the first place? She thinks it was because *he holds that her soul is worth saving as well as richer people's* (line 290). Do you agree?
5   How do you explain the difference between the way the curate speaks and the way Mrs Chundle speaks? Copy down some examples. What does it tell us about their social class?
6   At the end of the story, the curate kneels in the dust of the road for several minutes (line 299). What do you think he is doing? Why? In what ways does this show that he has changed?

#### Mrs Chundle
1   What is Mrs Chundle's attitude to the curate at the start of the story? Why does she have this attitude towards him?
2   How and why does her attitude to him change? Do you think she found a *real friend?*
3   Choose six to ten adjectives from the following list that best describe Mrs

Chundle at the start of the story. Find evidence to support your views.

| | | | |
|---|---|---|---|
| independent | cantankerous | uneducated | sensible |
| sensitive | grateful | friendly | generous |
| outspoken | indifferent | religious | common |
| respectful | cynical | cheeky | sarcastic |
| deceitful | hard-working | modest | proud |

Now find six to ten adjectives that describe Mrs Chundle towards the end of the story. They might be the same as before or different. Again, find evidence to support your view.

## Marian

1 First make a note of all the facts you know about Marian: her age, her social class, her interests, her appearance, etc.

2 What do the following situations tell us about Marian? Look at: *a*) what she says to the nurse on reception (lines 12–25); *b*) her reasons for making the visit and bringing the flowers (lines 15–17; 114–119); *c*) her reactions to the old women (lines 45–63); *d*) her thoughts about the old women (lines 62; 96; 111); *e*) the way she leaves an apple under a bush before going in (line 204).

3 Why does Marian react to the old women in the way she does?

4 *It was the first time such a thing had happened to Marian* (lines 176). What has Marian learnt from the visit and how long will she remember what she has learnt? Will she try to claim the points for the visit? Why?

## The old women

1 First make a note of all the facts you know about the old women: their names, ages, social class, interests, appearance, etc.

2 What do the following situations tell us about the old women? Look at: *a*) the way they are described (throughout); *b*) words used to describe the way they speak; *c*) the relationship between the two of them (throughout); *d*) what they say about each other (lines 120–185); *e*) any actions of theirs that stand out (lines 94; 111; 168; 179; 191); *f*) the way they both try to win Marian over to their side (lines 84–185); *g*) their final actions before Marian runs out (lines 179–195).

3 Both women claim that the other woman is either not well or out of her mind (lines 120–147). What are their reasons for doing this? What is your view of their health?

4 Is this an accurate picture of old people? Explain your answer. What do you think causes them to behave in this way?

## Themes and genre

Refer back to your notes that you made before you read the stories.

1 What are the points about the care for the elderly that Hardy and Welty want to make in their stories? Find evidence in each story for your answers. Which writer feels more strongly?

2 These stories were written both to entertain and to get across a certain point of view or message. Give each story a mark out of ten, where one means it was written solely for entertainment, and ten means it was written solely to get across a message. Explain the marks you have given.

3 Who benefits most from the acts of charity in these stories?

4 Which picture of old people do you find most realistic?

**Narrative structure and viewpoint**

Both writers use the third person to tell the story ('he' or 'she' instead of 'I'). This allows them to use a range of narrative techniques that have different effects on the reader.

1 Narrating the action: the writer writes only what characters do and say. The reader has to work out what they are thinking and feeling. For example: *Quite near him was a stone-built old cottage of respectable and substantial build. He entered it, and was received by an old woman.* (line 6–7 *Old Mrs Chundle*).
Which of the authors uses this technique the most? Find other examples.

2 Viewing the action from one character's point of view: the writer writes only what one character can see, hear, etc. The reader sees the story from their point of view. For example: *There was loose, bulging linoleum on the floor. Marian felt as if she were walking on the waves.* (line 26–27 *A Visit of Charity*).
Which author uses this technique the most? Find other examples. This technique also builds tension because the reader shares the uncertainties of the character in the story. Which of the stories builds up tension in this way? Provide examples from details in the text.

3 Writer's comments: the writer comments directly to the reader on the action. This helps the reader to understand what message the writer is trying to get across. For example: *It was the first time such a thing had happened to Marian.* (line 176). There can also be sarcastic or ironic comments about the characters, as if the writer is talking about a friend behind their back. For example: Hardy is being ironic when he calls his curate the *zealous young man*. Find other examples of authorial comment, and explain why the author makes them.

## Interim Activities

You can use these activities to consolidate knowledge about the stories and as additional pieces of coursework.

**Speaking and listening**
*Arguing, persuading, and informing:* produce a three-minute radio phone-in on the subject of the care of vulnerable people in society. Work in groups of four to six made up as follows:
□ the presenter of the radio phone-in
□ a representative from 'Help the Aged'
□ callers to the programme with different opinions
At the end of the show the presenter should draw conclusions from the range of views offered.

**Writing**
*Original writing:* write up the diary of the curate. Divide your diary into three entries:
□ the entry for when you first meet Mrs Chundle and find that she is lying to you
□ the entry when you discover what is wrong with the sound tube
□ the entry when you find out that she has died

## Wider Reading Coursework Assignments

### Foundation Tier

The main characters in these stories both learn something from the situations in which they find themselves. Which character, Marian or the curate, do you think learns the most from their experiences? You should consider:

□ what they are like and what they think at the beginning of the stories
□ the reasons why they get involved with the old people
□ what happens to make them change their outlook
□ what they are like by the end of the story
□ clues at the end of the stories which show how much they have learnt, and how deeply the message has sunk in

### Higher Tier

Both stories have a message or moral for the reader. What do you think the messages of these stories are? Which story is most effective in getting its message across? You should consider:

□ the main themes of the stories and the message that you draw from them
□ the intention that the authors had in writing the stories, linked to the social contexts in which they are set
□ how far you think the authors were trying to get a message across, and how far you think they were trying to write an entertaining story
□ the narrative techniques used to convey the message
□ the way the characters change (see the Foundation Tier question)
□ the endings of both stories
□ each author's comments on the action of the stories
□ the point of view from which the stories are told
□ your own opinion on the themes in the stories

# Castles in the Air
## *The Poor Relation's Story* and
## *The Secret Life of Walter Mitty*

### Understanding the Stories

Work on this section in pairs or groups, but keep detailed notes of your answers. They will be useful for your coursework assignment later.

### Before reading

1   Do you ever day-dream about what your life would be like if you could make certain changes to to it? What do you day-dream about?
2   What would you like to change about yourself: your appearance, your confidence, your friends, where you live? What prevents you from making these changes?
3   In what ways do the time and place that we live in make us the people that we are? Think about how young people were expected to look, think, act, and speak in the Nineteenth Century. How are these things different now?

## Social, historical, and cultural context

Charles Dickens (1812–1870) is one of the most famous English writers of the Nineteenth Century. A period of poverty as a child while his father was in a debtor's prison is an experience that emerges quite often in his writings: for example, the workhouse in *Oliver Twist*, and in his social comments about the difficult lives of poor people in *Hard Times* and *Dombey and Son*. However, his writings also contain a great spirit of optimism and of good winning out at the end, particularly in his Christmas stories. Scrooge's reversal of character in *A Christmas Carol* was extremely well received by readers when first published, which led him to produce other stories in a sentimental style. *The Poor Relation's Story* (1852) is one of these.

James Thurber (1894–1961), an American humorist, wrote essays and stories and drew cartoons for the *New Yorker* magazine. His stories and cartoons show a rather sour view of married life, with both husbands and wives complaining or bossing each other about. He often depicts a day-dreaming man pestered by an exasperated wife, as in *The Secret Life of Walter Mitty* (1942). He described himself as 'crotchety', and he had a fine eye for the absurd.

## Plot

Here is a jumbled summary of the two stories. Separate out the statements by number, and then put them in order. Keep a copy of the final versions in your notes.

The main character (the Poor Relation, or Walter Mitty):
1  gets told off by his wife for sitting in the wrong chair
2  describes how his partner in business, John Spatter, agreed to be open with him and not to take advantage of him
3  gets told off for driving too fast
4  imagines that he is the pilot of a Navy plane
5  describes his friendship with his cousin, Little Frank
6  imagines that he is a world-class surgeon saving a millionaire banker
7  buys some puppy biscuits, then goes to wait for his wife in the hotel lobby
8  retells how he was cut out of his Uncle Chill's will
9  describes how his family and John Spatter's family often meet together
10 explains what his daily routine is supposed to be like
11 drives the wrong way into the car park and gets told off by the attendant
12 admits that he has been making the whole story up
13 imagines he is a first-world-war bomber pilot about to go on a mission
14 says he really lives in a castle
15 buys his overshoes, then imagines he is being questioned in the witness stand
16 agrees to start off the round of stories by the Christmas fire
17 describes how Christiana agreed to marry him
18 imagines he is facing a firing squad
19 drops his wife off at the hairdressers, then gets told off by a traffic cop

## Characters

### Michael, The Poor Relation
1  Reread the start of the story (lines 1–32). Find three references to Michael's lack of confidence in being the first to tell a story.
2  Find three references that show he knows what his family think of him (lines 1–32).

3   In what ways do his daily routine and his outings with Frank show: a) his lack of money; b) his lack of friends; c) that he has no fixed occupation (lines 35–107)?
4   In what ways is he well matched with Frank (lines 61–107)?
5   How does he view his contribution to the world (lines 94–107)?
6   He tells of the time his uncle threw him out of the house, which was a turning point in his life (lines 108–209). What was his life like before his uncle threw him out? Refer to his occupation, his home life, and his relationship with Christiana.
7   Why does his uncle throw him out? What mistakes has he made in his uncle's opinion (lines 108–209)? How do these mistakes confirm the opinion the rest of the family had about him earlier in the story?
8   The story he tells is what would have happened after his uncle threw him out if his fiancée and partner had acted differently. What did Christiana and John Spatter really do (lines 211–251), and how did their actions affect him?
9   Do you find this character sympathetic (you like him and feel sorry for him) or contemptible (you think he is ridiculous and pathetic)? Explain why.

### Walter Mitty

1   Choose six adjectives from the following list that you think best describe Walter's character. Give reasons for your choices.

| | | | |
|---|---|---|---|
| funny | incompetent | pathetic | shy |
| independent | escapist | stubborn | meek |
| mad | imaginative | aimless | lonely |
| ridiculous | harmless | clever | picked on |

2   How are Walter's actions controlled by his wife? Refer to: his health, his clothes, the speed he drives at, what he buys, servicing the car, and the way he waits for her.
3   How is Walter treated by others and why do people like the traffic cop and the parking lot attendant treat him in this way? How does he react?
4   How well does Walter communicate with others? Look at: a) his conversations in the car (lines 18–33); b) with the parking lot attendant (lines 70–77); c) in the A&P (lines 119–123); d) in the hotel (lines 156–163). Contrast these with the fluency and confidence of his day-dream thoughts (lines 1–15; 39–69; 98–114; 134–155; 169–174). What does the difference between the two worlds add to your knowledge of Walter?
5   How does Walter explain his behaviour to his wife (lines 161–162)? What does he mean by this and what does it tell us about his relationship with her? What is her reaction?
6   Is Walter deliberately vague or can he not help it? Look at what sparks off his day-dreams, and the way he finally manages to remember the dog biscuits (lines 114–115).
7   Compare the character that Walter presents of himself in his day-dreams with his real-life character. How do they differ? What does it tell us about how Walter would like to be?
8   Do you find this character sympathetic or contemptible? Explain why.

### Themes and genre

Both stories describe characters whose real lives are not as they would like them to be. They deal with this by creating a fictitious world or worlds.
1   In Michael's real life he has ended up poor and miserable due to being open and trusting, while the characters who deceived him have ended up rich and comfort-

able. In his fictitious world everyone ends up happy and comfortable at the end because they had all been open and trusting.

Why do you think Dickens has written the story in this way? Is it because: *a*) Michael's family are being criticized for not helping him enough; *b*) Michael has himself to blame for his own position; *c*) to get on in the real world you have to be tough; *d*) people should not take advantage of open and trusting people; *e*) if we all showed Christmas spirit all the time, then we would all be rich and comfortable; *f*) people should be more open and trusting; *g*) such a sad and sentimental tale would go down well with his magazine readers; *h*) a combination of some or all of these reasons. Find evidence to support your view.

2  For both Michael and Walter decide: *a*) to what extent he is responsible for his own position; *b*) to what extent it is other people's fault; *c*) what steps he could take to change his life, considering the time and the place in which the story is set; *d*) what he could do if the story was set in modern times.

3  Is Thurber making any comments about how a man should act? Does he think that men should: *a*) be tough and inscrutable; *b*) do as they are told; *c*) know what they want in life; *d*) be in charge in a marriage; *e*) just be interested in adventure and having fun; *f*) grow up; *g*) a combination of these characteristics? Find evidence to support your view.

5  *The greatest pistol shot in the world thought for a moment. 'It says "Puppies Bark for It" on the box,' said Walter Mitty* (lines 122–123). What does this extract add to our understanding of Thurber's view of Walter?

### Narrative structure and viewpoint

1  Both stories contain two main narrative strands. These could be called 'real life' and 'invented life'. For example, *The Poor Relation's Story* begins in real life as the whole family sits round the fire ready to hear Michael's story. It continues in real life as he explains his day-to-day routine, and how he was cut out of his uncle's will.
Finish analysing the story in this way and then do the same for *The Secret Life of Walter Mitty*. In what way is the structure of the two stories different?

2  How are the invented sequences of these stories introduced? How do you know when you are reading an invented sequence? Which of the writer's techniques do you prefer?

3  Both writers use language well for different narrative effects. Reread lines 139–153 of *The Poor Relation's Story* where Michael goes down to breakfast with his uncle after giving him the letter about his proposed marriage. How does Dickens create a cold atmosphere in the breakfast room? Look at the contrast between the house and the outside world, the heating and lighting. How do these reflect Michael's feelings?

4  Now reread the end of the story (lines 320–348). How does Dickens create a happy welcoming atmosphere at this point?

5  Thurber's presentation of Mitty's dream-world character is also very powerful, as a parody of adventure writing. How does Thurber give us the impression of an authoritative figure who is heedless of danger in each different dream sequence? Look at Walter's tone of voice, confident speech, and the adverbs that describe his speech; the technical details of planes, medical equipment, etc that show his expertise; the contrast with other weaker men; the increasingly dangerous, difficult and dramatic situations he is involved in; and the occasional presence of an attractive woman.

## Interim Activities

You can use these activities to consolidate knowledge about the stories and as additional pieces of coursework.

### Speaking and listening
*Explaining, describing, and narrating:* script and perform a scene between Walter Mitty and his wife based on the story. Show how Mrs Mitty gets increasingly annoyed with her husband, as he will not talk to her and does not seem to listen.

### Writing
*Original writing:* write your own life story with the changes that you would like to make. Use the same technique as Dickens to introduce your story: you are sitting with friends, telling each other about your lives.

## Wider Reading Coursework Assignments

### Foundation Tier
How well do the Poor Relation and Walter Mitty relieve the boredom and restrictions of their everyday lives? You should consider:
☐ what their normal lives are like
☐ how their invented lives are different and better
☐ how much their inventions help them to put up with their everyday lives
☐ your opinion of each character

### Higher Tier
Why do the Poor Relation and Walter Mitty choose to escape from reality in the way they do? How successful are they? You should consider:
☐ what their normal lives are like
☐ the reason why their lives are like they are, their own awareness of how this has happened, and the choices they could make to change their lives
☐ the way they escape from reality, and the vividness of their invented lives
☐ how much their imagined lives help them to put up with their everyday lives
☐ how the writers use different narrative techniques to depict their characters' real and imagined lives
☐ how these characters are used to convey an authorial comment
☐ your opinion of each character

# Hero Worship
## *The Sexton's Hero* and *The Will*

### Understanding the Stories

Work on this section in pairs or groups, but keep detailed notes of your answers. They will be useful for your coursework assignment later.

### Before reading

1 What is the modern idea of a hero or heroine? Do you think these definitions have changed over time?
2 How easy is it to stick to your principles? Under what circumstances might you forget your principles and follow the crowd?
3 How big a part in your life does religion play? Think about how your behaviour is affected by your religious beliefs and the beliefs of wider society.

### Social, historical, and cultural context

Elizabeth Gaskell (1810–1865) wrote many short stories and novels about the industrial and farming communities around Manchester. This was where she lived with her husband, a church minister. Besides containing strong storylines, her writing also shows the social concerns she worked for in life. These included the improvement of the understanding between the respectable and the outcasts in society. *The Sexton's Hero* (1847) reflects many of these aspects of her life and works, combining a portrayal of an outcast in a community near Morecombe Bay, a dramatic storyline, and a religious theme.

Mary Lavin (1912–1996) was born in America, but grew up in Ireland from the age of 10, and follows in the great tradition of Irish short story writing. Her stories contain sharply-drawn views of middle-class Irish life, often showing characters who feel isolated by what they see as the stifling restrictions of society and religion. *The Will* (1944) explores the reactions of an estranged daughter to the death of her mother. The daughter has been left nothing in the will of this wealthy woman. Now widowed and struggling to bring up a family, she believes that her mother will be tortured in Purgatory because she did not forgive her before she died.

### Plot

#### The Sexton's Hero
Here is a jumbled summary of the story. Put the events in order and keep a copy of the final version in your notes.
1 They later find out that it was true that his religious principles prevented him from fighting.
2 They are almost drowned by the incoming tide; Gilbert saves them, but is drowned himself.
3 Two friends talking in a churchyard are interrupted and told a story by the Sexton.
4 Gilbert refuses to fight because of his religious principles, even when Letty asks him.
5 The Sexton's wife and daughter die soon afterwards; he leads a sad life ever after.
6 The whole town turns against Gilbert, and Letty marries the Sexton.

7   When the Sexton first moves to Lindal he falls in with a gang of rough youths.
8   The Sexton and Letty go to a wedding across the sands and are late returning.
9   Two years later Gilbert Dawson arrives in Lindal and they become friends.
10  They both love the same woman, Letty, so the Sexton tries to pick a fight with Gilbert.

## The Will

The following is an incomplete summary of the story. Fill in the missing parts with as many words as you want.

The story starts after the reading of Mrs (1) ____'s will. (2) ____ is surprised that their mother felt so bitter about (3) ____ that she did not (4) ____. The other children are concerned about this, but (5) ____ just wants to know if her mother (6) ____ before she died. According to (7) ____, she once mumbled something about (8) ____. This reminds Lally of her wedding day. At this point, (9) ____ offers her (10) ____ from the three of them, but Lally refuses because it is not what mother wanted. She says she manages to keep her family by (11) ____. The others do not approve of this, and would like her to stop. (12) ____ suggests that she stay the night, but she refuses this too. She must return home that night because (13) ____. The others agree to let her go, but begin to feel resentful, especially because she refuses to (14) ____ to the station. Eventually, (15) ____ leaves. Before she gets to the station, she calls on a priest. She asks him to (16) ____ and insists that it is paid for (17) ____. On the train home she becomes worried once more, and decides to (18) ____ as soon as she gets back to the city.

## Characters

### Gilbert Dawson

1   What background details about Gilbert Dawson does the Sexton give at the start of the story (lines 54–90)? Look at: his size, his occupation, his manner, the way the Sexton reacts to him, and his leisure activities.
2   What is it that sparks off the Sexton's anger, and what does he do as a result (lines 78–98)?
3   Gilbert refuses to fight and asks the Sexton's pardon (lines 94–122). How easy was it for him to do that? Find evidence to support your answer.
4   How does his manner change after the village begin to pick on him (lines 123–181)? Look at: his mood, the way he walks, his sporting activities, his friendships, his appearance, his spirit.
5   Explain how Gilbert is on hand to rescue the Sexton and Letty (lines 257–266). Why do you think he does this? What does this say about him?
6   Describe his manner during the rescue (lines 257–286). Look at the speed of his actions, the way he speaks, the way he takes charge. Is there any sign of resentment?
7   Describe the condition and the contents of the Bible that the Sexton receives from Gilbert's sister (lines 313–322). What does this tell you about him?

### Lally Conroy

1   Explain how long ago and why Lally and Mrs Conroy had fallen out with each other (lines 1–85). What has happened to Lally's husband since then (lines 238–240)?
2   What evidence is there that Lally is less well off than her family? Look at: *a*) the way she has to make money (lines 140–144); *b*) her children's education compared

with Kate's children's (lines 190–195); c) her appearance (lines 241–268); d) her clothes (lines 303–308; 429–430).

3   How does Lally react to being left out of Mrs Conroy's will (lines 19–34)?

4   Lally says, '*The only thing I regret was that I didn't get here before she died.*' (lines 28–29). Why did she want to see her mother? Is it: a) to ask her mother's forgiveness before her death; b) to persuade her mother to include her name in the will; c) because she just wanted to see her mother before she died; d) because she still loved her despite the quarrel they had had; e) to talk about the good times they had before the quarrel; f) a combination of these reasons? Find evidence to support your view.

5   Why is Lally so keen to know if her mother mentioned her name (lines 47–64)? Is it that: a) she hoped she still meant something to her mother; b) she hoped her mother still loved her despite the quarrel; c) she hoped her mother had forgiven her; d) a combination of these reasons? Find evidence to support your view. Now turn back to the point that Lally finds out that her mother had actually mentioned her (lines 250–255). Does this change your answer?

6   The rest of the family try to persuade Lally to do several things: to accept money (lines 90–137); to stop taking lodgers (lines 138–174); to stay the night (lines 170–259); to open a hotel (lines 197–259); to use the family car to go to the station (lines 287–328). For each one of these note down: a) the reasons why she does not accept their offers or suggestions; b) the way in which she responds; c) what her answers and her responses tell us about her character.

7   When she runs out of the house (line 318), what causes *the beat of blood in her temple and the terrible throbbing of her heart* (lines 343–344)?

8   Lally is determined to get what she wants from the Canon (lines 372–463). Identify words and phrases from her conversation with him to show how determined she is. Look at: the way she approaches the house and asks to see him, the way she talks to the housekeeper, the way she speaks to the Canon, her emotions, and the way she insists on paying him herself.

### Themes and genre

Gaskell defines heroism in *The Sexton's Hero* by saying that a hero *acts up to the highest idea of duty he has been able to form, no matter at what sacrifice* (lines 26–27).

1   In what way does Gilbert Dawson fit that definition of heroism? What is his idea of duty and what sacrifices does he make?

2   In what way could Lally Conroy be said to fit the same definition? What is her idea of duty and what sacrifices does she make to fulfil it?

3   In both cases their senses of duty make them act differently from the way they are expected to behave. How is Gilbert expected to behave in Lindal? Look at: a) the behaviour of other young men (lines 62–67); b) the village reaction to his refusal to fight (lines 123–132); c) Letty's actions when he refuses to fight (lines 133–151); d) how difficult Gilbert finds it to refuse (lines 109–122).

4   How was Lally expected to behave in her home town? Look at: a) the reaction of her mother to her marriage (lines 1–78); b) the reaction of the rest of the family to her lodgers (lines 140–170); c) their response to her way of dressing (lines 241–311); d) to her not wanting to stay the night (lines 181–251); e) to her refusing the car (lines 292–302); f) Kate's reaction to the way her nephews and nieces are being brought up (lines 190–195); g) the comment the priest makes about Lally (lines 402–404).

5   What role does religion have in the way both these characters act?

### Narrative structure and viewpoint

We expect to come across heroes in the genre of adventure stories. Adventure stories create suspense in the mind of the reader by giving clues about the growing danger the characters are in. As readers we can recognize the danger signs that the characters seem to miss.

1   Which of these stories makes use of an adventure story structure? What evidence can you find to support your answer?

2   One way to show how heroic a character is, is to show how much they suffer as a result of their heroic actions. A good writer will give the reader a strong sense of the difficulties they face. Gilbert faces the difficulty of the incoming tide (lines 183–299). How well does Gaskell depict the great danger it presents? Refer to: *a*) the build-up from the journey away from the wedding; *b*) the state of the Sexton's horse; *c*) what the Sexton and his wife think and say; *d*) the descriptions of the sands, the sky, and the speed of the tide; *e*) the sounds they hear and the weather.

3   Because of her decision to leave home, Lally's life has been made more difficult than it might ever have been. How well does Lavin show the hardships that Lally has faced because of her decision? Look at: *a*) how poor she looks (see character questions on pages 135–136); *b*) the contrast between her now and her as a young woman (lines 318–371); *c*) her brother and sisters' reactions to the way she has aged (lines 241–249); *d*) how the priest sees her (lines 429–430).

4   Both writers also give a sense of the strength of feeling their characters have for what they believe in. How does the reader learn how strongly Gilbert Dawson feels about not fighting?

5   Lavin links the fire in the Canon's house and the train with Lally's thoughts about her mother in Purgatory (lines 406–494). What impression does this give the reader of Lally's strength of feeling?

## Interim Activities

You can use these activities to consolidate knowledge about the stories and as additional pieces of coursework.

### Speaking and listening
*Discussing, arguing, and persuading:* role play the occasion when the Sexton tries to pick a fight with Gilbert.

### Writing
*Original writing:* write a script of the conversation between Lally and her mother when Lally goes to explain who she wants to get married to and why.

## Wider Reading Coursework Assignments

### Foundation Tier
What pressures are on Gilbert Dawson and Lally Conroy to conform? In what ways do they stick to their principles despite these pressures? You should consider:
☐   the expectations of the societies of both characters
☐   the way both characters behave that goes against the expectations
☐   the reason why each behaves in the way that they do
☐   the way they treat people who have mistreated them when opportunity arises

- ☐ how far each sticks to their principles
- ☐ how well the authors show the intensity of the pressures to conform and the difficulties of withstanding them

**Higher Tier**

Which character, Gilbert Dawson or Lally Conroy, acts in a more heroic manner? You should consider:

- ☐ different ideas of heroism
- ☐ the expectations of the societies of both characters, the way both characters go against expectations, and the reasons why they do this
- ☐ how well the authors show the intensity of the pressures to conform and the difficulties of withstanding them
- ☐ the way these characters treat the people who have mistreated them when the opportunity arises
- ☐ to what extent and in what terms these characters are heroes
- ☐ how the structure of the stories adds to the impression of these characters' heroism
- ☐ conclusion: which character is more heroic in your opinion.

# Into the Unknown
## *The Superstitious Man's Story* and *Night-Fears*

### Understanding the Stories

Work on these questions in pairs or groups, but keep your own detailed notes of your answers. They will be useful for your coursework assignment later.

### Before reading

1  Name some good horror films, TV programmes, and books. What ingredients do they have in common? Think about storylines, surprises, the supernatural, characters, atmosphere, and endings.
2  Why do you think horror stories are still so popular today, despite our scientific knowledge and understanding of the world?
3  Do you have any superstitions and beliefs that you know are not rational but in which you still believe?
4  Where do fears come from? Do they come from within or from outside us?

### Social, historical, and cultural context

Thomas Hardy (1840–1928) was born and brought up in the small village of Higher Brockhampton in Dorset. Great changes that were affecting Britain at the time, such as the coming of the railways and the development of industry, came quite late to Hardy's home village. This meant that folk traditions and superstitions survived longer here than in other areas. Hardy liked to include these superstitions in his stories and novels. *The Superstitious Man's Story* (1894) is one such story. It comes from a collection called *A Few Crusted Characters*, which are supposed to be tales told by a group of travellers on a stage coach on its way to Longpuddle. The tales are for a fellow traveller, John Lackland, who is returning home after 35 years abroad.

L.P. Hartley (1895–1972) was the son of a solicitor turned company director, and had a wealthy and privileged upbringing, educated at Harrow and Oxford. His stories and novels often deal with the difference between reality and what people think is reality. He also uses symbolism, where a person or thing can stand as a symbol for something else. This may help to explain the character of the stranger in the story, *Night-Fears* (1924). This story is set after the First World War, when people no longer readily believed the kind of superstitions found in Hardy's story. The western world was more confident in its scientific knowledge and understanding, and the psychological works of Freud had shown that such fears and paranoia could come from within us.

## Plot

### The Superstitious Man's Story
1   What is the first clue that something bad is going to happen in the story?
2   According to Betty Privett, what did her husband do the night she was doing her ironing? Where does William say he was?
3   What does Nancy Weedle see that night and where? Why is she there?
4   How can Betty guess what Nancy is going to tell her?
5   How does William die and who discovers his body?

### Night-Fears
1   What does the night-watchman have to guard during the night?
2   At first he was uneasy about the job? What aspects of the job made him uneasy? Has he got over it now?
3   To help raise his spirits the night-watchman thinks about the good things in his life. What are they?
4   Who does he think the stranger is at first?
5   What does the night-watchman find unusual about the stranger?
6   What is it that drives the night-watchman to commit suicide?
7   What happens to the stranger?

## Characters

### William Privett
Remember that one of the points of this story is to show the superstitions in action in a community. Because of this, detailed and complex characters are not necessary. However, Hardy does give us some idea of the individuality of the characters in the story.
1   What was unusual about William, according to the person telling the story (lines 1–4)?
2   What clues are there in the story that William is a reserved man, preferring to keep himself to himself?
3   What habits and routines does William have?
4   What is his relationship like with his wife, Betty?
5   What do we learn about past incidents and periods in his life? How do they help explain what happens on the day he dies?

### The night-watchman
1   The first three paragraphs are important in helping us to understand the character, and so explain what happens at the end (lines 1–43). What do you learn

about the night-watchman from the following: *a*) his initial impressions of the job; *b*) his attitude to it now; *c*) his defensive nature; *d*) his domestic background; *e*) his relationship with his wife?

2   In what ways is the night-watchman already feeling the strains of this job (lines 1–43)? Look at: *a*) his loneliness; *b*) the vividness of his thoughts; *c*) his difficulties in sleeping; *d*) the lack of things to keep him occupied during the night.

3   In what ways is the appearance of the stranger (line 50) both welcome and unwelcome? What early signs are there of the night-watchman's unease?

4   The stranger slowly undermines the night-watchman's confidence in each of these aspects of his life: *a*) his relationship with his workmates (lines 82–89); *b*) his ability to pay for his family's needs in the future (lines 90–114); *c*) his ability to withstand the strain of working at night (lines 115–125); *d*) his relationship with his children (lines 126–135); *e*) the memory of his father (lines 136–144); *f*) his concerns for his own health (lines 145–150); *g*) his relationship with his wife (lines 151–166).

For each of these aspects explain in what way the stranger undermines the night-watchman's confidence and how the night-watchman reacts.

### The stranger

1   How is the stranger made to seem sinister and threatening? Look at: *a*) how he first appears; *b*) how his words sometimes have more than one meaning; *c*) his knowledge of the night-watchman's affairs; *d*) the way he sits; e) the control he has over the night-watchman's thoughts; *f*) the way he speaks and the authority in his voice; *g*) his reaction to the night-watchman's suicide; *h*) the way he leaves at the end of the story; *i*) anything that makes him seem supernatural.

### Themes and genre

1   List the supernatural events that take place in *The Superstitious Man's Story*, and explain the meaning these events have in the minds of the villagers. For example, when the church bell suddenly became heavy and difficult to ring, the sexton thought it meant that somebody local was going to die.

2   What logical or rational explanations can you give for these events? Remember that the story takes place in an isolated countryside community in the first half of the Nineteenth century.

3   What do you think Thomas Hardy believes?

4   What is the supernatural element in *Night-Fears*?

5   What logical or rational explanation can you give for the supernatural element in *Night-Fears*? Remember that this is fiction and that objects (such as the coke-brazier) and people (such as the stranger) can be symbols for other things.

6   What is the similarity between the coke-brazier and the miller's-moth?

7   Look back at the list you made of the conventions of horror stories. Does either or both of these stories fit your list? If there is a match, find quotations and examples from the texts to prove this.

### Narrative structure and viewpoint

1   *The Superstitious Man's Story* is supposed to be an oral story – a story that one of the characters in the story is telling to another. Find signs in the text that *a*) someone is supposed to be speaking the story and *b*) there is someone listening.

2   What effect does this narrative technique have on the reader?

3   *The Superstitious Man's Story* is also told in episodes. The action in the story

takes place over several days and several places. What are the different episodes? What effect does this technique have on the reader?

4   How would you describe the mood or atmosphere of *The Superstitious Man's Story*? Is it scary, matter-of-fact, intimate, distant, comforting, tense, sympathetic, or something else? How does Hardy manage to achieve this mood?

5   *Night-Fears* is mostly told through the thoughts, feelings, and words of the night-watchman, for example *he valued the brazier primarily for its warmth. He could not make up his mind whether he liked its light.* (lines 2–4). Find more examples of this from the text. How does this technique help to create the tension in the story?

6   Sometimes the author adds comments of his own on the action in *Night-Fears*, for example *(the night-watchman had not mentioned a contract)* (lines 163–164). Again, find other examples of this and explain the effect they have on the reader.

7   *Night-Fears* is not told in episodes, but takes place in one place and at one time. How does this technique help to build tension in the story?

8   How would you describe the mood or atmosphere of the story? Is it scary, matter-of-fact, intimate, distant, comforting, tense, sympathetic, or something else? How does L.P. Hartley manage to achieve this mood?

## Interim Activities

You can use these activities to consolidate knowledge about the stories and as additional pieces of course work.

### Speaking and Listening
*Explaining, describing, narrating:* produce a report on the death of William Privett for a TV programme, such as *Strange but True*, that investigates unusual phenomena. Include interviews with key witnesses, such as Betty, Nancy, and John Chiles.

### Writing
*Original writing:* write your own psychological horror story. Concentrate on creating a tense atmosphere by describing the setting in detail and showing the effect it has on the mind of the main character.

## Wider Reading Course Work Assignments

### Foundation Tier
Which story do you find easier to believe and why? You should consider:
- ☐   how the supernatural is used in both stories
- ☐   how easy it is to believe the supernatural parts of the stories, and why
- ☐   how convincing the main characters are
- ☐   how the way the stories are written help to make them easy to believe
- ☐   conclusion: which story is more believable

### Higher Tier
Which story is more effective as a horror story? You should consider:
- ☐   what makes an effective horror story (with examples from stories, films, etc.)
- ☐   how these stories conform to the conventions of the horror genre
- ☐   how effective they are and the impression they make on the reader
- ☐   what the authors' intentions were in producing the stories
- ☐   conclusion: which story is more effective

# Rites of Passage
## *Malachi's Cove* and *Eveline*

## Understanding the Stories

Work on this section in pairs or groups, but keep detailed notes of your answers. They will be useful for your coursework assignment later.

### Before reading

1   What are the ingredients of a good love story? What would you say are the typical obstacles in love stories that prevent true love blossoming, such as feuding families? Does a love story need a happy ending?

2   What roles do women play in today's society and in modern literature? Think about women's occupational roles, family roles, and the portrayal of women in the media. How have these roles changed in the last 50 years, or in the last 100 years?

3   In what different ways does society mark the marriage of a man and a woman? Why are special ceremonies used to mark this occasion?

### Social, historical, and cultural context

Anthony Trollope (1815–1882), after a fairly poor and miserable childhood, worked his way up from being a clerk in the Post Office to become an important and successful civil servant. He wrote extensively at the same time, and is most remembered for the series of books known as the Barchester novels. These deal with middle-class and clerical life in the invented county town of Barchester. By contrast, *Malachi's Cove* (1867) is a rural love story with a difference. In this tale, Trollope shows the literary skills for which he was appreciated during his lifetime: the careful description of people and places, and the ability to tell a good story.

James Joyce (1882–1941) left his native Ireland in 1902 for a year to escape what he saw as the narrowness and restrictions of Irish Catholic life. He returned only for brief visits to his mother's funeral and to arrange the publication of his book, *Dubliners* (1914), from which the story *Eveline* is taken. This collection of short stories described ordinary people engaged in their everyday lives, using a then new technique of story telling which has become known as 'stream of consciousness'. *Eveline* first appeared in a magazine in 1904, one month before Joyce himself eloped with an unmarried woman, a Miss Nora Barnacle. In it, a young woman weighs up the arguments in favour of her running away from her restricted and difficult life in Ireland to get married, or staying and looking after her violent father, which as the oldest unmarried woman of the family, she regards as her duty.

### Plot

#### Malachi's Cove

1   The setting plays an extremely important part in *Malachi's Cove*. Describe the cove and the ravine, and explain how they have such an important role in the story.

2   Describe how Mally Trenglos makes her living, and explain how she comes to be doing that work in place of her grandfather.

3   Others come down to the cove to do the same work. How does Mally try to stop them?

4   Whom in particular does Mally dislike? How does she try to make his work difficult for him?

5   They both set out to gather seaweed on a stormy April afternoon. Who gathers the most seaweed, and how does the other react?

6   What does Mally do for Barty that she swore she would not? What does she do once she pulls Barty from the water?

7   Describe Mr and Mrs Gunliffe's reactions to the news of the accident. Are they what Mally expected?

8   What makes Mr and Mrs Gunliffe think better of Mally? How do they each show their appreciation?

## Eveline

This story describes Eveline's thoughts as she tries to decide whether to stay at home or to escape with Frank, and so it jumps from the past, to the present, to the future, and back again. However, it is still possible to pick out a storyline.

Many plots follow the pattern of 'situation, problem, resolution, and outcome'. For example in *Malachi's Cove*, the initial 'situation' is that a young woman, Mally, collects seaweed in a secluded cove. The 'problem' occurs when a young man, Barty, starts to collect the seaweed as well, threatening her livelihood. The 'resolution' of this problem is when Barty falls into the water hole and is saved by Mally. The 'outcome' is that the feud ends and the young couple get married.

Now explain what the situation, problem, resolution, and outcome are for *Eveline*.

## Characters

### Mally Trenglos

1   Trollope gives the reader a great deal of information about Mally Trenglos, reporting it as though he has been told by people in her community. He makes her sound a wild and unruly person, but someone with a good side. This good side is necessary, otherwise it would be hard to believe that Barty could fall in love with her. Reread lines 1–107 and make notes on Mally's physical appearance and her dress, her age, her relationship with her grandfather, her relationship with other people, her attitude to church-going, her ability to work. Divide your answers under the headings 'Mally's good points' and 'Mally's bad points'.

2   How does Mally react when she finds she cannot stop others from taking the seaweed (lines 108–162)? What does this tell us about her character?

3   In what ways does she show her quick temper and obstinate rivalry in her dealings with Barty (lines 154–320)?

4   Trollope says the thing that most disturbs Mally is the fact that Barty sees her working (lines 237–239). Why should this disturb her? How is Trollope hinting at the eventual outcome of the story by mentioning this?

5   At what point in the story does Mally's hatred for Barty turn to affection? What causes the change? Is it a sudden change, or has it slowly been building up?

6   After the rescue, her grandfather says people will think she has murdered Barty (lines 427–428). In fact, Mr Gunliffe (lines 475–476) and Mrs Gunliffe (lines 521–522) both accuse her of killing their son. What thoughts help Mally to cope with each of these accusations? What do these thoughts tell us about her?

7   What impressions of the farmhouse does Mally get (lines 618–674)? What do these tell us about her way of life?

## Eveline

1 Eveline is considering leaving home. What is it about her home life that makes her life difficult? Look at: a) the housework; b) her job; c) her relationship with her father; d) her health; e) her freedom of choice about the way to live; f) her relationships with Frank and with others in the story.

2 What is it about her home life that makes her want to stay? Look at: a) how familiar she is with the local people; b) how familiar she is with places and things ; c) the promise to her mother; d) the memories her home brings; e) her religious beliefs.

3 What is it about her mother's life and the way it ended that frightens her?

4 What is it about Frank that draws her towards him? What do his attractions say about her own life and character?

5 What is it that makes her mind up for her at the last minute? Is it that: a) the confusion at the docks frightens her; b) she feels that it is her duty to stay with her father; c) the thought of leaving makes her ill; d) she does not like the way that Frank is forcing her to go; e) she wants to devote herself to a life of self-sacrifice; f) she does not love Frank enough; g) she prefers to stay with what she knows than to enter the unknown; h) a combination of reasons. Find evidence in the story to support your view.

6 Select six adjectives from the list below that you think describe Eveline. Choose episodes from the text to support the adjectives you have chosen.

| | | | |
|---|---|---|---|
| trapped | dutiful | independent | hardworking |
| meek | tough | self-sacrificing | loving |
| bold | quiet | victimized | passionate |
| pathetic | impetuous | confused | indecisive |

## Themes and genre

1 Love stories come in all settings and genres, but they always have two characters who want to be together and who are usually prevented from being so. What are the obstacles that prevent Mally and Barty and Eveline and Frank from getting together?

2 Historically, women's role in society has been defined by their relationship to a man. For example, until recently a young woman was expected to pass from the home of her father or guardian to the home of her husband with no independent life in between. Looking at the stories, how far is the behaviour of Mally and Eveline and their place in society dependent on the men in their lives? Consider: a) each character's social class; b) her job; c) her freedom of movement; d) her relationship with others; e) her use of leisure time; f) how people address them. Are they treated with respect equal to or less than that given to men?

## Narrative structure and viewpoint

1 Both stories build up to a moment of dramatic tension, when the problem facing one of the characters reaches its resolution. Identify the moment of dramatic tension in each story.

2 Each writer uses different techniques to build up to the moment of tension. Trollope follows the traditional narrative technique seen in other stories in this anthology. He describes the setting and the characters. He explains what the problem is, then builds up to the dramatic moment. Reread lines 240–418 and explain how Trollope increases the tension in this section. Look at: a) his description of the weather and sea conditions; b) Mally's skill; c) the difficulties Barty faces and

the way Mally reacts; *d*) the description of the water hole and Barty's attempts to get seaweed; *e*) the difficulty that Mally has pulling him out of the hole; *f*) the danger that they are in.

3  Joyce uses the stream of consciousness technique of story-telling. The whole story is told through Eveline's thoughts, and what she sees, hears, and feels. Reread the story and show how Joyce builds up the tension. Look at: *a*) the atmosphere of the room and Eveline's mood; *b*) the pressure of time passing; *c*) the way her thoughts keep returning to similar themes, showing the difficulty she has in coming to a decision; *d*) the change from inaction to action; *e*) the use of breaks in the narrative to show her strength of emotion; *f*) her jumbled feelings at the docks and the influence of the confusing surroundings on her.

## Interim Activities

You can use these activities to consolidate knowledge about the stories and as additional pieces of coursework.

### Speaking and listening
*Explaining, describing, and narrating:* conduct an interview with Barty Gunliffe and Mally Trenglos for the local newspaper about the remarkable rescue and even more remarkable marriage. Work in groups of three, taking on the roles of the reporter, Mally and Barty.

### Writing
1  *Original writing:* write your own love story using the pattern of situation, problem, resolution, and outcome.
2  *Original writing:* write the letter that Eveline writes to Harry or to her father explaining why she has decided to leave.

## Wider Reading Coursework Assignments

### Foundation Tier
Both Mally Trenglos and Eveline Hill have marriage in mind at some point in their story. Explain the obstacles that they face and why Mally decides to get married while Eveline decides against it. You should consider:
☐   the setting and the context of both stories
☐   the difficulties both characters face
☐   the decision that both characters make about marriage
☐   the reasons why they make those decisions
☐   your opinion on whether they made the right decision

### Higher Tier
*Malachi's Cove* and *Eveline* show how conflicts of interest could arise when a woman leaves her family home for the home of her husband. Which writer brings out the tension in this conflict more effectively? In addition to the bullet points in the Foundation Tier question you should consider:
☐   the place of women in society then and now
☐   the role of the men in both stories
☐   the narrative techniques used by these writers

# Winners and Losers
## *The Bottle Imp* and *The Rocking-horse Winner*

### Understanding the Stories

Work on this section in pairs or groups, but keep detailed notes of your answers. They will be useful for your coursework assignment later.

### Before reading

1 What is a fable? What is the purpose of a fable? Can you name some famous fables? What are the ingredients of a fable? Think about settings, characters, story-lines, and language. Can fables be set in modern times?

2 What would you sacrifice your soul for? For money, for love, for your family, for yourself, or for a particular cause?

### Social, historical, and cultural context

After training first as an engineer and then as a lawyer, Robert Louis Stevenson (1850–1894) began his career as a writer. He was a determined man, battling against tuberculosis to write many books. He travelled widely in search of clean air and a climate that would help his condition, eventually settling in Samoa in 1889. There he became known as 'Tusitala' – the teller of tales – never taking his skill seriously, but just delighting in spinning a yarn. He wrote dramatic adventure tales, such as *Treasure Island*, but also stories with a sense of lurking evil, such as *The Strange Case of Dr Jekyll and Mr. Hyde*. *The Bottle Imp* (1893), published simultaneously in English and Samoan, reflects a range of Stevenson's interests: magical fables, like the *Arabian Nights*, traditional Western story-telling, the Samoan oral tradition, and his own travels among islands in the Pacific.

D.H. Lawrence (1885–1930) was one of five children born to a miner and an ex-schoolteacher near Nottingham. Very much influenced by his mother, Lawrence survived a poor childhood and tuberculosis. He managed to avoid working in the mines and became a teacher. Soon he left this job because of ill health and began his career as a writer, travelling widely and writing extensively, producing novels and poems as well as short stories. He never did live a settled life, plagued as he was by money worries and constant bad health. His work reveals a passionate and intense nature with an accurate eye for detail. Often autobiographical, his writings also show his close relationship with his mother, and a sensitivity about his poor working-class background.

### Plot

#### The Bottle Imp
Here is a jumbled summary of the story. Put the events into order and keep a copy of the final version in your notes.

1 He meets Kokua and she accepts his offer of marriage.

2 Keawe marries Kokua. He is not happy, however, because he still has the bottle.

3 He discovers he has leprosy, and so he tracks down the bottle and buys it for one cent.

4   Keawe gets tricked into buying a bottle in San Francisco.

5   He makes a wish for a house, but gets it through the death of his uncle and cousin.

6   Keawe sells the bottle to Lopaka, after making the imp appear before them.

7   Keawe gets a sailor to buy the bottle to sell back to him, but the sailor refuses.

8   Keawe tells Kokua about the bottle, so they try unsuccessfully to sell it for four centimes.

9   Kokua makes an arrangement to buy the bottle without Keawe's knowledge.

10  He tests the bottle's powers then shows it to his friend Lopaka.

### The Rocking-horse Winner

1   The house whispers, *There must be more money.* Why is there not enough money in the house?

2   Paul asks his mother why they are the poor members of the family. What does she tell him and what does he decide to do as a result?

3   What does Paul do to find luck?

4   What makes Uncle Oscar take an interest in what Paul is doing? Who does he go to see?

5   What doubts or misgivings does Uncle Oscar have about becoming a partner?

6   When does Uncle Oscar begin to realize that Paul and Bassett are serious about Paul's ability to spot winners? What finally convinces him?

7   How does Paul help his mother? What effect does his money have on the house and what effect does the house have on him?

8   Why is the Derby so important to Paul?

9   How does his mother find out what has been going on?

10  What do you think causes Paul's death?

### Characters

#### Keawe

1   What do we learn about Keawe from the first paragraph of the story (lines 1–9)? How well equipped is he to deal with everything that will happen to him?

2   How does Stevenson stress that he is a moral and honest character? Look at: *a*) his first reaction to the bottle (lines 76–79); *b*) when his uncle and cousin die (lines 186–235); *c*) when he sells the bottle to his friend (lines 276–325); *d*) the way he does not say who he is to Kokua (lines 344–388); *e*) the way he will not marry Kokua until cured of leprosy (lines 419–461); *f*) what he says to the man from whom he buys the bottle the second time (lines 521–562); *g*) the way he tries to hide the knowledge of the bottle from Kokua (lines 584–626); *h*) the way he is ready to save her soul at the end (lines 904–980).

3   How does he treat Kokua when he manages to get rid of the bottle the second time (lines 803–881)? In what way is this out of character? Why does he behave in this way to her?

4   On a scale of 1 to 10, how realistic a character do you find Keawe? Explain your choice of number.

#### Paul

1   Look at the conversation between Paul and his mother, Hester (lines 55–98). What does the reader learn about his character at this point in the story? Look at: the kinds of questions Paul asks and the way he asks them, his limited understanding of the family situation, and his understanding of his mother.

2   Why does Paul go in search of luck? Is it a) because of the house's voices; b) because his family is not lucky; c) because he wants to win his mother's love; d) because he wants his mother to believe him; e) another reason, or f) a combination of reasons. Find evidence in the story to support your view.

3   As soon as he begins to look for luck, Paul's character changes (lines 96–121). How does it change? Look at: his changing relationship with his sisters, his nurse, and his mother, the way he treats his horse, and his manner as he searches.

4   Find at least three reasons why he agrees to make his Uncle Oscar a partner (lines 122–286). What do these reasons tell you about Paul's attitude to his plans? Is what he is doing right or wrong?

5   How would you describe Paul's state of mind at this point? What clues are there that there is something wrong?

6   Paul wants to help his mother but does not want her to find out (lines 286–320). Why not? Describe his manner. Can you explain his behaviour?

7   Towards the end of the story the changes in Paul's character become more obvious as more pressure is put on him (lines 362–424). Describe how he reacts to each of these pressures: a) the sudden influx of money into the house; b) his failure to find a winner; c) the passing of important race meetings; d) his mother's proposal to go away to the sea.

## Hester, Uncle Oscar, Bassett, and Nurse

Explain how these characters contribute to Paul's death. For each character consider specific points.

1   Hester: her relationship with Paul; the lifestyle she expects to have; her relationship with her husband; what she does with Paul's £5,000.

2   Uncle Oscar: the way he keeps Paul's secret; how he encourages Paul; how he makes money from Paul's skill.

3   Bassett: how he keeps Paul's secret; the way he makes money from Paul's skill; the way he presumes Paul's skill is heaven-sent.

4   Nurse: her growing inability to control Paul.

## Themes and genre

Fables are short stories that carry a moral lesson. Aesop's animal fables are perhaps some of the best known. Fables often combine everyday settings with a fantastical element, and are written in a distinctive style using straightforward vocabulary and sentence structures. They are a traditional form of story, but have been used by modern writers when they want to make a particular point. They were especially popular in the 1920s and 1930s.

1   Skim read lines 1–54 of *The Rocking-horse Winner*. In what ways does this story seem like a fable? Look at: the opening; how characters are introduced and named to the reader; the introduction of a fantastical element; and the vocabulary and sentence structures used.

2   Only the start of *The Rocking-horse Winner* is written in this style. Why has Lawrence chosen to start his story in this way? What will the style help the reader to accept?

3   Skim read *The Bottle Imp*. In what ways does this story seem like a oral fable? Look at: the opening; how the main character is introduced; how the setting is made to seem normal and everyday for its expected audience; the introduction of the fantastical element; and the vocabulary and sentence structures used.

### Narrative structure and viewpoint

A fable allows a writer to put over a particular moral point of view. Both of these stories show characters who gain money and advantages from a fantastical source, but they also show that the characters suffer disadvantages because of this.

1   Is the ultimate source of the money and advantages in each story good or evil? Do the writers approve of these sources of money? How can you tell?

2   Which characters end up as overall winners at the end of the stories? Which end up as overall losers?

3   What are the points that these writers wish to make? Select from these: *a*) you should make sacrifices for your loved ones; *b*) you should work for your living and not expect miracles; *c*) do not live beyond your means; *d*) people are more important than money; *e*) you should try to live your life honestly, even if you sometimes do get things wrong; *f*) it's all right to do wrong if you can pass the punishment onto someone else; *g*) poverty forces people to act in dishonest ways; *h*) don't store up evil for yourself; *i*) greed will never prosper, only love and kindness. Find evidence to support your choices.

4   Which writer feels more strongly about the point he makes? Why?

5   As well as getting a point across, both writers are trying to entertain their readers, but they do it in different ways. Read this list of entertaining writing techniques. Decide which writer has used which techniques.

☐   leaving large gaps in the narrative to build up to a dramatic moment of tension
☐   drawing out the story to increase suspense
☐   leaving clues in the text about the ultimate tragic ending
☐   using fantastical descriptions and imagery
☐   writing a dramatic ending
☐   introducing everyday descriptions and conversations to contrast with a fantastical element
☐   creating a good character who is obviously doing the wrong thing

Now find evidence of each technique in the stories.

## Interim Activities

You can use these activities to consolidate knowledge about the stories and as additional pieces of coursework.

### Speaking and listening

*Discussing, arguing, and persuading:* role play the following conversation in pairs. Imagine one of you is the boatswain who bought the bottle off Keawe for two centimes. You have woken up sober in the morning and now realize the true meaning of the bottle. Try to persuade Keawe to buy the bottle at one centime, reminding him of the promise that he has made.

### Writing

*Original writing:* write your own modern fable to get across a point that you feel strongly about. Pitch your story at a level that 10 or 11 year-old children will be able to understand.

## Wider Reading Coursework Assignments

**Foundation Tier**

Consider the way the characters of *The Bottle Imp* and *The Rocking-horse Winner* end up. Do they get what they deserve? You should consider:

☐ the moralizing nature of fables

☐ the way both of these stories could be considered fables

☐ the moral standards of the characters, and the way they end up: Paul, his mother, Uncle Oscar, and Bassett; Keawe, Kokua, and others who handle the bottle

☐ conclusion: do the main characters deserve the ending they get?

**Higher Tier**

Which of these stories should be taken more seriously? You should consider:

☐ what fables are and the purpose of writing them

☐ the entertainment value of these stories in terms of their structure, suspense, surprises, writer's style

☐ their seriousness value: impact of the fantastical elements on the characters (see Foundation Tier question), the message each writer wants to get across, how strongly the writer feels about the subject

☐ conclusion: which story should be taken more seriously and why?

# Wider Reading

The main purpose in providing this Wider Reading list is for you to take your enjoyment of any of the stories or themes explored in this anthology further. However, you can also develop your analytical talents by asking yourself a few questions while reading. The suggested list is grouped under the six theme headings of this anthology.

First under each heading come collections of short stories by the authors featured in the anthology, marked with an (a). As you read these stories you can try to work out if the author has a consistent 'voice' in their stories. Ask yourself:

1  Is there any similarity of style between these and the story featured in the anthology? Look at: the sentence structure; the use of vocabulary; the use of images; and the use of narrative techniques.

2  Are there similarities in the stories' characters, settings, storylines, and themes?

3  Are there any similarities in the values and beliefs that are implicit in the author's stories?

Second in each group come stories or novels (shown by an (n)) that are related to one or both of the featured short stories in each pairing through subject, theme, or genre. These texts are marked by a (b). As you read these texts compare the way they deal with a topic with the way the authors in this anthology deal with it. Ask the same questions as listed above and decide which author's treatment you prefer and why.

### Care in the Community

(a)  *Life's Little Ironies*, Thomas Hardy, Sutton, 1983
   *Wessex Tales*, Thomas Hardy, ed. Kathryn R. King, OUP, 1991
   *Changed Man and Other Tales*, Thomas Hardy, Macmillan, 1966
   *The Collected Stories of Eudora Welty*, Eudora Welty, Penguin, 1989

(b)  *The Darkness Out There*, Penelope Lively, included in the 1998 and 1999 NEAB Anthology: old age
   *Time*, H.E. Bates, from *A Day Saved and Other Modern Stories*, ed. Peter Taylor, CUP, 1979: old age

### Castles in the Air

(a)  *The Christmas Books*, Charles Dickens, Penguin, 1994
   *My World and Welcome to It*, James Thurber, Mandarin, 1993

(b)  *Mr Reginald Peacock's Day*, Katherine Mansfield, from *The Complete Stories of Katherine Mansfield*, Golden Press in association with Whitcombe and Tombs, 1974: a false sense of reality
   *Billy Liar* (n), Keith Waterhouse, Longman, 1989: a false sense of reality

### Hero Worship

(a)  *Cousin Phillis and Other Tales*, Elizabeth Gaskell, ed. Angus Easson, OUP, 1981
   *My Lady Ludlow and Other Stories*, Elizabeth Gaskell, ed. Edgar Wright, OUP, 1989
   *The Long Ago and Other Stories*, Mary Lavin, Michael Joseph, 1944
   *Family Likeness and Other Stories*, Mary Lavin, Constable, 1985

(b)  *The Half-Brother*, Elizabeth Gaskell, Penguin 60s, 1996: self-sacrifice
   *The Parvenue*, Mary Shelley, from *Collected Tales and Stories*, ed. Charles E. Robinson, John Hopkins University Press, 1976: self-sacrifice

*The Son's Veto*, Thomas Hardy, from *Life's Little Ironies*, Thomas Hardy, Sutton, 1983: self-sacrifice

*Resurrection*, Richard Rive, from *African Short Stories: An English Anthology*, Macmillan: family split at a funeral

## Into the Unknown

(a) See list of Hardy's short stories above

*Night-Fears and Other Stories*, L.P. Hartley, Putnam's, 1924

*The Complete Short Stories of L.P. Hartley*, Hamish Hamilton, 1973

(b) *The Turn of the Screw*, Henry James, J.M. Dent, 1993: pyschological fear

*Pollock and the Porroh Man*, H.G. Wells, from *The Plattner Story and Others*, Methuen, 1897: driven to death by supernatural causes

*Harry*, Rosemary Timperley, from *Roald Dahl's Book of Ghost Storoies*, Jonathan Cape, 1983: fear of the dead

*The Only Story*, William Trevor, from *The Oxford Book of Twentieth Century Ghost Stories*, ed. Michael Cox, OUP, 1996: driven to suicide

## Rites of Passage

(a) *Lotta Schmidt and Other Stories*, Anthony Trollope, Penguin, 1993

*Malachi's Cove and Other Stories and Essays*, Anthony Trollope, ed. Richard Mullen, Tabb House, 1985

*Dubliners*, James Joyce, Jonathan Cape, 1967

(b) *The Captain's Last Love*, Wilkie Collins, from *Victorian Love Stories*, ed. Kate Flint, OUP, 1996: love/adventure

*Jane Eyre* (n), Charlotte Brontë, Penguin, 1996: love/drama

*Rebecca* (n), Daphne du Maurier, Victor Gollancz, 1992: love/drama

*Going into Exile*, Liam O'Flaherty, from *Classic Irish Short Stories*, ed. Frank O'Connor, OUP, 1985: Irish emigration

*Turned*, Charlotte Perkins Gilman, included in the 1998 and 1999 NEAB anthology: independent woman

*A Man Can Try*, Eldred Durosimi Jones, from *African Short Stories: An English Anthology*, Macmillan: a relationship ends

## Winners and Losers

(a) *The Supernatural Short Stories of Robert Louis Stevenson*, ed. Michael Hayes, John Calder, 1976

*The Prussian Officer and Other Stories*, D.H. Lawrence, Penguin, 1995

*The Woman Who Rode Away and Other Stories*, D.H. Lawrence, Penguin, 1996

(b) *Visitors*, Brian Moon, included in the 1998 and 1999 NEAB anthology: real life with fantasy

*Examination Day*, Henry Slesar, included in the 1998 and 1999 NEAB anthology: real life with fantasy

*The Lifted Veil*, George Eliot, Penguin 60s, 1996: real life with fantasy

*Metamorphosis and Other Stories*, Franz Kafka, Minerva, 1992: real life with fantasy

*The Mortal Immortal*, Mary Shelley, *Collected Tales and Stories*, ed. Charles E. Robinson, John Hopkins University Press, 1976: real life with fantasy

*The House of Eld*, R.L. Stevenson, from *The Weir of Hermiston and Other Stories*, ed. Paul Binding, Penguin, 1979: fable